Murder Most Welcome

D1630712

NORTH EAST LINCOLNS
LIBRARIES

WITHDRAWN
FROM STOCK

AUTHORISED:

NORTH EAST
LINCOLNSHIRE
LIBRARIES

CLE	LCO
GCL 7/10	NUN
GCR	SCO
GRA	SLS
HUM	WAL
IMM 7/19	
LAC	

Murder Most Welcome

Nicola Slade

LARGE PRINT

Oxford

Copyright © Nicola Slade, 2008

First published in Great Britain 2008
by
Robert Hale Limited

Published in Large Print 2009 by ISIS Publishing Ltd.,
7 Centremead, Osney Mead, Oxford OX2 0ES
by arrangement with
Robert Hale Limited

All rights reserved

The moral right of the author has been asserted

British Library Cataloguing in Publication Data
Slade, Nicola.
    Murder most welcome
    1. Widows - - Fiction.
    2. Family secrets - - Fiction.
    3. Romantic suspense novels.
    4. Large type books.
    I. Title
    823.9'2–dc22

ISBN 978–0–7531–8366–3 (hb)
ISBN 978–0–7531–8367–0 (pb)

Printed and bound in Great Britain by
T. J. International Ltd., Padstow, Cornwall

Acknowledgements

Murder Most Welcome owes a debt of gratitude to my favourite Victorian novelists, Charlotte M Yonge and Mrs Henry Wood whose work I've plundered shamelessly for period details — although they should not be blamed for the liberties I've taken with nineteenth century mourning. I'm also grateful to the friends and relatives who read the book in its early form, especially Olivia Barnes, Ruth Beaven and Monica Mitchell. Thanks, too, to the Scribblers, particularly Jo Frith, Linda Gruchy, Sally Zigmond and Jane Smith for their encouragement, and to my family for all their love and support.

DRAMATIS PERSONAE

CHARLOTTE RICHMOND
A colonial with light fingers and a dark secret, who is only too happy to be the widow of:

MAJOR FRAMPTON RICHMOND
A surprisingly lively corpse

FANNY RICHMOND
A dear, sweet little mother with a well-oiled wheelchair

REVD HENRY HEAVITREE
Half-brother to Fanny. A vicar with a sideline in wholesale slaughter

BARNARD RICHMOND
A side of beef on two legs who thinks he is the heir

LILY RICHMOND
His wife, a girl with gums, who is determined he *will* be the heir

LADY FRAMPTON
A titled grandmother whose h'aspirants are 'ard to 'ear

AGNES RICHMOND
A spinster

REVD PERCY BENSON
A curate

KIT KNIGHTLEY
    A Jane Austen hero, married to:

ELAINE KNIGHTLEY
    An interesting invalid

LANCELOT DAWKINS
    A young man who is too friendly by far with a corpse

LADY WALBURY
    A mother with a mission

COLONEL FITZGIBBON
    A man who has something nasty to tell

A MYSTERIOUS INDIAN GENTLEMAN
    An Indian gentleman who is mysterious

DR PERRY
    A man who knows many secrets and confides only some of them to his wife

JOB HOXTON
    Did the butler do it?

OLD NURSE
    A prophet of doom

PRINCE ALBERT
    No, not that one; a fat spaniel

Assorted neighbours, villagers, animals, servants and dead people

CHAPTER
ONE

LATE SPRING 1858
in the south of England

As she laid out the body, Charlotte Richmond made two surprising discoveries.

The first of these led her to suspect that the man on the bed had been murdered. *By* whom, she had not the slightest notion. *To* whom she was profoundly grateful.

The second discovery confirmed what she had known all along: the deceased — late and far from lamented — had not possessed the habits of a gentleman.

As this was the second time in less than a year that he had apparently been murdered, Charlotte felt she might be forgiven for not falling into a paroxysm of grief; indeed, strong hysterics might, she considered, be a more appropriate reaction.

Hysterics not being in her nature, she merely veiled his face decently with a linen cloth and wondered what to do with the object she had so surprisingly encountered. "Well, well, well," she murmured. "Here you are, dead *again*, I see. I wonder what is to become of me now?"

A few short weeks previously, Charlotte, who was waiting with some trepidation in the entrance hall at

1

Finchbourne Manor and trying to overcome her anxiety by observing the ancient, dark oak of the panelling, the extreme chill of the flagstone floor and the picturesquely leaded windows that let in so little light, had overheard her mother-in-law express a similar sentiment.

"Oh, that *dreadful* Mutiny, what *will* become of that unfortunate child, poor, dear Charlotte?" she had enquired, allowing an artistic sob to colour her voice.

"Well, Mama," answered a prosaic female voice. "I understand that Charlotte is even now on her way home from India to Finchbourne. If you recollect it was your own suggestion, when we heard of dear Frampton's sad death, that she should make her home here with us. And after all, there is no reason to believe that Charlotte is a child; remember, dearest Frampton was thirty-seven and his letters made no mention that his bride was much younger than he was himself."

"Oh, do hush, Agnes dear!"

In spite of the nervous tension that had her sitting ramrod straight on an uncomfortable oak settle, blackened by age, Charlotte listened, with wry amusement, to this conversation. Shifting very slightly in her seat, she felt a twinge of guilt as she recollected how differently Frampton Richmond's "sad" death had been viewed by her military acquaintances in India. I must say nothing, she thought, shaking her head. I have seen the damage caused by a stray shell fired into the midst of the market place, who am I to lob a shell of my own and destroy their illusions about their lost hero — and for what? Rumour? Speculation? No, not I, my part

2

is to play the grieving widow and ingratiate myself into their home and into their affections, to make a settled home for myself at last. Besides, she reminded herself, I dare not raise any spectres from the past. What if they found out about me?

At this point the butler broke into her deliberations, ushered Charlotte towards the drawing-room door and coughed loudly.

"Mrs Frampton Richmond, madam."

"What? Who? Oh my goodness, Charlotte, my poor, dear sister!" Agnes Richmond broke into the moment of astonished silence and leapt to her feet, arms outstretched, ready tears flowing. "Oh, you poor, dear girl, why did you not let us know when to expect you? And on such a nasty wet day. Why, goodness, you're absolutely soaked. Here, come to the fire and let us get you warm."

"Thank you, you're very kind." Charlotte Richmond felt the tension in her shoulders relax as she smiled at the large, eager young woman whose embrace, offered with such awkward enthusiasm, had made her stagger back a little. "You must, I think . . . I believe you must be Miss Richmond?"

"Indeed, oh yes, indeed." Agnes was overcome by a further cascade of tears. "But you must call me Agnes. We are sisters now, after all, and I never had a sister . . ."

"Oh, do hush, Agnes dear," came her mother's command. "Stop being sentimental. Poor dear Charlotte can have no desire to be wept over by you. Are you a little warmer yet, Charlotte? Then come here, my dear and let me greet my poor boy's heartbroken, widowed bride."

Stiffening her shoulders, Charlotte allowed herself to be led past a welter of red hangings and upholstery by the fluttering Agnes to the woman, who, swathed in overpowering mourning — bombazine, braid, beading, bugles alike, all of deepest, darkest black — sat in what looked, at first sight, like a cane bergère chair beside the fire, until one noticed its wheels. While Agnes plumped up the bulging, gold-tasselled cushions of purple brocade the two Mrs Richmonds appraised each other, Mrs Richmond senior with a mournful curiosity, Mrs Richmond junior with a wary reserve.

Fanny Richmond must be in her late fifties at least, judging by what Frampton had let fall, Charlotte thought, though she looked younger, just a slight frost of silver on her dark hair, a plump, pretty woman marooned in her invalid chair. A hunting accident, Frampton had told her.

"Broke her back and damned near broke her heart but Mama's a game bird. Sent for a wheeled chair as soon as she was able and whizzes around like one of those old Greek fellows in a chariot, propelling herself, don't y'know. Yes, you always know when Mama's about, you hear the wheels squeaking long before you see her. Damned handy, sometimes, having advance warning. The dear, sweet little mother."

Yes, thought Charlotte, standing meekly to attention while she was scrutinized. I can see where Frampton might have been glad of a warning of her impending arrival, in spite of the hasty but dutiful comment he had tacked on to his description.

"Give me a kiss, my dear," came the soft command, and Charlotte bent to comply. "Welcome to your new home. Are you quite well? Such a long, sad journey. I trust you kept in good health?"

"Thank you, I am usually in excellent health," Charlotte replied, and was surprised to see the delicately arched brows meet in a swift frown as Mrs Richmond examined the tall girl beside her, then gave a gusty sigh of disappointment.

"Ah, well." Mrs Richmond lifted her eyes to gaze at a nearby portrait, which Charlotte recognized with a moment's instinctive recoil as that of her own late husband. After several more heartfelt groans which accompanied a period of reverent contemplation of the portrait's black silken veiling and the wreath of immortelles set on it at a rakish angle, the bereaved mother applied a wisp of lace handkerchief to her eyes and, addressing Charlotte once more, said, "You are very slender, my dear. I had hoped . . ."

Shaking her head, Mrs Richmond turned rather briskly to practical matters. "My dear, should you be too fatigued to join us for dinner tonight? No? Brave girl, brave girl. Agnes will take you to your room to make your toilette. We have only our neighbours joining us tonight, delightful people, nothing formal, old friends merely, but they will be arriving shortly and I

5

should not like to keep them waiting. If you are quite sure you are not too overcome?"

Charlotte responded with an obedient nod, trying to suppress the kaleidoscope of impressions that assailed her — of loud aristocratic voices, sombre mourning and crimson furnishings. So far so good, she told herself; at least she hadn't been shown the door and sent packing. She followed meekly in Agnes's wake, to be led up the impressive staircase of blackened oak that dominated the hall. At the top, the stairs branched off into a pair of half-flights. According to her guide, one led to the original house and the other, which they now followed, to what was known as the Queen Anne wing.

"What a fortunate circumstance it is that your room is ready and waiting for you, dear Charlotte," gushed Miss Richmond. "Mama wanted you to be put in poor, dear Frampton's room but I thought you might find it too distressing a reminder of your great loss so I've put you next to me. I hope that will be acceptable. I could easily instruct them to —"

"Thank you, you're very kind," Charlotte interrupted in an attempt to deflect another flurry of tearful twittering. "That is just what I should like, to be near you. I never had a sister either. Or a settled home," she added.

"Oh, my dear, how delightful. This is your home now and you are my dear, *dear* sister." Agnes was clearly charmed and she tucked her hand into Charlotte's and drew her new sister into a small bedroom painted in delicate blue tints. "We are rather a long way from the main part of the house but I feel sure you won't find it too fatiguing."

"No, indeed." Charlotte smiled at the notion. "I'm used to exercise and plenty of it. I found the sea passage sadly restricting. Nothing to do but pace round and round the deck all the time and back again by way of variety."

While Agnes fussed around the room, Charlotte stripped off her bonnet, tidied the glossy brown hair which was arranged in demure plaits and topped it with a plain black silk cap, then she draped her mantle on the bedpost and splashed her face vigorously in the bowl of hot water brought by the maid.

"Should I change?" she asked, looking doubtfully at her plain black cashmere dress. "I do have a black silk though I'm afraid that I have very few clothes; at one place on my journey to the Indian coast I escaped the mutineers with only the muslin dress on my back along with a shawl that belonged to my mother. Luckily I managed to replenish my wardrobe thanks to the kindness of various chance-met acquaintances." Indeed, she bit her lip ruefully, some of those ladies were more generous than they knew, but she was sure they would have spared a petticoat here or a camisole there, it was just that she'd never actually asked them. To fend off another moist embrace, engendered by her tale of hardships encountered, she hastily rummaged in her valise. "Look, Agnes, perhaps I could just pin on a fresh collar? Would that be acceptable to your mama? I should not like to keep you all waiting for your dinner, especially when you have guests."

7

"Oh, it is just our neighbours from the Hall." Agnes dismissed her qualms and employed her handkerchief vigorously. "A fresh collar will be quite sufficient, dear. They will understand; we do not stand upon ceremony. Do you have one to hand? I could fetch one in a trice."

"No, please." Charlotte put out a restraining hand. Really, Agnes Richmond was *too* eager to please. It was going to be exhausting if she carried on like this at all times. "Here we are, I have one here in my dressing case. I'll just pin it in place."

"Oh, what a sweet brooch. Is it a family piece?"

Charlotte glanced down at the small gold spray of acanthus leaves.

"In a way," she replied. "It was a gift to my mama from my godmother, Lady Margaret Fenton. She and Mama were close friends for many years and she was very kind to me."

True enough, she thought, Lady Meg was nothing if not a kind woman. In fact kindness had often been her undoing, especially when narrow-minded citizens had frowned upon Meg's particular notion of generosity.

"What a *dear* girl you are." Agnes patted her with bashful affection. "Oh, what a wistful expression — do banish it at once, you are at home now. Here, let me take a proper look at you. Why, you look quite delightful: a charming addition to our family here. What a handsome young woman you are, my dear."

"Hardly." Charlotte laughed aloud then made amends as Agnes looked crestfallen. "My dear Agnes, you're too kind to say so, but I know it's only your fancy. I'm too tall, too gawky and my complexion is so

8

brown as to put me beyond redemption. If you expected a beauty to arrive from India I fear you must be sadly disappointed."

"Oh dear." Agnes dashed a tear from her slightly bulging brown eye. "What a sentimental old silly I am, to be sure, crying so at the least little thing. What must you be thinking of me! Come downstairs before Mama has occasion to fidget."

"I think you are a kind and generous woman," Charlotte assured her in a burst of confidence, adding mendaciously, "No wonder Frampton was so fond of you." A fresh storm gathered. "Now, now, remember your mama is waiting."

Hampered by Agnes who, wallowing in sentiment, was now clinging fondly to her, Charlotte made her way downstairs again. The hall, as she had observed earlier, was unmistakably Tudor, with its dark oak gate-leg tables, carved chests and stiff wooden settles, together with gloomy velvet hangings in a dusty crimson. There were crossed pikes, suits of armour, displays of what looked like mediaeval instruments of torture and ancient banners sprouting from the panelling, their tatters hanging limply. The drawing-room, however, opened out from the newer wing and Charlotte paused on the threshold, stunned by what she saw.

"Ah, there you are, my dear." Mrs Richmond held up her face for a further round of kisses as she herself wheeled her chair towards the door to greet them. "I see you are admiring my drawing-room. A particularly handsome one, is it not?"

Charlotte gazed round in some astonishment. On her arrival, nervous tension meant that she had scarcely taken in her surroundings; now, however, she had leisure to inspect the full panoply of Finchbourne Manor's main reception room. Although generously proportioned the room gave the appearance of being poky because of the clutter filling it to the ceiling. A rosewood étagère supported flowers in bulbous pots and a burrwood what-not was heavy with marble busts. Card tables, sewing tables, occasional tables, draped with chenille, lace, velvet or beribboned muslin, each held its full complement of porcelain figures, stuffed birds, clocks, albums, silver picture frames and waxed flowers under glass domes. A rather strident red wallpaper could be glimpsed in the gaps between the massed ranks of ugly dark oil paintings of ugly dark people, in ugly dark heavy frames, and the tall windows were lavishly draped in suffocating folds of velvet, again in the prevailing crimson, albeit of a slightly different, clashing shade. Still more overpowering reds, in yet other tones, figured again in the upholstery of the gargantuan chesterfield sofas, the chaise longues and the button-backed chairs.

Charlotte could only wonder at the dexterity with which her mother-in-law whisked about the room in her wheelchair (silently, she noted — the chair must have been oiled since Frampton's last visit home). Mrs Richmond maintained an impressive turn of speed, managing not to disturb a single ornament or collide with what appeared to be a breeding colony of footstools, but as her hostess shot her a frowning glance of enquiry Charlotte hastily summoned up a murmured, "Charming, so many delightful objects," which seemed to pass muster.

"Thank you, my dear." Mrs Richmond preened then rather pointedly remarked, "How prompt you have been, such a refreshing change," a comment which Charlotte assumed was directed at the plump girl in lavender who was glowering at her from the other end of the long room.

"Now, let me look at you, dear Charlotte." Once more Mrs Richmond directed that same hungry stare at Charlotte and once more shook her head in obvious disappointment as she surveyed the slender figure now free of outer wrappings and shawls. "Ah well, you must know, my dear," she confided. "I had allowed myself to nourish foolish hopes that as it is only six months since that direful day when my poor boy met his Maker in that terrible Mutiny . . . But, alas, I see it is not to be, heartfelt though my prayers have been."

Her face took on a glow of almost religious fervour as she continued, her voice rising to a throbbing note that sounded, to Charlotte, dangerously close to hysteria. "An heir." She gave a gusty sigh. "To carry on the sacred Name of Richmond, a grandson, an heir to the property, how dearly have I desired it, *yearned* for it, *prayed* for it, my poor boy's child."

"*Really*, Mama-in-law." The protest was made in a plaintive little voice which nevertheless carried a steely undertone. "I was under the impression that you already *had* an heir to the property in the shape of my husband. Also your poor boy, in case you had forgotten."

The interruption masked Charlotte's instinctive shudder at Mrs Richmond's suggestion and she straightened her shoulders as she regained her usual calm reserve. At the same moment Agnes left off her ineffectual poking at the fire smouldering in the vast black marble fireplace. Charlotte eyed this monstrosity with interest. Modelled possibly after Adam and *not* one of his better designs, at that, she thought, remembering her godmother's views on, among other things, art, music, architecture and furniture design ("*the more you appear the complete bluestocking the less anyone will suspect you if there's trouble, Char*"). Agnes reluctantly surrendered her place to the superior parlourmaid who now entered, casting a withering look at the almost defunct fire. As the fire sprang magically to life under these expert ministrations, Agnes, looking rather dispirited, seemed suddenly to become aware of the small, plump girl who was now frowning in fury at Mrs Richmond.

"Oh, Lily, dearest Lily." She uttered soft cries of delight and rushed forward in an attempt to press unwanted kisses on her victim's round, pink cheek.

Mrs Richmond Senior gave Lily a sweetly mournful stare while her daughter-in-law fussed with the flounces on her hooped skirts as she sat down on the nearest chair (an ugly spindle-legged object covered in a shiny brocade in an unattractive shade of maroon, strongly suggesting raw liver). Making great play of looking to see if Agnes had left sooty handprints on her lustrous

12

light-coloured silk folds, Lily ignored the other three women in the room. Only when she had satisfied herself that not a speck of soot adhered did she lift her eyes, to find Agnes eagerly hovering once more at her side.

"Oh, Agnes, sherry, how thoughtful you are to me," Lily said by way of forgiveness in her little-girl voice, taking the crystal glass which Agnes was now offering. "Oh, it is quite like Papa's sherry that we used to have at Martindale when dear Mama was alive. Oh, how happy we were then, I could almost fancy myself there. Only, of course, the drawing-room at Martindale is a much grander room than this, though this is well enough, dear Mrs Richmond."

She sipped daintily at her sherry wine and bestowed a gracious smile upon the head of the household.

"Now, what were we saying? Oh yes, an heir to Finchbourne. What did you mean, Mama-in-law? I do not understand."

Ignoring both the mortified groans from Agnes and any possible embarrassment that Charlotte might feel (though in fact Charlotte had herself in hand now and was watching the scene with some amusement), Mrs Richmond replied in tones quite as plaintive as those of Lily.

"I merely speculated that dear Barnard might not, in fact, have been my heir. That it could have been the case — quite within the realms of possibility — that Charlotte might have been in a delicate situation, even yet."

13

Paying no attention to Charlotte's stiff but fervent denial, young Mrs Barnard Richmond sat bolt upright, her shoulders stiff, her spine poker-straight. An angry scarlet flush stained her plump young cheeks and her fine dark brows met in a straight line above her little retrousse nose.

"I hardly think so, Mrs Richmond." She spoke coldly. "I hardly think that could be so." She glared at Charlotte and turned again to Mrs Richmond. "I don't believe it. I *won't* believe it."

"Lily? Why are you looking like a thundercloud, my dear?"

At this juncture, a large, beefy man walked into the drawing-room, rubbing his hands with pleasure at the sight of the now crackling fire.

"Good evening, Mama." He bowed to Mrs Richmond. "Agnes." He kissed his sister with affectionate gusto. "And this must be . . .?"

"Charlotte, my dear," interposed Mrs Richmond. "Allow me to present your brother Barnard, dear Frampton's younger brother. That's right, Barn, give your sister a kiss."

Charlotte submitted to a bashful salutation, accompanied by a fervent pressing of her hand.

"Delighted, delighted. Poor old Framp, dear old fellow."

Barnard retired in confusion to wipe the manly dew from his eyes as his mother sighed then, with a sniff and a look of disdain, beckoned to her other daughter-in-law.

"Barnard's wife, Lily, my dear."

14

Lily Richmond bared her large white teeth and rather more of her large pink gums in a chilly smile as she stood on tiptoe to greet her new sister.

"Gracious, how tall you are, Charlotte! You make me feel such a little thing. My papa always called me his Little Lily, you know."

"How charming." Charlotte bared her own teeth in reply, mindful that while they were equally pearly, she was, thankfully, much less prodigally endowed with gums.

"Now, Lily." Barnard stowed his large red spotted handkerchief into his pocket, harrumphing loudly to cover his emotion. "What's all this? You look just like one of the stable kittens that's about to scratch, my dear! What has ruffled your fur so?"

He laughed heartily at his own pleasantry, repeated it several times, rolling it around his tongue; still finding it apt, he then took the glass held out to him by the eagerly attendant Agnes and sat down on an oak stool beside his wife's chair.

"It is just that Lily took exception to my notion — alas now discovered to be unfounded — that Frampton's widow might yet become the mother of Frampton's child," said his mother in an injured voice as she applied the linen and lace handkerchief to her eyes once more.

"I'm sure I meant no word against you, dear boy, merely that I should have been so happy to have a remembrance of your poor brother to carry on the sacred line."

"A child?" Barnard's bluff, bronzed face beamed rosily round at them. "Capital, a capital notion. What a thing it would be, would it not, Mama? Dear old Framp a father, hey?" The pleasure was slowly replaced by a puzzled frown. "Old Framp, eh? I don't know . . . Mama, are you sure? I mean, old Framp, y'know, not a ladies' man, not at all . . . not by any means."

His voice tailed away under his mother's woebegone gaze and his wife's narrowed eyes. He swivelled his head still further and took in Charlotte, with her slender figure, quite unmistakably unmaternal.

"No, no, Barnard." She took pity on his bewilderment. Really, she thought, compared to his brother, the poor creature seemed rather slow-witted. She shuddered a little as she remembered Frampton's vicious tongue and thanked God that he was dead. "It is no such thing. It was merely conjecture on your mother's part."

"Oh, what? Ah, yes, conjecture, quite so, thank you. Still" — he cast a suddenly shrewd glance of warning at his wife, still glowering around the room — "it would have been a delightful thing if it were so, delightful."

"Well said, Barnard." His mother dropped a crumb of approval in the direction of her remaining son. "I am pleased to see that one of you, at least, feels the correct sentiments."

Quietly assuring Agnes that her feelings were not hurt, Charlotte sipped her sherry thoughtfully and watched with interest as Lily sank back in her chair, apparently absorbed in pleating the heavy black fringe on the half-mourning lavender silk flounces, her small, plump face carefully devoid of expression. Mrs Richmond diligently applied her handkerchief again, a heart-rending picture of bereft maternity, while Barnard drained his glass and held it out for a refill.

Charlotte considered her new situation. This was what she had always wanted, she reflected. Respectability, wealth, comfort, and a family — it was all within her grasp and for a moment the prospect terrified her. What if she put a step wrong? What if she spoke out of turn and it all came tumbling down about her ears? Then her native commonsense and optimism reasserted itself.

The size of the house had surprised her, as had the number of servants coming and going about their duties. The house, she reflected, would certainly do. Living at Finchbourne Manor, respectability would be hers without question, wealth and comfort too. But could she bear the family?

As though in response to Charlotte's thought, Agnes paused to pat the younger girl's hand as she carried the decanter towards her brother. Charlotte flushed slightly. I should be ashamed by such kindness, she reproved herself; the question should rather be can they stand me?

Agnes reached her brother's side in response to his cajoling smile. "Here you are, Barney dear, though it will soon be time to expect our guests. Will Grandmama be joining us tonight, does anyone know?"

"She certainly will," boomed a female voice from the doorway, and in came an elderly woman whose bulk was not minimised by the profusion of mourning jet which armour-plated her monumental bosom.

"Grandmama." Barnard rose hastily and placed a substantial chair, heavily encrusted with carving, near the fireside. "Here, old girl, sit down here."

"Old girl, indeed, you saucy boy!"

The scolding was accompanied by an indulgent tap on the shoulder from her fan as the old woman lowered herself carefully on to the ruby velvet cushion, causing the stout blackened oak of the legs to buckle slightly while the carved lions on the arms appeared to groan and writhe in protest.

"Well, well, this is cosy, is it not?" She nodded round the room, apparently not noticing a stranger and speaking in an accent that Charlotte, to her surprise, immediately recognized as Cockney. "Fanny, 'ow are you tonight? You're looking well."

Mrs Richmond sniffed at this provocation. "Thank you, ma'am, I am feeling a little fatigued, so foolish of me. My poor back, you know, is a constant trouble to me, though naturally I never distress my dear ones by complaining, and of course I am still subject to fits of overwhelming grief."

"Grief? What in the world . . . what, for Frampton?" The old lady pursed her lips and struggled, making an effort at the last, to bite off the remark that obviously hovered on the tip of her tongue. "Well, poor lad, per'aps it was for the best."

"How can you say so, ma'am?" Mrs Richmond retorted angrily. "My son's death may have been glorious but that is as nothing to the shining light of his

18

life and the loss to his honoured and ancient lineage. Nay, the loss not only to his family, his regiment, but to his country . . ."

Charlotte blinked in astonishment at this pronouncement but her surprise turned to guilty shock as the old lady changed the subject with some haste.

"Well, what about this so-called wife of his, eh? A man of the cloth and a governess, I believe you said her parents was. All well and good, I dare say, if that's the truth. But did I not 'ear that they had come from h'Australia? Mark my words, you'll find that they were transported, like as not."

"How *dare* you!" Her sudden spurt of anger (quite unjustified, as she admitted inwardly) surprised her, and in the moment following her outburst Charlotte was overcome by a feeling of shame at her own hypocrisy. But she had a part to play, she reminded herself hastily, and that part surely required indignation at this point.

"Eh? What? What's that?"

The old lady started up in her chair, noted the angry glitter in the strange young woman's hazel eyes and sat back, unusually abashed.

At that point the butler, Hoxton, coughed discreetly.

"Mr and Mrs Knightley, madam."

Agnes and Barnard, who had stood frozen in the appalled silence that greeted their grandmother's unfortunate gaffe, leapt forward, Barnard looking genial, Agnes babbling with incoherent embarrassment as she attempted to apologize for her grandmother.

19

"It was naughty, I know, dreadfully naughty," she gasped. "But truly, Charlotte dear, she did not know you were there, and, well, she *is* eighty, after all."

Charlotte had herself in hand once more and made haste to reassure her. "I should not have reacted so strongly," she whispered. "I was too quick to take offence. I believe that we Australians may be too sensitive on the topic as I know that many people in England fail to recognize the difference between free-born settlers and the convicts."

A flurry of welcome met the newcomers, a tall, brown-haired, broad-shouldered man who was tenderly supporting a delicately lovely woman whom he then deposited gently into a chair beside the fire. A few moments' talk ensued then Mrs Richmond beckoned Charlotte to her side.

"Ah, yes, pray allow me to introduce my daughter-in-law, Charlotte, arrived only this evening, from India. Mrs Knightley, Mr Knightley."

"Mr Knightley?" Charlotte's demurely dropped lashes flew up and she gazed with interested amusement at the guest. "*Really* Mr Knightley? Of Donwell Abbey?"

"Alas, I fear not." He smiled, revealing a twinkle in his blue eyes and the suspicion of a dimple in his cheek as he shook her hand and led her to his wife's chair. "Christopher Knightley, or rather Kit, merely of Knightley Hall just two miles away from Finchbourne. Let me present you to my wife. Here, my dear, another admirer of Miss Austen for you."

"How delightful." Mrs Knightley's large grey eyes glowed with pleasure in her too-thin, too-pale face, the forget-me-not silk of her dress accentuating her ethereal fairness. "Kit measures people by their reaction to his name, you must know." She held Charlotte's hand in a friendly grasp. "If they make no comment he dismisses them as of no importance. But if they react as you did they are friends for life! Though Kit's father would have been more correctly of an age to be Emma's Mr Knightley."

As Charlotte's place at Mrs Knightley's side was taken by Lily Richmond, a large, trembling hand was laid on Charlotte's sleeve and she turned to see the old lady who had risen with some difficulty from her lion-carved throne and was gazing at her with pleading eyes.

"And I'm Frampton's old granny, me dear." The old woman heaved her bulk gratefully on to another chair, of flimsy gilt and cane this time. "And you must grant me pardon for my thoughtless words for I had no thought of 'urting your feelings. I would not do so for anything in the world, that I would not. Come now, do you forgive me, hey?"

"Why, of course I do, ma'am," Charlotte said warmly, and was clasped heartily to the vastness of whalebone and jet. "I'm afraid I did not catch your name. You are . . . ?"

"My mother-in-law, Lady Frampton," Mrs Richmond said with a languid wave of her plump white hand, with its weight of mourning bracelets and rings in jet and pearl and plaited hair.

"Lady *Frampton*?" Charlotte was momentarily at a loss.

"Ah yes." Mrs Richmond heaved a mournful sigh. "The Richmond name, my own I am proud to say — glorious, unsullied and unstained! — has always been of paramount importance — *paramount*, I say — and I, alas, was my father's only child. My husband took my surname upon our marriage so I felt it only right to give his patronymic to our eldest son."

She broke off at the blank look on her new daughter's face.

"His patronymic, my dear. His surname, in other words." She gave a tiny sigh of disappointment at the philistinism of the colonial-born. "Otherwise it has long been the custom for the first-born son in my family to take as his given name his mother's maiden surname. My own father was christened Arlington."

Mrs Richmond smiled her sad, sweet smile, this time tinged with satisfaction as she manifestly cast a possessive eye back down the serried ranks of the generations, heroes one and all, but she looked up with faint hauteur as Charlotte answered her with a smile quite as sweet though without a trace of sadness.

"Really? Then perhaps it is a fortunate circumstance that I am not, after all, in an interesting situation."

"Why, pray?" Astonished, Mrs Richmond forgot to exclaim at this lack of modesty before guests. "I was under the impression that your maiden name was Glover? A worthy enough name, surely?"

"No doubt, ma'am," came the demure answer. "Glover was my stepfather's name, however, though I have often used it."

"And your father's surname?"

"It was Lucy, ma'am."

Charlotte bit her unruly tongue as Mrs Richmond stared at her in surprise and the elegant Mrs Knightley hastily fanned herself with great vigour. Although Charlotte could not quite see her face, she gained the impression that the lady was smiling while her husband had hastily retired to the chimney breast, apparently to admire the leaping flames in the grate while he tried to pretend that his shout of laughter had been a cough. His tanned, pleasantly rugged face creased into laughter lines and as his eyes met Charlotte's with an even more pronounced twinkle, he raised a quizzical eyebrow and smiled warmly at her.

Agnes fussed about him, offering a glass of water, or Old Nurse's particular horehound and honey mixture to ease his cough, as well as a seat well away from the draught, but he shook his head and was smiling kindly down at her when Mrs Richmond placed herself firmly once more into the centre of attention.

"Do stop fussing around poor Mr Knightley, Agnes," she scolded, and when her daughter slunk submissively to Charlotte's side, her mother struck again. "And do leave poor, dear Charlotte alone, Agnes, for heaven's sake. Let her come here and talk to Mrs Knightley." When Charlotte obeyed she found she had nothing to say, however, merely to listen as Mrs Richmond rehearsed once again the tragic tale of her eldest son's demise.

"How charming," put in Mrs Knightley, obviously in a kindly attempt to deflect the monologue and to spare

Charlotte's supposed feelings, "to find a new daughter in the midst of your tragedy."

"Indeed, indeed." Gratified by this evidence of sympathy, Mrs Richmond settled to her tale. "Alas, dear Frampton, how surprised we all were to hear that he had married poor, dear Charlotte so suddenly, when we had all but given up hope of his ever finding a woman worthy of him. And so opportunely too, with his promotion to major coming hard upon the heels of the wedding. I am sure he never showed any interest in young ladies before. Indeed I was used to despair, but there, the dear boy always insisted that he had never met a woman to measure up to his own mama!"

Charlotte sat demurely, hands folded tightly in her lap, lips folded tightly in her impassive face. At Mrs Richmond's last remark, Charlotte glanced upwards and intercepted a significant look between her new brother, Barnard, and the pleasant Mr Knightley. As Barnard shifted his feet awkwardly and Mr Knightley looked away with a frown, she wondered if, as seemed possible, the two men had their own conjectures regarding Frampton Richmond's long-drawn-out bachelorhood; had perhaps speculated also on the topic of the rapid promotion arriving so promptly in the wake of that timely wedding.

Poor, dear Charlotte indeed. She grimaced inwardly as she politely turned her attention once more to her mother-in-law's history.

"Poor girl." The tone was lowered and confidential but Charlotte could still make out the words. "She and her father had but recently arrived in Meerut, you know, on their way to Mr Glover's new church. Such a courageous act, to accept an appointment in such troubled times."

"It was a fever, was it not?" Elaine Knightley included Charlotte in her kind smile, but Mrs Richmond was not to be cheated of her narrative.

"Indeed," she repeated, applying her dainty lace handkerchief to a melancholy tear. "They had been there a mere week, was it not, Charlotte, my dear? Awaiting safe conduct to the hill station, but most happily dear Frampton was at hand and formed an attachment to the dear girl at once, so in the midst of her grief, poor, dear Charlotte found joy. A very quiet wedding, of course, in the circumstances, and soon, so very soon afterwards . . ."

The lace handkerchief fluttered violently, the maternal voice failed utterly.

"Mama." Agnes was fluttering, dutiful and distressed, at her mother's side. "Oh, pray do not distress yourself so. Shall I fetch the sal volatile? Or call Old Nurse?"

"Oh, do hush, Agnes dear." The command was muffled with motherly tears and in the slight pause which ensued, Mrs Knightley addressed Charlotte.

"I believe you have still no details of what occurred, of how Major Richmond met his death, have you, my dear?" Her low, sweet voice held only kindness and concern and Charlotte warmed to her.

Mrs Richmond cast aside her handkerchief to answer before her daughter-in-law could open her mouth. "Alas, no," she sobbed, with a shudder of anguish. "Not even a grave to call his own. Identification was . . ." Her voice sank to a hoarse, dramatic whisper. "*Difficult.*" She rallied and raised glowing eyes to her son's portrait. "He must be counted a hero," she thrilled. "Along with his fallen comrades — the most noble, the *most* noble scion of the family of Richmond."

Charlotte was relieved to find herself seated beside the amiable Mr Knightley and the relentlessly fussing Agnes when they were announced into the dark panelled cavern of the dining-room with its billowing draperies and chair seats of dark and dusty green plush checkered with purple to form an unlikely tartan. More heraldic banners decorated the room, together with animal heads of every kind anchored to the walls. ("Dear Grandpapa was exceedingly fond of animals," confided Agnes proudly as Charlotte looked askance at the stuffed polecat that glared directly opposite her). A meal partaken beside Lily Richmond would give her galloping indigestion, she decided, while Agnes, on the other hand, appeared to be a kind and harmless enough creature. A distinctly irritating one, in truth; she had to admit to a modicum of sympathy for Mrs Richmond's automatic. "Oh, do hush, Agnes dear!" which continued to ring out at regular intervals.

Bearing in mind yet another of her godmother's maxims — "*eat what you are given no matter how unpalatable, it may be the last food you see for many a day*" — Charlotte quietly worked her way through the substantial dinner, manfully indifferent to the prevailing brown hue of the food — brown soup, an unidentified brown-tinged fish, boiled fowl in a brown onion sauce, brown cauliflower cheese (though in this case the dark

26

colour was evidently due to scorching), ending with brown batter puddings. While she was thus employed she cast unobtrusive glances round the room at the assembled company. Used to summing people up rapidly or rue the consequences, she knew herself to be a fairly accurate judge of character at first sight.

So, whom have we here? Mrs Richmond, Frampton's dear, sweet, little mother. Hmmm, yes, I can see why he thought so, she decided, looking under her lashes at her mother-in-law. It must have been devastating to her, an active woman and the "lady-lord" of the manor, to have her freedom snatched away by a horse's false step. It argued considerable strength of character to take up her life again as she had. But sweet? Hmm, we'll see.

At this point Charlotte realized, to her mortification, that she had absent-mindedly palmed the silver salt cellar, in the shape of a shell, that had reposed on the snowy linen in front of her. Frowning at such a slip, she contrived to retrieve the charming trifle and, feigning nonchalance, replaced it on the table under cover of her napkin. She held her breath for a moment half expecting an uproar — shock, horror, condemnation and the summoning of a constable — before continuing with her observations.

Lady Frampton? Well, now, there was a surprise. Not quite the aristocratic lineage Frampton had led her to expect. Obviously the title was a knighthood, or Frampton would have been *Sir* Frampton or something of the sort, wouldn't he? A nice enough old woman, but distinctly smelling of the shop. Charlotte had met plenty like her; she would have flourished in the colonies, taken it all in her stride.

Unlike Agnes perhaps. Or perhaps not. Plenty of clinging ivies turned into hearty oaks when they had to. A tiny chuckle escaped her lips — what a ridiculous mixed metaphor.

"I suspect, Mrs Frampton Richmond, that you have been having something of a game at the expense of your new family. Come now, confess that you have a wayward sense of humour which is likely to get you into all kinds of hot water."

Mr Knightley spoke quietly as the elder Mrs Richmond turned her attention from him to her second son. Charlotte looked up at him with a slight, guilty smile.

"I fear you are only too correct, Mr Knightley. Pray do not encourage me to be uncivil to my hosts, it would be quite shocking behaviour in me."

"Indeed it would," he agreed seriously, echoing her prim manner. "Indulge me by telling me just one thing, though. Was your father's name really Lucy? Or was it merely the inspiration of the moment?"

"The latter, I fear," she admitted. "But please don't disgrace me by telling anyone. I don't know what my . . . I mean, my father died when I was an infant and I have been called by my stepfather's name for almost as long as I remember."

He gave no sign of noticing the slight stumble and turned the conversation to Miss Jane Austen and her novels.

"I know that you have read *Emma*," he remarked. "I obviously have a particular interest in that novel, but what of Miss Austen's other novels? I must confess to a fondness for *Mansfield Park*."

"Oh, no," she exclaimed eagerly. "That's my least favourite. Emma and Lizzie Bennet were always my heroines." She composed herself and continued. "We had very few books," she told him. "But, as a girl, my godmother, Lady Margaret Fenton, met Miss Austen when the countess, Meg's mother, was taking the cure at Southampton, not long before Miss Austen's untimely death. That led to Lady Meg purchasing every one of Miss Austen's books and she would never be parted from them, carrying them years later all the way to Australia with her, so I was able to devour them as soon as I was old enough." She smiled at him. "I believe I knew them almost all by heart when I was younger."

He seemed touched by the wistfulness of her tone.

"I had not realized that you were an Australian, Mrs Richmond." He spoke with friendly warmth. "You must have some interesting stories to tell. What a very large swathe of the globe you must have seen in such a short lifetime."

As she was about to respond, she caught a glimpse of herself in a mirror, partly obscured by the stuffed animal opposite her. Who could this confident, laughing young woman be, with her angular features softened by a smile and a slight flush brightening her brown complexion? As she stared, the smile vanished and a guarded expression took its place. The colour deepened in her cheeks as she looked away.

"How very tactful." She had regained her composure, smiling again but ever watchful. "But it's not so short a lifetime indeed. I'm twenty-four years old, you know."

"Do, pray, accept my apologies." He laughed down at her, looking amused at the sparkle in her clear hazel eyes. "A hoary old age indeed. But I must repeat myself, that seems a mere child to an elderly gentleman of ten years seniority."

Across the snowy linen of the dining table, Charlotte noticed that Elaine Knightley was watching them with an indulgent smile as she listened to Barnard's plodding account of the spring sowing, until something, an unhappy thought or a sudden discomfort perhaps, wiped away the smile as she hunched her shoulders a little and, frowning, bit her lip. Charlotte felt a moment's anxiety but Mr Knightley claimed her attention once more and when she looked again at his wife Mrs Knightley's serene smile was once more in place, that greyish tinge to her skin quite vanished.

"Pray allow me," he was saying to Charlotte, "just this once, to convey our condolences, my own and my wife's, on the sad loss of your husband. I am better acquainted with his brother, Barnard, as it happens — we were at school together — but I always found Frampton an amiable enough fellow."

"You are too kind." She was serious once more, looking earnestly up into his friendly blue eyes. "I fear I scarcely deserve such generosity, for I myself was barely acquainted with Frampton, you know."

He looked taken aback at her frankness but apparently decided that he liked her for it as he gave her a nod of approval.

"I am afraid Mrs Richmond Senior was much distressed by circumstances, the difficulty in identifying the bodies, I mean."

"Yes," she answered him very gravely. "In fact, it was decided — by the colonel, I believe — that there should be a memorial service which encompassed all the fallen, for there was only one survivor of the ambush and he was sadly wounded. In fact, they say he may never recover his wits from a savage blow to the head. The colonel was most kind to me, but I know he was greatly disturbed by the whole affair. Indeed, there were shocking rumours flying around in the bazaars and in the cantonments."

He expressed surprise and she continued in the same low, confidential voice, making sure that Agnes and her mother-in-law could not hear.

"Indeed, although, of course, hysteria was running very high at the time, I myself heard every rumour under the sun, ranging from talk of incompetence to treachery." She shuddered slightly. "I cannot forget that once, when I entered a room unexpectedly, a conversation was hastily choked off." She shook her head slightly, raising a hand to shade her eyes for a moment. Meeting Mr Knightley's grave but friendly gaze, she whispered: "The man who was speaking, I think he was a major, was saying that murder had been done."

CHAPTER
TWO

Charlotte was glad to follow the household custom and retire early. "Oh yes." She gave a weary sigh when Agnes accompanied her to the cosy bedroom along the corridor. "It has certainly been a most exhausting day."

She unpinned the severely plain black silk cap that sat primly on her shining brown hair and laid it carefully on the walnut dressing table. Just because I seem to have landed in clover, she reminded herself, there is no reason to be careless with my clothes. It may all come unravelled at any moment and I'll be back where I was before, relying on my wits as usual.

"You should have telegraphed to us," Agnes scolded fondly. "Fancy coming all the way from Southampton today. And straight off the boat, too. Why did you not spend the night at some hotel?"

"It is hardly 'all the way' from Southampton, Agnes, it is less than twelve miles, after all. Besides, I couldn't afford a hotel," came the blunt reply.

"But surely, dear Frampton . . .?"

"Frampton's affairs were left in such disarray" — Charlotte frowned as she stared in the mirror — "that it was not possible to make out just what I was entitled to, so the colonel simply made me a small allowance from Frampton's pay until things could be settled. Besides, the state of unrest in the country made everything ten times more difficult. That is why I have taken so long to reach England." No need, at present, to mention the nebulous whisper she had heard, about funds missing from the officers mess, or that other whisper, even more nebulous, concerning the truth of Frampton's death.

"Oh, oh yes, I see." Agnes plainly did *not* see but Charlotte did not enlighten her. "We did wonder, dear. After all, it is nearly six months since . . ."

Charlotte turned to her with an apologetic smile.

"Indeed I did not mean to be so dilatory in making myself known to my new family. But with the Sepoys on the rampage and all communications broken down, it simply wasn't safe to travel far. I spent the time making my way to the west coast whenever I could find an escort, stopping at settlements on the way and helping with the nursing where and when I was able. Besides all the wounded, there was an outbreak of cholera, you see."

She stood up and gave Agnes's shoulder a squeeze.

"I'm a capital nurse, you must know. We lived in such remote parts all my life that I had to learn to be doctor and nurse together. If you are ever taken ill, I promise you I'll nurse you splendidly back to health!"

With these encouraging words, she propelled Agnes gently towards the door and out on to the landing.

"There now, I'm sure you are just as tired as I. It's plain to see that all the management and worry of the house falls on your shoulders. Off to bed now, and thank you for my kind welcome."

As Charlotte closed the door firmly but gently on Agnes, she read first bewilderment in the plain, honest face, then a dawning realization. Oh dear. Charlotte frowned guiltily. I shouldn't have said that; Agnes is obviously a willing doormat and I may have sown the seeds of rebellion. I must watch my tongue, she scolded herself, it is no part of my plan to make myself unpopular with Mrs Richmond. I am to be meek and mild and dutiful; quite unexceptionable.

Alone in her own room at last, Charlotte undressed, feeling unutterably weary. She blew out her candle and climbed into the four-poster bed with its blue brocade drapery, while she struggled to call to mind something that had struck her about her new family's appearance. It was no use, the notion refused to reappear; as she had admitted to Agnes Richmond, it had been an exhausting day.

The previous night had been a sleepless one as the ship made her way across the Bay of Biscay and up the English Channel; many passengers had scarcely bothered to retire to their cabins at all, preferring to watch the coastline and pick out familiar landmarks in the shadowy greyness of early dawn. While they were thus preoccupied, Charlotte was tempted, impelled by habit and the lifelong, ever-present anxiety as to money, to flit from empty cabin to empty cabin, employing skills learned from her enterprising stepfather; a ring here, a few coins there, a brooch or two, calculating to a nicety the risks involved. She had actually opened her door when conscience intervened. No, that's all in the past, she vowed, life is different now and I want to be like other people. I'm going to be *respectable* from now on.

On disembarking at Southampton some time after noon, Charlotte had stowed her luggage safely for the time being while she bade farewell to her shipboard acquaintances.

"No, no," she assured more than one kindly enquirer, with scant regard for truth. "I am to be met shortly. No, thank you, I am not afraid to wait by myself."

Old habits died hard and Charlotte had been careful to make herself pleasant to the other passengers but to avoid intimacy.

"Don't get too friendly," *her stepfather always said*. "Keep a little distance. That way you can stick to a simple story and not forget which one you've told; let people get too close and you start making up more and more elaborate tales so you'll trip yourself up. Mark my words, Charlotte, that's the way to disaster. Always remember, love, keep it simple."

No danger of forgetting, not ever. Will Glover's words had been dinned into her since childhood so she turned on her heel with a friendly nod and wave of farewell and made her way into the anonymity of town, with a definite end in sight.

On the way up the High Street, her eyes darted from side to side, taking in the terrain, shrinking a little at the press of people while marvelling at the size and bustle of the city and pausing now and then to admire the grey stone of the mediaeval walls with the great arched gateway that was the Bargate, as a passerby told her, visible in the distance. Yet another of the abiding watchwords of her upbringing: "*Always take notice of your surroundings,*" Lady Meg used to say. "*A sensible woman will always know where to find a church, a bank, a pawn shop and the nearest stagecoach stop in case embarrassment forces an early retreat.*"

Charlotte hesitated outside a wide-fronted building at number 57 High Street, but it proved to be the offices of the Peninsular and Oriental Steam Ship Company and she was disconcerted to be hailed by one of the officers from the ship. He seemed disposed to linger so she gracefully side-stepped his conversation and admiring glances and with a hasty nod of farewell soon found what she was seeking, yet another imposing building that must certainly be a bank, flanked by an equally large building that was evidently an inn. She had already asked a porter where to find the railway station — Lady Meg's advice needed to be revised as her own hurried departure from England had pre-dated the spread of the railways — and that sudden gleam was surely caused by sunlight breaking through the murk of a nearby alley to shine on to the golden balls of a pawnbroker's shop.

As for some of Lady Meg's other precepts, she would make use of them all in good time as need arose.

"Business first, then something to eat," she determined and headed down the alley, whisking her mother's rose-patterned shawl around her shoulders and hastily tucking a matching velvet rose into her bonnet. Her appearance thus altered (just in case), another of Will Glover's exhortations, she assumed an air of tremulous respectability as she entered the dingy emporium and spun the pawnbroker a tale of a deceased grandmother and an ailing mother fallen on hard times, displaying the spoils of her anxious journey through India to the coast and safe passage to England.

"You wish to sell some jewellery, young lady? Might I see the pieces, miss?"

The shopkeeper perused the documents of owner-ship — letters from a fond parent detailing a bequest — and, finding them satisfactory, handed Charlotte the modest sum they agreed. I should hope so too, she thought with quiet satisfaction, those letters are a convincing touch, they took me hours to write on the voyage home and even Pa would have been proud of such workmanship. And I didn't even steal those brooches and rings. She smiled faintly, remembering the abandoned baggage cart she and her escort had discovered. You couldn't call it stealing, just picking things up by the roadside.

Once out of sight of the shop, she removed the shawl and the velvet rose and tucked them into her carpet bag, before making her way, with the firm and measured tread of an unobtrusive, well-born, though grief-stricken young lady, up the steps to the banking house.

"A deposit, madam? It is a little unusual, madam, for an unaccompanied lady. Is not your husband . . .? Oh my goodness, pray, madam, do not distress yourself. Ah, Mrs Frampton Richmond of Finchbourne? *Most* certainly, Mrs Richmond, pray take a seat for a moment." Mention of Finchbourne and the Richmond name eased the transaction considerably and the tearful mention of her recent widowhood evoked manly sympathy.

"We do not ourselves have the honour of providing banking services for Mrs Richmond and Mr Barnard Richmond, but in the circumstances there can be no difficulty, no difficulty at all."

There was indeed no difficulty and Charlotte, glowing with the unaccustomed comfort of security in the bank — enough to live on for a while if the Richmonds turned her away — took herself next door to The Star to order a light meal before tackling the journey to Finchbourne and confronting the next stage in her new existence.

"You went into a public *house*?" Agnes had moaned when Charlotte sketched out her day's activities. "And a *bank*? Oh Charlotte, dear Charlotte, pray do not mention this to Mama, she would be so dismayed." She fluttered and twittered for a good ten minutes before plucking up courage to caution her headstrong colonial sister. "Perhaps, indeed I am sure, things are different in other parts of the world, but here — oh dear, pray, do not take it amiss, dear Charlotte — here, a young lady may not enter the portals of a place of business without the support of a gentleman of her family.

Indeed, even then it would be a most extraordinary proceeding. Pray, pray, do not let Mama — or Lily, *especially* not Lily — know that you did so."

Finchbourne was a world way from the eucalyptus gums and the wattle and the emptiness of her native haunts; a long way, too, she hoped, from the constant removals and the fear — usually a certainty — of discovery and disgrace. As for that moment of temptation on the ship last night, she frowned. Thank God I stopped myself in time. I'm a different person, in a different life, she reminded herself, I must never, ever think of such a thing again, no matter what. Sitting up in the handsome four-poster bed with its figured brocade hangings, she considered her future. Whatever the state of Frampton's finances there would, she thought, be at least a small, regular income for her, and that would be riches indeed compared to what had gone before.

Restlessly she plumped up her pillows and considered her situation. I've never had a real home, she thought, never had a corner of the world that I could call my own, but this shall be it and I'll do nothing to jeopardize it. I'm young Mrs Richmond of Finchbourne now, and here I'll stay.

Yes, she mused as she lay back in her clean, soft, *expensive* linen sheets, I've come a long, long way. Look at me, Ma, I'm a real lady now!

Next morning, Charlotte was summoned to Mrs Richmond's bedchamber by a servant who announced herself as Old Nurse, sole prop and mainstay to the afflicted mistress of the house. This worthy officiously plumped her mistress's pillows and removed to a small side table a tray containing the remains of a slight, nourishing breakfast of haddock, stewed mutton kidneys, bread and butter with marmalade and what looked like a now empty vat of porridge.

"Being such a poor, sad creature I have to take my breakfast in bed, you see." Mrs Richmond Senior touched a dainty napkin to her lips, sighed and smiled her sad, sweet smile, inviting Charlotte's sympathy. Her lips tightened slightly when Charlotte responded briskly.

"Very sensible, ma'am."

"My nights, you know, are so long, so disturbed by grief and nightmare, that I am of no use at the breakfast table, such a cripple as I am . . ." As Charlotte maintained her polite smile, Mrs Richmond seemed to feel herself to be at a loss, even more so when Charlotte continued in that same pleasantly practical vein.

"How may I be of service to you, ma'am? I'm exceedingly grateful to you for offering me a home and I hope you will make use of me. I'm a good nurse. I was telling Agnes last night that living in such a vast, empty country accustoms one to making do. I'm also an economical housekeeper and quite a good farmer and gardener, though I do concede that I know nothing about English flowers or crops. But I do want to make myself useful to you and I hope you will make use of me."

Mrs Richmond blinked.

40

"I hardly know . . ." she groped for words. "But my dear child . . ." she temporized in order to overcome her surprise. "You are dear Frampton's widow, there is no necessity for you to be of service, none whatsoever. You are my daughter now and must make your life here with us and have a good, long rest. Later perhaps you might busy yourself with some of my many charity works — Agnes can assist you there. You must know that I concern myself passionately with many of the ills of today's world, the *sins*, the *degradations* . . ." The dangerously hysterical throbbing note that Charlotte had previously remarked returned to her voice as she spoke, and she pressed her fingers to her temples, but after a pause she continued more calmly. "My dear, there can be no question of nursing, or — or farming!"

Charlotte swallowed the comment that sprang to her lips and Mrs Richmond nodded, apparently approving her reticence.

"For today, dear child, I suggest that Agnes might show you our church, where for generations the Richmonds have lain in all their glory, such a noble, noble race. I have caused a stone tablet in memory of dear Frampton to be placed above the Manor pew. I cannot, myself, see it except through a veil of tears." She paused, giving way to a melancholy sob and Charlotte silently passed her a clean handkerchief from the bedside table crowded with medicine bottles and miniatures as well as small marble hands and feet. What in God's name could they be *for*? Charlotte wondered.

"Thank you, dear child. As I was saying, *I* am such a poor wretched creature that I am totally undone whenever I think of my poor boy, but I dare say young people are made of sterner stuff."

As Charlotte turned soberly towards the door, Mrs Richmond sniffed and added a parting thrust.

"I must say, dear, that you seem to have recovered remarkably — indeed, *astonishingly* — well from such a punishing blow. I suppose I must be glad to see you in good spirits though of course, as I say, as a mother I am totally suspended by grief."

Her face suddenly impassive, Charlotte looked back at the woman in the bed.

"I cannot tell you, ma'am," she said in a level voice. "I cannot describe the emotions I experienced when I heard that my husband would not be returning to me."

Charlotte closed the door quietly behind her and leaned back against the solid oak, feeling drained. No, she shuddered, nothing would, nothing could, ever come close to the relief of learning that Frampton Richmond was dead.

It had been an arranged marriage in every sense of the word, she recalled wryly. She had needed a husband's protection, Frampton had needed to parade a semblance of marital bliss. As if I cared about his way of life, she thought now, with a tolerance borne of a wide experience far beyond the reach of most grown men, let alone so young a woman. Frampton might have lived his life as he pleased for all I cared, she frowned, as long as he let me alone and maintained a veneer of respectability to pacify the regiment. But he didn't keep to his side of the bargain . . .

Time to pull yourself together, Charlotte, she scolded herself briskly. And now she came to think of it, Mrs Richmond hadn't felt it necessary to apologize further for Lady Frampton's gaffe of last night. Perhaps she knew Agnes did it for her or perhaps she simply didn't care.

What Charlotte did mind, very much, was her own unguarded moment of anger at the old lady. Righteous indignation — especially so unwarranted — had no place in her role at present, time enough for that once she was established and accepted as young Mrs Richmond, the widow. Yes, she scolded herself, that was a near thing with Mr Knightley, too. She had nearly let slip too much about herself by far. Though perhaps he wouldn't care, she thought with a smile, recalling the intelligence and good humour that coloured Mr Knightley's every word. Still, even if it made no difference to him, she could think of others not so far away who would be much less tolerant if they knew all about her. If they knew everything about me, everything about Ma and Will, she reflected, I should be out of this house at once, marched off in disgrace to the nearest magistrate probably.

Conscious of a sudden chill, Charlotte set these thoughts aside and made her way to the breakfast parlour where the rest of the Richmond family were at the trough, shovelling in eggs and fish, stewed kidneys and bacon at a great rate.

"Charlotte, dearest!"

That was Agnes, of course, leaping fervently from her chair to embrace the new arrival.

"Sit down here beside me, dear. Hoxton . . ." She summoned the butler. "Help Mrs Frampton to some kedgeree. Did you sleep well, dear Charlotte? I do hope so. If not I will see about changing your room. Sometimes that room suffers when the wind is in the east —"

"Please, Agnes," Charlotte protested with a good-humoured pat on the other woman's shoulder. "I slept soundly all night, pray do not distress yourself. It was such a novelty to sleep in a bed that did not pitch and toss from side to side."

"Pitch and toss?"

That was the bovine Barnard, looking puzzled.

"The ship," Charlotte explained and he nodded, pleased to be enlightened.

"Never been on a ship, myself," he said smugly. "The Richmonds have always been land animals, you see. Poor old Frampton was always sick as a dog, he used to say, when he was on a transport ship."

Agnes cried out at this reminder of the dear departed and Charlotte had to spend a few minutes assuring her and the crestfallen Barnard that she could indeed bear to hear his name mentioned. All the while she watched them, a glance in the mirror opposite revealing a growing twinkle in her bright, alert, hazel eyes. Land animals, of course! That was just what they were, that was the likeness she had been struggling to make out.

Barnard was not the only bovine member of the family; they made up a herd, from the plump little dairy cow who was Mrs Richmond to big, beefy Barnard with his great shoulders, heavy haunches and long, weathered face. He and Agnes had inherited their shiny bulls' eyes from their mother and Agnes, too, was beef to the ankle under her horsehair crinoline, unless Charlotte was much mistaken.

The late Mr Richmond, né Frampton, had probably been of the same ilk. Like had married like, she mused, observing his mother as she mooed loudly at her grandchildren on topics ranging from her corns to the toughness of the toast she was chewing, while tossing scraps of meat from the vast serving platter before her to the indolent spaniel at her feet. She always relished her food, she had confided to her new granddaughter the previous evening after dinner. Indeed, she and her late husband, an elderly London merchant, had become acquainted over a roast mutton dinner she had served him in the chop house belonging to her aunt. It had been, she said, her healthy appetite as much as her lively cockney spirits that had captivated the old gentleman.

"Good morning, Charlotte. How are you today?"

That was her other sister-in-law, Lily. Silly little Lily to misquote Lily's revered papa. Presumably Lily had decided to be gracious to the newcomer; she was certainly baring her gums in what, one must charitably assume, was meant as a friendly gesture. Now *Lily* was less a cow than a plump, pink pig, from her dainty little trotters to her pert little turned-up snout.

Charlotte grabbed her napkin to her face to disguise her involuntary chuckle at the trend of her thoughts, pausing only to ponder on her own likeness. And what am I then, she wondered ruefully. A weasel? Or perhaps a snake in the grass?

"Mrs Richmond suggested I should take a walk around the village this morning." She turned to Agnes. "Would you like to come with me or shall I make my own way?"

"On no account!"

Agnes was scandalized and said so in several different ways. At last Charlotte could bear no more so she interrupted the usual welter of half sentences and little flutters of anxiety.

"What time would you like me to be ready, Agnes?"

"I hardly know, dear Charlotte. Would eleven o'clock be too early, do you think? I have to speak to Cook, you see, and Mama always likes to give me her commands too."

"I have some mending to do, so eleven o'clock will suit me excellently," Charlotte told her firmly, draining her cup and setting it down firmly on its delicate saucer. "Do you usually have family prayers?"

"Oh my goodness, do you think we should, dear?" Agnes began to flutter again, covered with mortification at this family shortcoming. "Forgive me, dear Charlotte, I had forgotten that your stepfather was a clergyman by profession. Naturally you are accustomed to a greater observance of religion. We must seem shockingly lax to you, dear."

"Of course I don't think so." Charlotte concealed a sigh and set about reassuring her sister-in-law. "In fact, I'm only too thankful to find that I shan't be expected to join in family worship every day. Will, my stepfather, used to say that family prayers flourished in the households of the ungodly and that living a principled life was much more acceptable to God than outward show." Lily merely shot her a scornful glance and Barnard appeared frankly puzzled at such a concept, while Lady Frampton was too absorbed in greedily shovelling a spoonful of sugar, sneaked from the bowl, into her mouth, to pay attention to anything else. Charlotte turned resolutely to Agnes. "I do look forward to visiting the church with you later on, though, dear Agnes."

She rose, pushed her chair firmly away and nodded pleasantly to the rest of the family as she left the room. Apart from their initial greeting, neither Lily nor Barnard had addressed any remark to her, while Lady Frampton had been too busy addressing her breakfast to suffer any interruption. The old woman must have the constitution of an ox — there it was again, that family likeness — to put away such gargantuan amounts of food and yet have survived to at least eighty years of age.

In spite of her brusque manner, the old lady rather appealed to Charlotte. Touchingly anxious to make amends for her unfortunate comments of yesterday, she had been kindness itself during an evening distinguished by its tedium. When the Knightleys had taken their leave, the old lady had remarked, in an audible aside to Charlotte, that she couldn't blame them for going so soon; she was longing for her own bed too. Yes, I've met your like, Charlotte nodded inwardly, at plenty of places from Sydney to Melbourne, from Adelaide to

Freemantle, and many a scrubby little settlement between them.

And some of those old ladies were by no means fools, she reminded herself; some of them saw through Will Glover where other members of the congregation could find no fault in him, bowled over as they were by the liveliness that sat so charmingly with his soulful blue eyes. Better keep an eye on Lady Frampton and beware, too, that shrewd old gaze.

It was a relief to step briskly out into the soft, spring beauty of an April day in the south of England and to stop for a moment to survey the old Tudor manor house with its grey stone front and crooked, haphazard roof, the Queen Anne wing tacked on at an angle, blending in now after 150 or more years, red brick mellowed now to a pleasing pink.

"I felt so cooped up on board that ship," Charlotte confided to Agnes as they set off on the grand circular tour of the small town. "I'm used to miles and miles of open country. You can't imagine how different and vast the sky is in Australia. This seems like a country in miniature."

Pausing to admire the ducks on the village pond, Charlotte waved a hand towards the main street. "Southampton, yesterday, was so vast I could scarcely take it in, but this is so — so cosy. You must understand, Agnes, that to me a town has nearly always meant a collection of tin shacks, but this is so pretty." She gazed round at the picture-book surroundings with satisfaction, noting the brick and flint cottages, and dragged Agnes across the road to stare at the large plate-glass windows in the draper's shop. "Look at that window, and oh! What's this next door? The chemist's? I've seen those coloured glass jars and bottles in Sydney, but never in a village."

Agnes looked delighted at such enthusiasm and patted Charlotte's hand. "A few years ago a speculator settled here and decided to transform the village into a kind of inland spa. The air is so very clear and fresh here, you see, with the pines and heaths, and there are the chalybeate spring waters not far away in Southampton. He thought it a settled prospect; we're on the junction line here, of course, and not far from Winchester." She sighed. "He introduced gas lighting too. Finchbourne was to be completely up-to-date and a show place, but unfortunately his bank failed. It was such a pity — several of the local gentry lost a good deal of money in his scheme, and it would have benefited the local people so greatly."

Charlotte listened with interest then dragged Agnes to admire a clump of primroses at the edge of the road and to marvel at the snowy drift of blossom decorating a blackthorn tree. "So much *green*! I am accustomed to dry, dusty earth, mile upon mile of it. You can have no idea what it is like to one who was brought up where the land can go seven years without rain! And even when I went to India . . . No, you cannot imagine and neither could I have done so, even though everyone tried to tell me what England was like."

"Perhaps you have the English countryside in your blood," suggested Agnes kindly. "Your mama was

English, was she not? What part of the country did she come from?"

"Somerset, I believe," Charlotte replied, knitting her brows. "I don't precisely recall that she ever told me the name of the town."

No, she hadn't, had she. "*Don't bother me, dearest,*" was her constant refrain. "*It's all ancient history now; let's look ahead to the next adventure!*" It had all been an adventure for Molly Glover, every last second of it, not excepting those moments that even an accomplished optimist like Molly had found hard to infuse with excited anticipation.

Charlotte angrily brushed a tear from her cheek, hoping that Agnes was too preoccupied with nodding to the various cottagers they passed on their stately progress around the village green. No such luck; here was Agnes with a handkerchief at the ready.

"Oh, Charlotte! Pray forgive me, I did not mean to distress you, and of course I've made you think of poor, dear Frampton, too."

"Nonsense, dear Agnes. I am quite composed, thank you. I don't know why I . . . It is nearly a year now since Ma . . . since my mama died."

"Was it quite sudden?" Agnes was clearly trying to be tactful.

"Yes," Charlotte said bleakly. "She died in childbirth."

"Oh! Oh dear." Agnes was nonplussed. "She must have been rather . . . I mean she cannot have been very young to be —"

"She was thirty-seven," Charlotte answered abruptly. "It was a breech birth, unexpectedly early, and there was no doctor near at hand. The midwife was drunk and she botched the job. My stepfather and I had been visiting an outlying farm and arrived barely in time to bid her farewell."

"*Look after your little brother and love him,*" Molly had panted, weakly tugging at her daughter's hand. And Charlotte, dry-eyed and with a cold stone in place of her heart, had promised, even as she looked across the room at the waxen little corpse in the makeshift crib. Will Glover had wept bitterly but Charlotte had not shed a tear when they buried mother and son in the little township on the south coast of the Australian continent, and she had remained dry-eyed all through the journey north to Freemantle and throughout the business of obtaining Will's appointment to the Indian station.

I cried for Will, for Pa, she thought now in astonishment, and I cried for myself when I married Frampton. But this is the first tear I've shed for Ma.

Agnes was eyeing her charge with affectionate anxiety as she steered the younger girl towards the church. "Come and sit in the porch, dear," she persuaded her. "It's nice and cool and you can compose yourself. What a sad tale, your poor mama, and so young. Why she must have been . . ." Agnes did some arithmetic on her fingers and gasped. "Why, she must have been nothing but a child when you were born!"

Charlotte nodded, struggling with the tears that again threatened to overcome her.

"There now." Agnes had settled the matter to her own satisfaction. "She and your papa must have been desperately in love to marry at such an age."

"Yes indeed." Charlotte had pulled herself together now. "I think *desperate* might well be the word Mama would have used at that time. Now, won't you show me the church, Agnes? *Agnes?*"

Agnes was not paying any attention. Her bull's-eye gaze was aimed at the lych gate through which a young man in holy orders was making his way. Charlotte shot a glance at her sister-in-law and was not surprised to see an unbecoming crimson suffuse her cheeks. Oh, for heaven's sake, she sighed. She might have known Agnes would be in love with the curate. Oh well, let's take a look at him. Hmm, well, there's a surprise, balding and spindly, no accounting for taste; though, to be fair, she's probably never had much to choose from.

"Oh! M-m-miss Richmond! I did not see . . . I mean . . . how do you do?"

"Oh! Mr Benson! How very . . . are you . . .? I thought . . ."

Charlotte looked on benignly as the curate stammered and Agnes fluttered until she thought it was time to take a hand.

"Agnes?" She nudged the other woman with a firm though gentle elbow.

"Oh, oh, of course, how remiss of me. Charlotte, this is Mr Percy Benson, curate to Uncle Henry."

52

"How do you do, Mr Benson." Charlotte shook the curate's limp and clammy hand. "Uncle Henry?"

"M-m-miss Richmond's uncle, the Reverend Henry Heavitree, vicar of this parish," explained the curate, his Adam's apple bobbing and his gaze straying respectfully towards Charlotte's companion.

"Uncle Henry is Mama's elder brother, her half-brother, I should say," Agnes explained. "My maternal grandmother was a widow, a Mrs Heavitree, with a small child — that was Uncle Henry — when she married my grandfather."

Charlotte nodded, waited for some initiative from her companions, shrugged at the lack of it and penetrated the gloom of the ancient porch by herself, to open the door into the church, admiring, as she did so, the enormous iron ring which lifted the latch. Agnes and Mr Benson made no move to follow her and she caught snatches of their stilted conversation as they stood in the porch like waxworks, Agnes still with that unbecoming flush mottling her cheek, and the curate gaping like a mooncalf at her. Oh well, let them be, she thought tolerantly, wondering if Mrs Richmond knew about this.

Inside the church Charlotte paused and stared about her in delighted awe. Accustomed as she was to the corrugated iron shacks common in the townships, a genuine twelfth-century church built of stone was a revelation to her.

"Oh! Oh, but this is wonderful," she gasped aloud as she gazed at the cool simplicity of the grey walls, the plain but elegant font and the ancient oak of the rood screen, all of it lit by the incredible glowing light streaming from the stained glass in the windows.

"I think so too, so I'm exceedingly glad to hear you admire it," chimed in a familiar voice, and when the startled Charlotte looked around her she saw Mrs Knightley, her fellow diner from the previous evening. She was sitting in a pew at the front of the church, just below the pulpit and she smiled and beckoned to Charlotte.

"Do come and join me, won't you? I'm afraid I can't get up and come to you — my legs won't carry me so far."

Charlotte hurried down the aisle and sat beside the woman she had liked on sight.

"I'm so sorry," she began. "I didn't realize that you . . ."

"That I was such a poor, sad creature?" Elaine gave a sudden peal of delighted laughter. "There, I sound just like your dear mama-in-law, don't I?" She covered her mouth, looking like a guilty child. "Oh dear, what will you think of me?" She sobered a little and patted Charlotte's hand reassuringly.

"The truth is that I have never been very strong and for the last few years my health has been rather poor. I had — I had a baby but something went badly wrong and the baby did not live, and I . . . well, never mind, I go along very well, after all."

Charlotte was moved by the blend of sadness and bright courage in the older woman's voice and in mute sympathy she squeezed the too thin, too delicate fingers that still held hers in a cool, friendly clasp.

54

"Still, enough of being morbid." Elaine spoke lightly and her eyes began to dance. "Surely you are not here alone? I expected to see you escorted by Agnes at the very least so that Mrs Richmond may hear every detail of your response to the sacred shrine of the Richmond family and particularly to Frampton's memorial tablet."

"Oh Lord." Charlotte jumped up in haste. "Thank heaven you reminded me. Where is it? I had better go and admire it and see if I can squeeze out a tear or two." She moved into the aisle and cast an enquiring glance around the building. "Where is it, please? She has already expressed astonishment that I can be so composed in the face of my great tragedy, but she supposes, charitably enough, that a mother's grief is the greater wound."

Elaine flashed her enchanting girlish grin at the deadly parody of Mrs Richmond in her best martyr mode and nodded towards the north wall.

"There, just beside the window with the primroses on the sill. But you have not answered me. Surely you have not shaken off Agnes?"

"Oh no." Charlotte was marvelling at the florid prose that commemorated her late, unlamented spouse. "We encountered the curate, and Agnes and he were instantly turned into pillars of salt; they were in the porch last time I looked. No doubt it was reprehensible of me to leave them unchaperoned but it seemed a kindness. She is scarcely a young girl, after all."

She paused in her exploration of the church to wrinkle her nose. "Heavens! What is that smell?"

"Incense," Mrs Knightley told her. "We are very high church indeed in Finchbourne. The village adores its saints' days and rituals and so forth. The vicar fell under the influence of Dr Pusey some twenty years ago . . ." She smiled as Charlotte paused in her progress up the aisle and looked at her, a question hovering on her lips. "Dr Pusey is a leading light of the Oxford Movement," she explained. "He and others are trying to bring the ideals of an earlier age into the Church and this is their way of doing it. It works very well in the village. The people feel there *should* be mystery and pageant and colour and uncanny goings-on. It makes a nice change from everyday life."

Elaine seemed about to make some further comment when the ancient tranquillity of the church was doubly disturbed. The west door creaked open to reveal Agnes and the curate as they entered with due diffidence and reverence, at the same time as the vestry door crashed open, shuddering back on its hinges, and in roared a minotaur in clerical garb, with a shotgun on his shoulder and several dead magpies on a string in his other hand.

Good God, thought Charlotte in amusement. It's a bull in a surplice, another side of beef on legs. It must be Uncle Henry Heavitree — it can surely be none other.

"Who's that?" roared the vicar, his head thrust belligerently forward as he charged towards the body of the church. "Is that you, niece Agnes? What the devil do you think you're doing, dallying there with my curate, hey?"

56

"Oh, Uncle Henry," twittered Agnes, wringing her hands and ducking her head in confusion, evidently trying to distract her uncle's attention from the wretched Benson, who was sidling away towards the bell-tower. "I brought dear Charlotte. Mama wished her to see dear Frampton's memorial."

"Who? What's that you say? Charlotte? What d'ye mean, girl? Speak up! Who the devil is Charlotte?"

"Oh, Uncle Henry, Uncle Henry! Of course, you have not heard. Here is our poor, dear Charlotte . . ." A sob rose and Agnes had to gulp convulsively. "Poor, dear Frampton's brave young widow, who arrived in Finchbourne only yesterday. Charlotte, let me present dear Mama's brother."

Charlotte held out her hand and dropped a demure curtsey to the bulky monster before her.

"How do you do, sir. How very much you resemble your late nephew Frampton. The likeness is startling."

In fact the resemblance was only apparent at close range. Henry must weigh half as much again as the late Frampton and was twice as broad, but the likeness was sufficient to give Charlotte an inward shudder.

"Frampton, hey? That damned whelp threatened me with the bishop when he caught me with the archdeacon's wife, damned trollop. Pusillanimous non-conformist. Good riddance, I say. He was a damned Bulgarian, young Frampton. Never forgave me for peppering his breeches with shot when he was up to no good with —"

The Reverend Henry Heavitree broke off his remarks and took stock of his new niece and his eyes lit up suddenly with a gleam she found all too familiar in men. Not *that* much like his nephew after all, she sighed, firmly disentangling her hand from his fervent, sweaty grasp.

"Well, niece Charlotte, do you ride then? Do you hunt, hey? Well, girl, cat got your tongue? D'ye shoot, I say?"

"No, indeed I do not." Charlotte spoke decidedly. "Hunt, that is; hunting has not come my way. I can shoot, sir, and I ride, of course. One can scarcely travel about in Australia without a horse, at least in the parts where we lived."

As for hunting, she shrugged inwardly, she had far too often been the quarry herself, or at least Will had been, for her to enjoy the chase. Let others do as they would. To deflect the interrogation she foresaw, she drew the vicar's attention to his own catch.

"Are you aware, sir, that your magpies appear to be bleeding all over your surplice?"

"Bleeding?" he bellowed. "Bleeding? God's nightgown! Of course they're bleeding girl — the miracle would be if they did *not* bleed, considering I've just shot them! The thieving bastards deserve to bleed!"

"Oh do pray hush, Uncle Henry." Agnes was tugging clumsily at the vicar's sleeve, desperately trying to silence his bellicose outcry. "You have not said 'How do you do' to Mrs Knightley."

"What? Oh, hah, beg your pardon, ma'am. How do you do? I did not see you there."

Mrs Knightley gave him her hand but was spared the rigours of a conversation by the arrival of a footman come to carry her out to the landau. She was looking pale and tired but she made her graceful farewells, with a particular smile to Charlotte and a promise that they should meet again soon for a good long talk. "You must come to call on me very soon," she suggested. "Don't stand on ceremony, you'll always be welcome."

Charlotte took a further turn round the church, struck once more by the serenity and the austere beauty of the place.

"How lovely this is," she remarked to Agnes. "I have seen nothing so wonderful in my whole life."

"It's only a little country church." Agnes halted and turned to stare at Charlotte, her plain face creased in a surprised frown, obviously puzzled by such enthusiasm. "I believe it is well thought of by artistic people but I have always found it quite commonplace. We must take you to see the cathedral at Winchester soon. Now that is truly a magnificent building."

Charlotte smiled slightly and allowed herself to be taken outside.

"We should be making our way home." Agnes was beginning to fuss. "We usually have luncheon soon and Mama will be put out if we are late. You will have ample opportunity, dear Charlotte, to visit the church again. Perhaps you would like to help with the flowers?"

She looked hopeful as Charlotte agreed, with reservations.

"I know nothing about English flowers, Agnes," she warned. "I might do something shocking like filling a vase with weeds."

"Oh no, dear," Agnes began, then a slow smile spread over her face. "Why I do believe you are teasing me, Charlotte, are you not? No matter, whatever you do to the flowers will be more artistic than my own attempts. I have no taste whatsoever, and my flower arrangements often cause grief to poor, dear Mama."

Charlotte was heartened at this glimpse of humour and the prospect of a more congenial Agnes and answered by tucking her sister-in-law's hand into her own arm. They had bidden the vicar and the curate farewell inside the church when Uncle Henry had frustrated his assistant's attempts to escort the ladies to the gate by the simple expedient of bellowing at him not to be such a damned fool, looking damned spoony over a damned woman, and his (Henry's) own damned niece to boot, and to damned well go and count the damned hymnals.

Quite in charity together, the Richmond ladies were shutting the gate behind them, when a gauntly haggard figure in black hailed them from the lane to the side of the church.

"Halt there! Can this be the widow of that monster?" The scarecrow figure of a middle-aged woman approached unpleasantly close and thrust her face, wild-eyed and staring, into Charlotte's. As Charlotte recoiled, the woman nodded. "Well may you look appalled, madam. And well may you thank the Lord thy God for the blessed release that He gave you by ordaining the death of that abomination of desolation!"

Charlotte stood frozen to the spot, too surprised to do anything but inwardly agree with her assailant. Agnes burst into tears and dragged ineffectually at Charlotte's sleeve, frantically trying to tug her away from the woman, and uttering soft cries to try to placate her.

"Oh indeed, Lady Walbury, *pray* do not speak so! Poor, dear Charlotte is but newly arrived in Finchbourne, pray do not discompose yourself so. Oh Charlotte, dearest, do come away at once, you must not stay."

"I suppose they have not told you?" The woman had ceased her rant and spoke in a more or less rational manner as she scanned Charlotte's face, apparently to her satisfaction for she continued in the same conversational tone.

"You look a sensible young woman. Why did you let him bamboozle you? Did they not tell you that the creature you called husband has another, more terrible name? That of murderer?"

"Oh, I could sink into the ground in shame," gasped Agnes. She and Charlotte were hurrying up the Manor drive with as much dignity as they could muster in the circumstances.

"Pray do not mention this to Mama, it could bring on one of her spasms; nor to Grandmama, she would be much distressed. Better not let Lily hear of it either, she would only make a fuss and write to her papa. And perhaps we should not tell poor Barney, he is such a good, bluff sort of fellow, he finds scenes so difficult."

"Of course I won't mention it," Charlotte panted as they hurried through the side door and managed to reach their bedroom floor without being detected. "But

61

you must tell me. Who is that woman and what in the world was she talking about?"

"Here, wash your hands and tidy your hair while I tell you," Agnes urged, all her flutterings and indecision vanished for once. "That's better, now let me borrow your hairbrush, thank you."

"Agnes, if you do not tell me, I'll scream," threatened Charlotte in an agony of curiosity. "Is she a madwoman?"

"No, that is, yes, in a way." Agnes evidently took note of Charlotte's exasperated frown and hastened to explain. "She is Lady Walbury, widow of a local landowner. Her daughter, Emily, was about my age but we were never friends, she was always very modish, and of course they spent much of the year in London." She paused to fiddle with her cuff buttons, then resumed her story. "Last time Frampton was home on leave, about two years ago, was just after Lord Walbury had died and the family were down in the country. Mama likes to believe that Frampton never paid any attention to any young ladies and in general that was true but that last leave he did spend time talking to Emily and I think she believed he was courting her. I don't think he was, though Lily says he was after Emily's money, but she is such a spiteful little cat and in any case, she was scarcely betrothed to Barn, so what would she have known?"

An over-enthusiastic twiddle resulted in a cuff button coming adrift in her hand. "Oh, *bother!* Anyway, Frampton returned to India and shortly afterward we heard first that Emily was ill, and then that she had — had drowned herself in the lake at Walbury!"

Charlotte made a shocked sound and hugged the wretched Agnes. "Well, what had that to do with Frampton?" she asked. "Believe me, Agnes, he had no . . . interest in young ladies. I mean —" She improvized rapidly as Agnes gave her a startled look "I mean he was, er, very shy, yes, that's it, much too shy, though he may well have been attracted to her money, much as I hate to agree with Lily. He was in a very expensive regiment."

Agnes nodded and wiped her eyes with the handkerchief Charlotte proffered.

"That's what we thought," she whispered. "But the day after the funeral Lady Walbury burst into our drawing-room. Poor Lady Walbury, she should have been prostrate with grief upon her bed but she made the most terrible scene, screaming in front of the whole roomful of morning callers that Frampton had led Emily on to expect marriage and that he had done wrong by her."

Agnes paused to tweak her handkerchief from her pocket and apply it to the inevitable tears streaking her face. "She said . . . Oh, it was terrible, she was frothing at the mouth and absolutely demented, shredding into tatters a bouquet of flowers that she actually plucked out of one of our vases, there and then. She said, right there in public, not caring who heard — and the bishop there, too — that Frampton had — that Emily was going to have a baby and that Frampton had callously abandoned her. And that's why Emily had drowned herself."

The sobs burst out again and Charlotte could scarcely blame Agnes for her distress.

"What a ghastly thing to happen," she said quietly. "But Agnes, I really do not believe, I *cannot* believe that Frampton . . . that he would have done such a thing. Truly I don't." No, she considered. He was callous and dissolute, he was a monster, he might even have been a — what did that poor demented soul call him? *An abomination of desolation.* But she did *not* think he got that girl with child.

"Mama would be horrified if she knew I had mentioned it," cautioned Agnes. "She thinks I don't understand but I do know that to — to have a baby without a husband is wicked. Besides, you're a married woman so it's all right to tell you."

Charlotte was relieved of the necessity of answering by a clamour from downstairs.

"There's the gong. Come along, Agnes. Here, splash some cold water on your face and compose yourself. I'll think up some explanation if any is required. Just follow my lead."

"Ah, there you are, dear Charlotte." Mrs Richmond waved the two young women to the table, looking keenly at Agnes. "Have you been crying, Agnes?"

"Agnes and I were at the church, Mrs Richmond." Charlotte's voice was composed. "She showed me Frampton's memorial tablet. We were both much moved."

64

And so we were, though not by the memorial, she thought complacently, especially as Mrs Richmond, with a sad smile of satisfaction, reached out to pat her hand.

"There, there, dear Charlotte. I knew you must feel it just as you ought, indeed as I do, when you saw his name and that dread date carved in stone. The Richmond men have all died with honour, there has never been a coward amongst them. Why, I believe their very bones would cry out should that ever happen!"

Throughout the meal the Richmonds conversed in what Charlotte was coming to recognize as their characteristic manner. Mrs Richmond pronounced, Agnes fluttered, Lily sniped, Lady Frampton said not a word but smacked her lips over her victuals while Barnard carried on a sensible conversation with himself, a most satisfactory auditor, if none other offered. Just now, Charlotte pricked up her ears, he was talking about poor relief.

"I'd like to set up some alms houses." He was gratified at her interest. "And some provision for orphans, as well as general relief. You will not be aware, Charlotte, that ten years ago the harvests failed year after year, sickness was rife, with famine in Ireland, and something not very far from it in this country too, besides revolution all across the Continent."

"Yes." Charlotte was intrigued by this glimpse of a different Barnard, not just the hearty John Bull he presented to public view. "We heard of it from the emigrants and of course my stepfather worked amongst them. One of the convicts, I understand, confessed to

Mr Glover that he actually committed some petty crime in order to be transported, deeming that a preferable fate to starvation at home."

"Enough of political talk, if you please." Mrs Richmond looked displeased. "I trust your stepfather was not a radical, my dear Charlotte?"

"Indeed not, ma'am," Charlotte returned meekly, and the elder lady nodded, well pleased. We had no time for political discussion, Charlotte reminisced silently. It was possible that Will Glover might have been called a radical, she thought with one of her inward smiles. Certainly he believed in the Robin Hood principle of stealing from the rich and giving to the poor, but his identification of "the poor" was elastic and, on many occasions, purely subjective.

As if reading her thoughts, Agnes wondered diffidently what Christian works of charity Charlotte and her mother had undertaken. "Did you have much opportunity, dear?" she mooed. "I do so like to help with visiting in the parish. We hold an annual bazaar for the poor — it's in ten days or so."

"Agnes likes to hold the hands of the old people as they lie a-dying," remarked Lily with a tinkling laugh. "I'm afraid the cottagers find her a decided nuisance. And of course she simply loves visiting the new babies and showering their ungrateful parents with gifts."

Charlotte saw Agnes wince at the cruelty in Lily's voice, but she replied with dignity, despite a heightened colour.

"It is true, Lily dear, that I particularly enjoy the new babies. They are so very sweet. I do indeed love to knit

66

and sew for them. They have little enough to look forward to, some of them, so it's the least I can do."

"It wasn't always possible to be consistent," Charlotte tried to explain as she deflected attention from the hapless Agnes, while seething inwardly at Lily's downright unpleasantness. What was the matter with that wretched girl? Why must she constantly dig at Agnes? "My stepfather was always moving about from one parish to another, he was much in demand." (And *that* is certainly the truth, she thought, suppressing another inward chuckle). "Something like a bazaar would not have been easy to arrange, although we used to sew and knit when we could and Mama tried always to provide food for the very needy. Certainly Pa, Mr Glover, my step-papa, believed in charity." Yes, indeed, particularly that which began at home. That wasn't strictly fair. Will would have given the shirt off his back to a man down on his luck, and frequently had. Dear Will, she sighed fondly, and Agnes clumsily changed the subject, clearly aghast at causing her poor Charlotte to dwell on what she surely supposed to be tender memories.

After luncheon Agnes contrived to speak to Charlotte alone. "I should have warned you, dear Charlotte," she hissed, her large, homely face aglow with kindly concern. "Don't speak to Mama about that speculator I spoke of, the one who brought gas lighting to the village. She and Frampton were vociferous in their opposition to his schemes. It would only upset her to be reminded." She bit her lip. "There's something else. Among the persons who lost money in his venture was Lord Walbury . . ."

Charlotte began to detect a glimmer of motive in the mad widow's accusations. "You mean that not only does Lady Walbury blame Frampton for her daughter's disgrace and death, she also has reason to blame Mrs Richmond and Frampton for their opposition to the speculation? And for its failure and her husband's losses?"

"Precisely." Agnes seemed relieved to find Charlotte so acute. "I believe Lord Walbury had invested very heavily in the scheme and had his fingers badly burnt."

A day or so later when Charlotte dutifully visited Mrs Richmond's bedside, her mother-in-law had a commission for her.

"Ah, Charlotte. Hoxton tells me Mrs Knightley has been unwell again, so you and Agnes must call to enquire after her health. Pray see the gardener about some flowers."

Agnes evinced surprising resistance to this edict, though not in her mother's hearing.

"Oh dear," she complained with damp defiance. "I promised to look over the hassocks in church this morning; some of them are in urgent need of repair."

"Never mind," Charlotte consoled. "I'll visit Mrs Knightley and you go to the church. Who knows, you might encounter Mr Benson there."

"Agnes and the curate?" Elaine Knightley, newly risen from her sickbed, poured morning tea amid the flowers in the conservatory. "What a cliché. I suppose I've noticed them exchanging significant glances but thought little of it. And you say Mrs Richmond does not approve because the wretched Percy is merely the son of a bookseller? Sometimes I really think her passion for her illustrious family name topples over into mania."

"You may be right," sighed Charlotte, relaxing in the warmth of Elaine's gracious hospitality. "Those illustrious ancestors who, without fear or favour, declined every offer of a title because nothing could be better than their sacred name. I was treated to a lecture only yesterday on the valour of Geoffroi de Richmond who went on not one but two crusades, and slaughtered countless unfortunate infidels. As far as I can tell that's all the early Richmonds did, ransacking, pillaging and slaying."

Elaine laughed. "Most of the landed gentry in Europe did likewise, but their descendants don't indulge their ancestor worship quite so assiduously as your mother-in-law. She once informed me that the Richmonds eschewed the vulgarity of a title: 'Better a Richmond with honour, than the shame of strawberry leaves and ducal vainglory,' were her very words." After a moment's hesitation she held out her hand, with a cajoling smile. "Shall we be friends? My life is so circumscribed that I'm greedy for new experiences. My neighbours are so kind and so dull, so predictable." She moved restlessly, frowning. "How ungrateful I am. They're good creatures who never fail to ask after my health. And they never fail to ask me what I mean when I make a joke. How will you fare in that gloomy mausoleum, weighed down by the honour of the Richmonds?"

Charlotte smiled slightly. "You won't believe me when I say that in Finchbourne and the Richmonds I have found my heart's desire." She shook her head as Elaine gave an incredulous laugh. "Oh yes, a quiet, dull, *respectable* life is exactly what I crave."

"Oh my dear." Elaine's eyes softened. "You're so young. Dull respectability? Not for long, Charlotte. You will surely marry again. I'm sure you'll find love one day."

"No!" Charlotte's denial was harsh. "I beg your pardon, I should not be so abrupt. But marriage? I think not, my experience was not such as to encourage me to repeat the experiment. And as for love . . . I saw love in all its glory in Australia; one moment hearts and flowers and the next half-a-dozen children under five in a tin shack in the outback, the mother looking every day of seventy and the father taken to drink." She gave a cynical shrug. "Even my mother and stepfather . . . They loved each other dearly, madly even, but I'll willingly forgo that passion without a moment's regret if I can only have security and peace."

Elaine Knightley raised her eyebrows but made no further comment. After a moment she pressed home her plea for friendship with an even greater warmth. "Let me call you Charlotte — none of this formality for us — and you must call me Elaine."

"I should like that." Charlotte was rather moved by the offer. "I am a little lonely sometimes, though Agnes is always kind. A friend would be a new experience for me. '*Don't get too close, Char, you'll drop your guard.*' Will's words. But my family always called me Char."

"With a hard 'Ch'?" queried Elaine. "Not soft, as in Charlotte?"

"Short for Charlie," came the reply. "There were times — and places — when it was expedient for me to be a boy." Elaine exclaimed and Charlotte nodded, with a tight, reminiscent smile. "You can have no concept of the places I have visited, places where a young girl would have been no more than a lamb to the slaughter. Believe me, it was no mere masquerade when I dressed as Charlie and cut my hair short."

That afternoon Agnes, refreshed by a clandestine meeting with her curate, suggested a visit to Winchester. They delivered various messages then Agnes dragged a willing Charlotte to see the Norman Great Hall with its much-vaunted Round Table, and down the steep High Street into the Cathedral Close.

"You must visit the cathedral, Charlotte," Agnes insisted and, nothing loath, Charlotte followed her sister-in-law out of the sunlight into the sublime and shadowy perfection of the longest nave in Europe.

"Oh!" was all she said as she stood in awed wonder. And "Oh!" was all she could muster as she stood in homage at the tomb of Jane Austen and dashed away a tear of regret that Molly, her lightsome, loving little mother, could not be there to join in her rapture.

"I knew you would appreciate the cathedral." Agnes spoke with quiet satisfaction as she pointed out the ancient encaustic tiles, the tomb of St Swithun (the saintly weather forecaster) and a dozen other delights. She was just apologizing for the fact that they must leave a tour of the cathedral library till another day when she glimpsed an officer in scarlet uniform accompanied by a sedate lady. The soldier glanced at the two women, looked again with recognition and made as if to turn away. Too late. Agnes hailed him and the lady beside him with pleasure, dragging her reluctant companion towards them, gabbling an introduction that Charlotte, who was still in a dream of romance and history, did not hear, though she did manage to gather that the major and his wife were old acquaintances of Mrs Richmond.

Polite commonplaces were exchanged and Charlotte was aware that the soldier was eyeing her in some surprise and his wife with something like pity. When Agnes made some half-sobbing reference to Frampton's much lamented death, the puzzled expression on the major's face altered to something like contempt and he murmured a comment which only Charlotte caught, and that imperfectly: "Whoever killed him deserves a medal."

As she hurried, a little late, into the drawing-room that evening, Charlotte was preoccupied with the major's remark. Why had he said such a thing? What had Frampton done to deserve such censure? What kind of man had she married?

"An Indian, Barnard!" Lily's voice was shrill with excitement and Charlotte broke off her musing to stare at her sister-in-law's flushed and important face. "He was in the village, an Indian in a turban, asking about Frampton!"

CHAPTER
THREE

"What's that you say?" Barnard shook his head in exasperation at the female onslaught. "For God's sake, Lily, stop squealing. Agnes, you're bleating like one of my best ewes. Mama?" He appealed to his mother for assistance. "Won't you explain what they're making such a to-do about?"

Lily and Agnes seemed to have formed an unlikely alliance as they stood on either side of Mrs Richmond's chair, talking at Barnard. Charlotte shivered. Having dropped Agnes at the manor gates (allegedly to speak to a parishioner, though a black cassock glimpsed in the distance suggested another quarry), Charlotte had relished the hour of solitary peace in her room, hoping to gain strength to endure an evening of Lily's little trotters thumping away on the pianoforte, with Agnes reading aloud (badly) from whatever improving tome Mrs Richmond deemed suitable.

"Certainly, my boy." Mrs Richmond's porcelain complexion assumed a delicately complacent flush as she was thus appealed to, supplanting the claims of wife and sister. "But first . . . Ah, Charlotte, do come in and take a glass of sherry, won't you, dear child?"

Fond greetings over, Mrs Richmond continued her tale. "Hush, Agnes, do, Charlotte will be fretted to death by you. You're looking pale, Charlotte, drink your wine. Well, my dears, we were just coming home from calling on some old friends in Hursley. Now, what was I . . . Oh yes, as the carriage drove up to the church we saw Agnes just emerging from the lych gate. You were speaking to the curate, Agnes. I hope he was not making a nuisance of himself?"

"Mama, *really!*" Agnes was scarlet and mortified, with downcast lashes. Lily was champing at the bit to get the story told.

"No, Lily." Mrs Richmond spoke sharply. "Barnard asked *me*, if you recall. Anyway, as we stopped to pick up Agnes, a most singular figure came up to us. An Indian in a turban, would you believe?"

"Good Lord!" Barnard's response was suitably astonished, as was Lady Frampton's: "Well I never!" Charlotte shivered again, horrified, and said nothing.

"Yes, indeed. He was most civil, I must say. He bowed very low and asked, in excellent English, if he had the honour of speaking to ladies of the family of Major Richmond, late of India."

What could he possibly want? wondered Charlotte as she recalled the attitude of the soldier in Winchester Cathedral. Could there be a connection? She shuddered. Surely there could be no threat to her from beyond the grave? Why was there still so much interest in Frampton? Surely we should have heard something by now, if there were anything to know? Besides, she

74

reflected, if it turned out he *was* murdered, I'd willingly shake his killer's hand.

In the days that had followed the ambush in which so many, besides Frampton, had died, nobody had actually spoken directly to Charlotte about her husband's supposed misdemeanours but there had been rumours and counter-rumours as well as the hastily broken-off whispers when she entered a room. In those chaotic days she had dealt almost entirely with the military and it was then that an unguarded comment, hastily denied, had informed her of the rumour concerning the missing regimental funds.

But was that, she wondered now, what had made her husband so unpopular — understandably so — or was there something else involved? Something worse? As she had told Mr Knightley on that first evening at Finchbourne, an officer had said, in her hearing, that murder had been done. But what had he meant? He had denied saying any such thing when she had taxed him, but the fact remained that Charlotte had heard him with her own ears. Had he meant that Frampton had been *murdered*? And if so, how had he known? Could it be, she bit her lip, that Frampton had been killed by one of his own men?

"Did he say what he wanted?" Barnard echoed her own question.

"Just what we enquired." Mrs Richmond applied her ever-present handkerchief to her eyes. "He replied, most politely, that he was in pursuit of information about the circumstances of my dear boy's death and wondered if we had any more news. And most extraordinary of all, he wished to know whether my poor, dear boy's effects had been sent home to us."

"What the devil for?" Barnard's question was natural but blunt and he looked hangdog at his mother's pained sigh.

"I thanked him for his interest," she replied with martyred dignity. "And informed him that as a mere female — and one suffering the agonies of bereavement, at that — I was unable to discuss such painful matters but that he was at liberty to call upon you, Barnard dear, if he wished to pursue the question."

"Did he . . . did he say whether he had been acquainted with Frampton?" asked Charlotte diffidently.

"We asked him that," Lily burst in, unable to restrain herself any more. "And only fancy! He gave the most ferocious frown and said that his only regret was that he had been spared that pleasure as it would have given him great joy to horsewhip Frampton!"

After spending a day vowing one minute to seek out the mysterious Indian gentleman and tackle him about Frampton, and the next to avoid him at all costs lest he know some of her own closely guarded secrets, Charlotte threw herself gratefully into helping Agnes with preparations for the forthcoming bazaar. Her attempts to be of assistance to the members of her new family had met with astonishment.

"Oh no, Miss Char, Mrs Frampton, I *should* say," the cook had protested — once Agnes learned the nickname it had soon become common property amongst the household. "I couldn't dream of you making pastry, or baking a pie. The mistress would be most upset."

"Farming?" Barnard had haw-hawed at the suggestion, rubbing his chin as he stared down at her in perplexity when she cornered him in the stable yard one morning. "What would a pretty little thing like you know about farming, Char?" Fortunately his gaze was diverted elsewhere and he was spared the distress of seeing the frustrated scowl that disfigured the pretty little thing's mobile features. When he turned back to her he kindly patted her hand. "Suppose I look out a nice quiet hack, so you and Lily can enjoy some pleasant saunters?"

"What about your mama's charity work?" Charlotte had caught Agnes one weary, wet day. "She said I might be able to help you, that you would tell me all about it?"

"Oh, of course." Agnes was eager to offer Charlotte assistance. "Here we are, these are the pamphlets that Mama has sent from London. How like you, dear Char, to concern yourself with the unfortunates."

"May I?" Charlotte took a handful of tracts and scanned one or two briefly. "Mmm, good gracious, I think I begin to see the drift of her interest. Fallen women? Children of shame? And what's this? 'A dissertation upon unspeakable practices among depraved young men?'" A momentary gleam lit her face as she wondered if Frampton had been aware of his mother's crusading interests. Who knows, she shrugged, I dare say he would not have cared in any event.

"What exactly does your mama do for these people?" she enquired with interest. "I suppose I could help her distribute leaflets, collect monies raised. Indeed, I could actually help her to raise money for them, that would be diverting as well as useful."

She broke off in the face of Agnes's bemused expression. "Well? What is it, Agnes? Have I said something peculiar?"

"Oh, Char." Agnes smiled kindly and patted her hand. (Why *will* they keep doing that, Charlotte growled inwardly, as though I were a kitten to be placated?) "Mama doesn't do anything about these people, she merely has the tracts sent down to her from London. You could not suppose that she would take more than an, um, intellectual interest in them. She is far too delicate and sensitive for anything such as you suggest."

Charlotte stared at her sister-in-law. "What? Mrs Richmond just *looks* at the leaflets and then what? Doesn't she do anything practical for them, these fallen women and men with their unspeakable practices?"

Agnes seemed shocked at Charlotte's astonished scorn. "Well, of course, Mama does *pray* for them."

Swallowing the sarcastic rejoinder that sprang to her lips, Charlotte resolved to tackle Mrs Richmond on the subject, only to meet with the same explanation.

"Do something, my dear? Good heavens." Mrs Richmond held up her hands in scandalized horror. "What could I do? Raise money for such people? How can you say such a thing, Charlotte? I would not for the world promote such degraded, dissipated individuals."

78

She shuddered and the dramatic, throbbing note crept into her voice as she spoke confidentially. "My dear, as a married woman I can speak to you on such subjects as I cannot to Agnes. The women who lead astray innocent young men of good family are dreadful enough, and how thankful I am that neither of my own dear boys has ever given me a moment's concern; but you might not be aware that there are other, more heinous crimes — unspeakable practices — between men."

Plainly mistaking Charlotte's recoil at the older woman's dramatic gloating Mrs Richmond nodded. "Yes, I thought you would be surprised," she said, becoming the third person that day to pat Charlotte's unwilling hand. "I have only recently become aware myself of this, through these pamphlets that my brother's friend sends me, and the thought fills me with such revulsion that sometimes I cannot speak."

Charlotte finally encountered the mysterious Indian one morning as she came out of the draper's shop where she had been buying a new thimble. He came up behind her, unnoticed.

"I think, madam, that you are that man's widow?"

"What?" She jumped and turned sharply to face him. "I am Mrs Frampton Richmond," she admitted, with a wary note in her voice.

He was tall, turbaned, with fierce moustaches. He loomed over her, cutting out the light and Charlotte edged away from him, her skirt in her hand, prepared to run if necessary.

"Where is it?" he demanded in a rapid undertone. "You must let me have it. It was not his to keep. Had he not died I should have killed him, to atone the disgrace he brought —"

"Here? What's this?" Dr Perry, Mrs Richmond's physician, intervened brusquely. Charlotte swung gladly on her heel to greet him and saw that he was staring past her, brow furrowed at the Indian gentleman now disappearing with rapid strides towards the station.

"Are you all right, Mrs Richmond?"

Dr Perry took her arm and led her to a seat by the village pump. "What did that blackguard want with you?"

"I really don't know." She shook her head, dazed. "He wants something, and wants it urgently, but what it is I have no idea."

That afternoon Charlotte and Agnes worked at making up a heap of small flannel garments ready for the coming bazaar. When she had sewn up the sleeves on yet another little dress, Agnes almost snapped. "For pity's sake, Char," she said, pursing her lips "Go into the village or for a walk on the hills, or something. You'll ruin six months' work in an afternoon if you're not careful. What *can* be wrong with you?" Almost immediately, she was moistly contrite. "Oh, dearest Char, do forgive me, I can't think what came over me."

"You're quite right to scold," Charlotte apologized, thrusting her needle and thread into the sewing basket. "I'm all a-fidget and some fresh air would do me a power of good."

80

It was the work of a moment to run upstairs, find her boots and bonnet and cloak and set off joyously towards the Tudor staircase. A happy thought struck her and she manoeuvred the two half-flights and ran along the landing.

"Lady Frampton? May I take your dog for a walk?"

"Prince Albert? Why, my dear, I suppose you might." The old lady heaved her vast bulk around in her chair and stared at Charlotte's bright face. "The boot-boy takes him for a walk every morning, but I'm sure he would enjoy another, wouldn't you, Prince Albert, dear?"

Charlotte giggled at the lèse majesté. "Won't you come too, ma'am?" she coaxed as she lingered at the doorway. "The air is so clear and warm, I'm persuaded it would do you good."

"Get away with you, me girl." The old lady was clearly highly diverted by the irreverence. "I'd be out of breath before we reached 'alfway down the front stairs! Off you go and give Prince Albert a good, long run."

Charlotte sped lightly down the drive towards the village but hesitated at the gate. A little down the road she could clearly see the snowy turban of the strange Indian. What could it be that he was seeking? she wondered. He had called at the Manor, to be received by a puzzled Barnard, who informed his equally bemused family that the Indian had insisted on inspecting Frampton's effects. Barnard had obliged but the Indian had left muttering what had sounded like sinister threats. As Charlotte wavered now, he evidently spotted her and hastened towards the gates.

No, she thought. I have nothing to tell him, nothing to give him — and he makes me unaccountably afraid. He raised his hand to her. A gesture of greeting, or a threat? Casting dignity to the winds, she turned and ran, for once in agreement with her sister-in-law, Lily, in wishing for a longer carriage drive.

"Such a pity, dear Mrs Richmond," Lily had insinuated in her most sweetly pitying tone the day before, "that Finchbourne Manor is so closely adjacent to the main road and the village. At Martindale, of course, our drive is over a mile long, such a boon in keeping out undesirable persons. But of course, Finchbourne cannot be compared to Martindale . . ."

Charlotte grinned as she recalled her mother-in-law's expression of disgust. It was hard not to feel sympathy when Lily came out with one of her poisonous little digs.

"Indeed there can be no comparison," Mrs Richmond had replied in freezing accents. "Martindale, after all, was built a mere fifty years ago, whereas this house was built in 1520 and before that the noble Richmond family held these lands for generations right back to the days of the Saxons. An old and noble family, dear Lily, as you, alas, would not understand, has its obligations to its tenantry and relishes their proximity."

Magnificent! Charlotte applauded her now, feeling safer as she put more distance between her and the intruder, and headed across the garden and into the park. Lily had been temporarily routed. Agnes had confided that the mention of her family's recent acquisition of wealth was always a sore subject to Lily. Even more painful, according to Agnes, was the thought of her stepmother's fortune which depended unequivocally upon trade, the new chatelaine being the daughter of a Birmingham manufacturer, whose factory produced brass tubes. The worst affront of all, it appeared — and here Agnes had cast a fearful glance over her shoulder — was the existence of the lusty boy whose birth had removed all hope of Lily becoming the chatelaine, in her own right, of her beloved Martindale.

Enough of family squabbles. Here before her were the downs. She emerged from the small ring of woodland, with its hazy drift of early bluebells, at the base of the hill, and whistled to the black and white spaniel to follow her up the chalky path. The dog capered about the green banks, now running up to her with an amiable, lop-sided grin, uttering short, happy yelps. As Prince Albert rubbed his head against her, Charlotte patted him fondly, eventually giving complete satisfaction by throwing a stick for him.

An hour's exercise calmed Charlotte's restlessness and she headed for home, rounding the hill behind Finchbourne, stooping now and then to add another blossom to her nosegay of spring flowers. "Oof!" She grunted with satisfaction as she spread her serviceable brown cloak on the ground and sank down, hugging her arms about her knees as she gazed out over the little place — almost a town — and the manor house nestling snugly at its edge, under the hill. "Look, Prince Albert! There's home down there. Let's have five more minutes. Aren't you glad to be up here where a person can breathe?"

"I most certainly am," chimed in a man's voice in amusement. "But are you not being more than a little familiar in addressing His Royal Highness thus? What would our gracious queen say about that, do you suppose, Mrs Richmond?"

She started but on turning round was pleased to recognize Mr Knightley approaching over the brow of the hill, two black retrievers at his heels, rushing to greet Prince Albert with foolish, smiling faces, tongues lolling and plumed tails wagging. She laughed as he bowed politely to the panting spaniel and she waved her hand towards her spread cloak.

"Won't you sit down, Mr Knightley?" she offered. "His Royal Highness and I are far too out of breath to rise to greet you with proper ceremony, but we can offer you a comfortable seat, and there's an unparalleled view to be had."

"It is a marvellous view, isn't it?" he said eagerly, sitting down. "You can almost see my house from here, across the heath by Cuckoo Bushes copse. I've loved coming up here ever since I was a small child. It was always my refuge in times of trouble."

"Oh?" Her hazel eyes were warm with sympathy. "Is it a time of trouble now? Are you seeking refuge? I do hope Mrs Knightley is not feeling unwell?"

He shrugged and shook his head.

"No, I can't say she is unwell. Unfortunately I cannot say she is well, either. Perhaps the best I can offer is that she is no more unwell than usual." He heaved a sigh and gazed unseeing at the view he had confessed to loving so dearly. Charlotte touched his arm with mute sympathy then, when he turned his head to look down at her hand, she withdrew it with calm composure. He continued to stare at her hands, now folded together quietly in her lap until, with a sigh, he looked away and spoke again. "She has been so brave, you know. I understand she told you a little of our trouble when you met in the church not long ago. I was surprised for she does not speak of it to anyone but myself; you must have an exceptional gift for drawing out confidences from others."

She demurred with a tiny shake of her head, but did not speak and he continued after a few moments of companionable silence.

"She was always delicate as a girl — our families were well acquainted and I knew her as an infant — but she knew how much I desired a child and my father yearned for an heir, but not — *never* — at the cost of her health. If we had known . . ."

He shook his head in painful exasperation. "Hindsight is never a profitable exercise, so what is the use. Suffice it to say that the birth of the child so damaged her that the doctors forbade any further attempt on pain of her death and it left her as you see her now, condemned to lie forever on a sofa except for the brief, exhausting times when she insists that she can and *will* walk."

After a moment of silent sympathy, Charlotte's concern about Frampton's death weighed on her, overcoming her natural reticence, and she made up her mind to speak.

"Might I ask your advice?" she said abruptly. As he gave an immediate assent she knitted her brows again then plunged into a confidence. "It will sound ridiculous," she said ruefully, "but I cannot shake off the feeling that there was some scandalous mystery connected with Frampton's death." She explained about the mysterious Indian and related the unsettling tale of the encounter in the cathedral.

"Somehow I wasn't shocked at what that major said," she told Kit. "It seemed to tie in with the rumours that were rife in India when I left and there was that one, hastily suppressed, suggestion of murder. And do you know what is the most terrible thing about it?" Her sense of unease deepened. "Since I came here to live with Frampton's family I believe that the only person in the world who truly mourns him is his mother. The rest of the family, though they would be shocked to hear it, are all not exactly glad but certainly rather relieved that he's dead. So, if he *was* murdered by his own men, perhaps the military were also relieved."

"I think you should not let the rumours distress you." Kit Knightley spoke definitely. "If there were anything of that sort you would surely have heard by now." He paused and seemed to choose his words with care. "I will agree that Frampton was not . . . had not the knack of attracting friendship or respect, but . . . it seems a damning indictment of a man."

86

"Exactly." Charlotte turned to him eagerly. "And yet it's true that his family are better off without him. Barnard is now the heir and will be an excellent squire and Lily will eventually change the Richmond mausoleum into a home. And Agnes? Who knows, without Frampton to back her up, perhaps Mrs Richmond might eventually relent and allow poor Agnes to marry the curate." She shrugged with a slightly rueful grin as she said this. "I must admit, though, that I need to work on *that* particular problem. I've no real hope of Mrs Richmond's being reasonable unless I can somehow persuade her that I'm even more indispensable than Agnes."

She frowned as she gazed towards the horizon and returned to her argument. "Even Lady Frampton feared he would pension her off somewhere, I think, from remarks she has let drop and Uncle Henry's comments about him are positively sulphurous. In fact, apart from his mother I think the only person who would wish to see Frampton alive is poor, mad Lady Walbury and that only so that she could rip him limb from limb!"

"And you?" asked her companion, concern shadowing his face. "What of you?"

"I?" The distant chiming of the church clock recalled her to her situation and saved her from further discussion so she spoke lightly. "I can only say that widowhood suits me." She changed the subject firmly. "Oh dear, I must take Prince Albert home. Thank you for allowing me to express my foolish fears. I have so much enjoyed being up here under the sky where one can breathe. I find it very enervating being hemmed in down in the valley when I have been accustomed to so much space."

He rose and offered his hand to help her to her feet, looking down at her for a moment, his face unreadable. "I'll walk down with you," he said. "I need a word with Barnard and besides, what you have told me about this mysterious fellow is a little alarming. I'll have a word in the village constable's ear tomorrow. I cannot have you continually accosted."

They parted in the stable yard, Mr Knightley to hand over his dogs to a groom before calling on Barnard, Charlotte to slip indoors and relinquish to the boot-boy the weary but happy spaniel. She changed into her one simple black silk dress, splashed cold water on her sun-warmed cheeks and confined her glossy mane of dark brown hair into a netted snood, then pausing only to refresh her flowers in a glass of water, and to fasten Lady Meg's acanthus leaf brooch, she set her features into a decorous expression and took herself downstairs at the pace Mrs Richmond considered appropriate for a widow.

In the drawing-room Charlotte shook hands ceremoniously with Mr Knightley, who had just entered with Barnard. As Agnes pressed cups of tea on them and entertained them to an interminable story about one of the cottagers, an exclamation from Mrs Richmond brought all conversation to a halt.

"How extremely odd," she repeated, looking up from the letter the butler, Hoxton, had delivered on his silver salver. "This is from the mother of dear Frampton's fellow officer, Lieutenant Payton. She writes of the consolation she has derived from the visit paid to her by Colonel Fitzgibbon some two months ago, when he called to pay his condolences on her loss. It seems the colonel is presently home on leave." She scanned the letter once more, turning it this way and that, to make out a passage where her correspondent had crossed her lines.

"How extraordinary." Her face was shorn of all its customary artifice and for once expressed genuine emotion. "*I* have received no such visit from the colonel. Indeed, I have heard nothing from him or from the regiment since he wrote telling me of my sad loss."

Charlotte stood aloof from Agnes and Barnard's attempts to comfort their mother. Enough of hypocrisy, she thought. Stand back, Char, and let them get on with it. A casual glance at Kit Knightley made her stiffen. He was staring at Mrs Richmond, an arrested frown creasing his brow as he drummed unconsciously on the edge of the table in front of him, the brown fingers on his square, capable hands beating out a tune of sorts. As though he sensed her stare he looked up, caught Charlotte's eye and for a moment the frown deepened, then his shoulders moved in a very slight shrug and he rose to his feet, taking his leave of them in his normal friendly manner.

Charlotte slipped quietly out of the room behind him. Running after him, her skirts caught up to protect the hem from the straw and mess of the cobbled stable yard, she called out to him to wait.

89

"What is it?" she burst out, with no polite preamble, her hazel eyes wide with dismay, knowing, somehow, that she could trust him implicitly. "Why do you look so? Does it matter, except to *her*, that she has not been officially wept over?"

"I don't know." He made no pretence of not understanding her, or fobbing her off with platitudes. "I cannot say. It is unusual to say the least, I should have thought. After all, Frampton Richmond was the senior officer involved in the ambush, was he not?"

His voice tailed off. Charlotte met his eyes bravely and knew that the same impossible, unwelcome thought had struck them both, that her conjectures might, after all, be proved correct.

"No!" It was almost a cry of pain and she actually put up her hand as if to ward off an idea too terrible to contemplate. "No, I can't *really* believe it. He was a dreadful creature, a monster, Lady Walbury spoke of him to me as 'an abomination of desolation' but he was a competent enough officer. Besides . . ." She shook down her skirts and was again her usual composed self. "There must, surely, have been some communication from the army if —"

"If the authorities suspected him of gross incompetence or negligence." Kit Knightley completed the sentence for her. "They might have kept it quiet, bearing in mind the turmoil in the country, though when we first met, if you recall, you spoke of the rumours that were flying around the bazaars. Remember, it would be unthinkable to allow the men to lose their trust in their officers during a time of rebellion. And afterwards — well, he was dead, so perhaps they let it lie. As to your other conjecture, that Frampton might have been murdered by one of his own men — I don't know. How can we know? It seems far-fetched, to say the least."

"But . . ." He took her hand for a moment and gave it a little shake, adding in a bracing tone: "We're only guessing after all, Mrs Richmond. Charlotte, then," he corrected himself, as she made a gesture of protest. "It could explain the colonel's surprising dereliction of duty. Words of condolence would choke in *my* throat if I believed a man's incompetence to have caused so many deaths."

He released her hand and nodded in farewell. "Don't let it disturb you, Charlotte. I'll make enquiries about your mystery man tomorrow and as to the other matter . . . In all likelihood we shall never know, so pointless to start a hare without cause. In any case, we shall be utterly confounded if it proves to be purely an oversight."

A little comforted Charlotte nodded and watched his tall, strongly made figure as he walked purposefully to the loose box where his dogs were yelping at his approach. Pointless to worry, as he had said, until the facts were known, if they ever were. But we both had the same idea, the niggling persisted in her head. We *did* think it. What an epitaph for a man that such a spectre could be raised and not immediately dismissed. And there was that major too, in the cathedral. And the Indian.

Attendance at morning service in the little parish church came as a revelation to Charlotte. I believed I knew all there was to know about going to church, she thought, as she stood entranced during the singing of the first hymn on her second Sunday in Finchbourne. The first week she had still been too wracked with nervous tension after her arduous journey to appreciate the service. Now, she savoured it. Henry Heavitree was an experience to be relished as he ranted against everything and everyone under the sun from anarchists to the perils of educating women lest their inferior brains collapse under the strain, but Charlotte could close her ears to Henry's diatribe and let herself be overtaken by the ancient peace of the place, enjoying a time that was both calming and uplifting. No need here, or ever again, please God, to be on the watch for the troopers, or to keep alert for the beginning of a murmur about the church funds; no necessity of maintaining a valise packed and ready for instant flight when one of Will's more enterprising schemes came unstuck.

She found herself enjoying everything about the service, even the ineligible Percy Benson who had almost redeemed himself during the hymn singing with the revelation of a fine tenor voice. Charlotte found herself wondering how she could make poor Percy into an eligible party. Could he rescue Mrs Richmond from a runaway carriage? No, the curate, puny and short-sighted with a bobbing Adam's apple, was no natural hero. Besides Mrs Richmond would be far more likely to give him a tip after such a rescue than bestow her daughter's hand in marriage. The only thing, Charlotte speculated, that would weigh with the lady of the manor was for Percy to be the incognito son of a duke.

Only that morning Agnes had ventured the opinion that Percy was confident of winning Uncle Henry's approval of the match, that Henry Heavitree was bound to come round to it sooner or later. Charlotte, to Agnes's chagrin, had burst out laughing. "Win round Uncle Henry? As soon turn the pyramids on to their points! I can see only one solution, dearest Agnes. You and Percy will have to elope."

As the congregation spilled out of the cool cavern of the church into the spring sunshine, Charlotte realized that she was beginning to feel dangerously at home in this tiny corner of England. Nodding to this one, shaking hands with that, stopping to talk to Dr Perry who asked her if she was recovered from her encounter with the eastern visitor. Reassured, he nodded and walked on, leaving his wife to hover diffidently.

"My dear . . ." Mrs Perry hesitated then spoke decisively. "If you ever find you need a friend, at any time, pray call on me. I have known your mother-in-law since we were girls and I know what she . . . Oh well, never mind."

A curious thing to say, Charlotte thought at the time. What was she offering? Friendship merely? A shoulder to cry on? Does she think I shall need one?

Charlotte's friendship with the Knightleys, husband and wife, progressed daily. Kit Knightley's intervention seemed to have had some effect; the Indian gentleman had made no further attempt to question Charlotte, though he had called on Barnard three more times in one day, to no avail. Meeting Kit on the hills, when walking the elderly spaniel, Charlotte had thanked him and they had encountered each other several times since, walking the dogs together and discussing everything under the sun — *except* Charlotte's suspicions of her late husband's perfidy.

With Mrs Knightley too, she felt able to relax, calling informally, as Elaine had begged her to do. It was an inexpressible relief to be able to speak just as she pleased and to Elaine, she did, occasionally, speak of Frampton and the circumstances of her brief marriage. Some things, however, she did not discuss and Elaine respected her reserve though she must, Charlotte suspected, spend much time in speculation during her wakeful, weary nights.

For example, although Charlotte was quite forthcoming about life in general in Australia, she knew that Elaine recognized that these were edited confidences.

"Before Ma met my stepfather," Charlotte said on Tuesday, "we spent some time on the west coast. There are settlements out from Freemantle all along the Swan River. Ma travelled as Lady Meg's companion for many years, with me in tow. When Meg was in funds we lived high on the hog, and when she wasn't, Ma set up as a governess and kept us all." She sighed. "I loved it out west; Ma missed England and the seasons, but Lady Meg loved it and so did I. It's so . . . so alive, so vibrant and exciting, you can have no notion."

She jumped up suddenly and paced around the room, her movements coltish as she reached up to sniff

94

at a lemon-scented geranium trailing down from a cast-iron étagère bearing fragrant plants in pots from Minton and Wedgwood, touched the cheek of a Parian nymph by Copeland and Garrett, or paused to whistle to the pair of canaries shrilling in an elaborate wire cage.

"I declare," she exclaimed, "this birdcage is shaped like the Taj Mahal, imagine!" Her admiring gaze took in the elegant slenderness of the iron columns and wrought-iron decorative trim. "This really is a splendid conservatory, isn't it? How I wish Ma could have seen it. She would have loved your little fountain, splashing away in its mosaic basin and — what's this? Oh my, a miniature rock garden." Charlotte knelt in delight to stare at the pretty trifle. "It's a fairy place." *Oh, Ma.* She sighed, touching a tiny yellow-flowered sedum with a gentle finger. *It's so lonely without you. I'm trying, I really am, to settle down here and to make a place for myself, but I'd give it up in the blink of an eye if only you and Will could beckon to me.*

She stood up and braced herself as she turned back to speak to Elaine. "Now I see an English spring with my own eyes I can appreciate what Ma missed so badly. It's so truly different. Once Ma and Will were married we spent much more time in the outback where the heat is all-embracing."

Her eyes softened and Elaine Knightley nodded with the warm sympathy that was so typical of her. "You were very fond of your Godmama, were you not?" she asked with interest. "What happened to Lady Meg, when your mama remarried, I mean?"

Her face shadowed, and Charlotte answered briefly, with none of the vivacity that had earlier lit up her rather angular features. "Lady Meg died," she said quietly. "We were visiting Sydney at the time. Meg was seeking news from home. It was a — a happy passing, you could say. At least she was doing what she loved best. And yes, I loved her very much, so did Ma. Without Meg our lives would have been bleak. Indeed, after her death and without her protection Ma was near desperation, with no money and a child to support — I was just coming up to twelve at the time. Then Will came into our lives and transformed them."

She smiled affectionately at the memory. "He was so hugely alive, so bursting with vitality and energy and the joy of living. He had the effect of lifting one's spirits and of bringing sunshine into a room. A gathering with Will in it was lifted out of the ordinary into a special occasion, a celebration. He was a darling, wonderful man, was Will Glover."

She fell silent and Elaine patted her shoulder. "He must have been a rare gift to the parishes where he served," she ventured kindly. "What wouldn't I give for a vicar like that, rather than our own inimitable Henry Heavitree."

"I think *you* would have welcomed Will." Charlotte stifled a giggle and refused to elucidate. "I don't know about Mrs Richmond, though. His sermons verged on the inspired sometimes, particularly when it came to raising funds." Her voice tailed away as she remembered the downside of those inspiring sermons, the laden collection plates and the shame and anxiety that Molly had always felt. "Yes, well . . ." she sighed. "Sometimes it's better to have a rather *less* inspiring man about the place; Ma adored Will and so did I, but there's no denying he could be a handful and sometimes things grew to be a little too exciting —"

"My dear," Elaine broke in. "Your stepfather sounds both charming and intriguing." She laughed as Charlotte shrugged and bit her lip. "Don't worry, I shan't press you for details unless — or until — you wish to tell me." To Charlotte's surprise Elaine Knightley interrupted herself with a peal of laughter. "Oh heavens, do forgive me, but I have just recalled a favourite pastime of my governess's. She would, by way of encouraging discussion, ask my sister and myself to choose which characters from history we should like to entertain to dinner. I remember I scandalised her by suggesting Lord Byron."

"Oh *no*." Charlotte, always ready to be diverted, shook her head. "Meg said he was such a fussy eater. He'd upset the cook and leave you with a domestic crisis. I rather think Charles II would be an ideal guest — think how irresistible to the ladies." She raised an eyebrow as she glanced at her friend. "It's an interesting idea, I grant you, but I don't quite understand what this has to do with Will?"

"Merely that he sounds the kind of man one would *always* want at one's table, to charm the ladies, banter with the gentlemen and leaven the leaden," explained Elaine.

Charlotte laughed. "No fear that he would annoy the servants, either. He told me once that he was staying in a grand house when the cook dropped dead, and so he, Will, turned to and whipped up an impromptu banquet." She dwelt fondly for a moment on the vision of Will, let loose in this neighbourhood, joking with Mr Knightley, hail-fellow-well-met with Barnard, teasing Agnes and buttering up Mrs Richmond. Ah well, useless, pointless speculation. She shrugged and sighed and turned to her hostess.

"Tell me, what will be my duties at this bazaar tomorrow?"

"You will be required to do three things." Elaine made no comment on the abrupt change of subject. "Firstly you will be expected to wear your best bonnet to allow the population to inspect you as the latest-comer to the place; secondly you must dance attendance on your esteemed Mama-in-law as she wheels in state around the assembly room at the back of the Three Pigeons; and thirdly you will be needed to prevent Agnes Richmond from having a collapse of nervous exhaustion after doing all the work and receiving none of the credit."

"Is that all?" Charlotte grinned. "I can readily imagine that Agnes does all the work — I've seen her at it already — but tell me who claims the credit? No, don't tell me, I can guess. Never fear, I shall bring Agnes to everyone's attention, however much she bleats at me. As to the other conditions, I suppose I can bear to act as chariot slave to my mother-in-law. At least there will be plenty of diversions and I expect I can support the interest in me. I had better look out my best trimmings when it comes to the bonnet, though."

"The bonnet is actually a metaphor," Elaine laughed. "The bazaar is held late in the afternoon and carries on into the evening. The people look forward to it immensely as an unofficial ball and the local gentry turn out in force. So, when I said bonnet, I really meant you must wear something rather more formal — your prettiest evening cap, no less."

"Hmm . . ." Charlotte's eyes sparkled. "How diverting. But I shall never be allowed to indulge in something so frivolous." The gleam of excitement died as she shrugged. "It's of no use though, I have nothing to wear, apart from the deepest, darkest mourning for my dear departed. Besides, will Mrs Richmond let Agnes and me attend the dancing? No, she'd never permit the memory of the hero of the Richmonds to be tarnished by such a breach of etiquette."

"No, no." Elaine looked surprised and rather touched by this evidence of girlish disappointment in the usually self-contained and composed Charlotte. "You underestimate Mrs Richmond's feudal spirit and slavish adherence to tribal custom. She will put in a token appearance, staying for precisely fifteen minutes after the band strikes up." She smiled at Charlotte's surprise. "Neglect to attend the bazaar hop? She would sooner die."

Charlotte found Finchbourne in uproar with Barnard bellowing in panic and Lady Frampton wheezing alarmingly on a crimson, plush, button-backed sofa which was gamely bearing up under its heavy load. Agnes was fluttering ineptly, while Lily, attended by

Old Nurse at her most lugubriously doom-saying, lay draped across an elaborately carved walnut and puce silk chaise longue, looking as pale and interesting as it was possible for a stoutly-built, highly coloured young woman.

"Such an alarm . . ."

"Poor dear young madam, I feared it all along . . ."

"Fuss about nothing . . ."

". . . ask your advice, Charlotte?"

"Please!" Charlotte held up a hand to stem the flow and turned to Barnard, usually the most coherent reporter.

Not this time. He was reduced to stammering, anxiety plain upon his bluff, red face and with the Greek chorus, "Not long for this world, poor thing," from Old Nurse, her soft Hampshire tones ringing dolefully in his ears.

Charlotte turned with a resigned sigh to Agnes, her least favourite witness.

"Dear Lily, so pale, my heart was fit to burst, poor little thing."

"Let me try to understand." Charlotte interrupted the morass of half sentences. She cast a jaundiced eye at old Lady Frampton, who had managed to catch her breath and was able to tell the tale. She, it transpired, had been about to enter the dining-room when Lily was taken ill, first doubling up and vomiting into the imposing brass-bound, mahogany wine cooler in the bay window, and then surpassing this virtuoso performance by staggering into the drawing-room and collapsing in a dead faint at the glacé kid-clad slippers of her grandmother-in-law, narrowly missing, thankfully, the gouty, overhanging flesh. Charlotte thought ruefully that there might have been an even greater uproar had the old lady weighed in with some of her saltier exclamations from a less demure era.

Charlotte acted swiftly to restore peace and quiet.

"Barnard, pray fetch your grandmother a glass of port, and get one of the maids in the dining-room with a mop and bucket. Agnes." She sighed and handed her sister-in-law a further handkerchief to stem the flow. "Please stop crying and find a glass of water for Lily. You might have them prepare her bed, she should probably be lying down. And you, ma'am?"

Lady Frampton shook her head vehemently so Charlotte, trusting to the old woman's common sense, turned back to the heroine of the hour.

"Oh!" Agnes returned almost at once with a tumbler of water which she slopped against Lily's chin. "What can be the matter? Can it be the first symptoms of rapid decline?"

"Don't talk such nonsense." Charlotte snapped, stooping to speak to Lily who was agitatedly wiping water off her best guipure lace collar. "Now, Lily, tell me . . ."

She whispered in the little pink ear, nodding once or twice over the murmured replies, putting another question or two. "Just as I thought." She straightened up with a reassuring pat on Lily's hand. "Nothing to be alarmed about at all. It's good news. Lily is about three months pregnant."

101

"What's that?" Unnoticed, the silent wheels of Mrs Richmond's wheelchair had brought her into their midst. "Do my poor ears deceive me? An heir? At last, an *heir* for Finchbourne? Ah, Barnard, my own, dear boy, I had begun to fear that you were destined to suffer the torments of childlessness, to become ever more discontented and alone with your barren wife — let me remind you, your *own* choice of wife, dearest boy. But all such doubts must be set aside. Oh, joyful, wondrous news, the first to lighten the shadows of this, the hallowed home of the Richmonds for so long, since the dread tidings of your brother's martyrdom reached us!"

Allowing his overwrought parent to clasp him in a fond embrace, Barnard blinked at this peroration, as well he might, considered Charlotte, concealing her own sardonic appreciation of Mrs Richmond's performance. Just like Mrs Jordan at the play, Meg would have applauded. Meg had been privileged to witness several of that gifted actress's appearances both before and after the lady was abandoned by her royal lover, William, Duke of Clarence. Poor Mrs Jordan, who, Meg had reported, had supported her ungrateful prince financially while he fathered her multitude of children, and had then been discarded when the duke scrambled into marriage with kind, plain Princess Adelaide, in a doomed attempt to produce a legitimate heir.

"We'll drink champagne tonight —" Mrs Richmond broke off her gloating. "What's this? Going to bed, Lily? Really you should not coddle yourself, my dear. I myself bore six children and not a day's illness, although three of my little angels were taken cruelly from me and all I have to remember them by is their dear graves and the precious marble likenesses of their tiny hands and feet that I treasure at my bedside."

At this point Old Nurse burst into the conversation. "Oh ma'am," she groaned, first dabbing her eyes with her apron and then wringing her hands in woe. "She must lay down on her bed this instant with a bowl of gruel lest the shock cause her to have a mishap. Why, I remember my old mother did tell of a poor woman as saw her cow give birth to a two-headed calf on the very day she found she was in the family way, and lo and behold she went and —"

"That will do, Nurse." Mrs Richmond interrupted the prophet of doom. "Oh, very well, go to bed if you must, Lily, but for heaven's sake do not be setting yourself up as ailing. Nothing can be so calculated to turn a man's thoughts elsewhere."

The news of Lily's impending motherhood gave a welcome respite from Agnes's increasing hysteria about the next day's bazaar as, deflected for once from her parish interests, she was able to let her dreams take wing, hanging over Lily oozing solicitude and sentiment.

"Imagine, a baby!" She breathed the words in prayerful ecstasy as she and Charlotte sat after dinner, finishing off the last batch of fancy goods for their stall. "Oh, Charlotte."

Her hands rested for a moment on the tassel she was stitching on to the upturned point of an embroidered slipper, destined for some astonished gentleman. "A baby will make such a splendid new beginning for this sad old house and how Mama has brightened up since she heard the news. Why, she is almost her old self again."

Mrs Richmond's entire conversation during dinner had been a continuation of her paean of thanksgiving and showed no sign, as yet, of abating. Indeed, she had insisted upon visiting Lily after the meal to ensure that such an unworthy vessel was truly aware of the great responsibility and honour of bearing the heir to the Richmonds.

Her absence was a considerable relief to Charlotte, who found her mother-in-law's triumph hard to bear, grateful though she was to Lily for giving Mrs Richmond the opportunity to cease her occasional sighs at sight of Charlotte's trim, slim figure. "Ah me, what might have been," she would murmur, handkerchief to her eyes.

A welcome interruption came when the butler, Hoxton, presented Charlotte with a parcel, just arrived, complete with a note, from Knightley Hall. Charlotte tore open the letter. It was brief but redolent of Elaine Knightley's good sense and generous heart.

"After you left this morning," she wrote. "I recalled this dress which has been packed away in my cedar chest for two or three years. Why on earth I thought dark green silk would become me I cannot imagine. It made me look a hag, and a hundred to boot, whereas you, my dear girl, will look delightful. I believe it will fit you. Although I am such a scarecrow these days, I was once much the same size as you."

"Wear this as a symbol of the new beginning to your life and let me have no ladylike demurs. Our friendship, though but a recent one, has already given me a great deal of pleasure. Allow me the further satisfaction of giving you this dress."

"How fortunate," gasped Agnes, as Charlotte sat in mute contemplation of the shimmering folds of dark green silk. "What a stroke of luck, just when Mama has decreed that we may go into half-mourning so that no shadow must fall upon the heir of Finchbourne."

Dragging herself from her reverie Charlotte burst out laughing. "What? Lily's baby? Mrs Richmond takes a long view indeed, does she not? And what if the long-awaited heir turns out to be an heiress? It is not written on a tablet of stone that Lily will produce a boy."

"Oh, Charlotte!" Agnes responded with a comical cry of dismay. "Do not, I pray, let Mama hear you say so, or Lily either. She's already speaking of the child as her little Fairfax."

"Fairfax?" Charlotte dropped Mrs Knightley's note on to her lap and turned a laughing face to her sister-in-law. "But Lily's maiden name was Rowbottom, was it not? Where in the world did she discover Fairfax?"

"With some ingenuity." Agnes could show spirit when she chose. "Her father's name, as you say, is impossible and her mother's maiden name was Smith, also beyond the pale for a Richmond, as you may well imagine. I understand that she dredged up Fairfax from a cousin twice removed on her grandmother's side, or some such."

Elaine Knightley was helped into the assembly room to open the bazaar with a few words of welcome and exhortation to the guests, to spend freely in a good cause, and the Richmond ladies hastened to greet her.

"My dear." She surveyed Charlotte with proprietorial delight and a warm embrace, shaking hands with Agnes. "You look utterly charming. How well that green suits you, doesn't it, Kit? Kit? Where can he be just when I need him?"

It seemed that Kit Knightley had not heard his wife's laughing admonition although he was standing just behind her, staring in dismay at Charlotte Richmond as though wondering what lanky, laughing Char had to do with this polished, smiling creature, agleam in emerald silk with an almost eighteenth-century air about the cascades of lace, shining brown hair piled high and topped by a frivolous confection of the same lace.

Elaine, who was again urging him to speak, to admire her protégé, looked at him curiously and at last he managed: "Indeed, you are very fine today, Charlotte, very fine indeed." Charlotte winced at the stiffness of his tone and, with a droop of her slight shoulders, she retreated abruptly towards the trestle table of fancy goods that Agnes had allocated her, only to be accosted by Henry Heavitree.

"Well, well, Mrs Knightley." He addressed Elaine in a muted bellow, adjusted to suit the delicate ears of an invalid. "I hope I see you in improved health today? And what's this? God's nightgown, niece Charlotte, you're looking a damned sight better in that fine rig than in your usual mouldy black! A peacock today, not a damned crow, hey?"

He rubbed his hands together and thrust his face towards his niece. "Well, girl? Going to give your old uncle a kiss, are you?"

"Indeed not, sir." Charlotte recoiled from the enveloping brandy fumes and tried to conceal a shudder of distaste as she deftly disentangled his questing hand from her waist. "I have a slight cold and would not dream of passing it to you. Where should we all be without your sermon to keep us awake on Sunday if you were to lose your voice?"

At the end of two hours, the bazaar was just about played out with only the unsaleable remains scattered forlornly about the stalls. With a good deal of jostling and elbowing the tables were removed to the yard and set up again, to be spread with cold meats, bread, cheese, jellies and creams, together with pitchers of cider and ale. Tea and coffee were also on hand for the ladies and the fiddler was heard tuning up for the dancing.

Leaning heavily on her footman's arm, Elaine moved slowly towards the outer door.

"No, no, my dear," she laughed at Charlotte. "I have done very well, I assure you, but I know when to concede defeat. I'm only tired, not ill, do not distress yourself. Kit will stay and do his duty with the local ladies and the farmers' wives." She held out a hand in farewell, smiling very kindly. "Are you enjoying yourself, dear Charlotte?"

The colour deepened in Charlotte's cheeks and her eyes sparkled with green mischief once more. "Oh yes, so much," she laughed. "Did you hear what the blacksmith said to me? He was extremely bashful and wriggled a lot then he managed to come out with the loveliest compliment. He said: 'You'm looking just like a nice springy young hazel tree, Miss Char.' I don't think anyone has ever said anything so charming to me in my life."

"The blacksmith is a poet and a man of perception," declared Elaine, then she lifted her hand. "Listen, there's the fiddler striking up. You must dance, Charlotte, it's a waltz. Now who shall partner you? Ah, the very man. Kit, my dear, I am homeward bound but you must stay and twirl this dear girl round the floor."

As Kit Knightley demurred, pleading poor prowess as a dancer, and Charlotte flushed and shook her head, a ragged chorus of encouragement sprang up from the estate workers near the door. Emboldened by long draughts of ale one of the stable lads spoke up.

"Ar, goo on, Miss Char, you 'ave a dance with 'e. Do you take 'er, sir, pretty as a picture her be!"

Overcome by his own daring, he buried his face in his tankard of ale, drained it and shouldered his way to an obscure corner of the room, followed by jeers and cheers from his mates. Behind him Elaine shooed her husband and Charlotte towards the dancing with a wave of farewell, and with a slight shrug Kit held out his hands.

"Pretty as a picture indeed." He smiled. "I notice he called you Miss Char?"

She had accepted his hand rather shyly but now she smiled in reply. "I know," she answered proudly. "They all do it. They've caught it from Agnes. I keep telling them they should say Mrs Frampton but they forget. Besides, I like it. They're all so friendly and kind, they almost make me feel that I belong here."

"Belong? You're part of us, Char, of course you belong." He smiled down at her. "Here, wipe your eyes, there's a good girl, no need to cry about it. What would we do without you now?"

"No." She was more moved than she could have thought possible. "I don't belong, not really." She hesitated, uncertain whether to continue. Kit raised an eyebrow and she went on, speaking slowly as though thinking aloud. "I don't belong here, or anywhere. I never have but in this lovely, lovely place I'm happier than I've ever been, so I'm afraid."

"Afraid?" he asked gently leading her in a flourish past the fiddler's rostrum.

"I'm living in a bubble," she said sadly. "And I'm afraid that it may burst at any moment. I can't help it." She raised serious hazel eyes to his. "Whenever Ma and I felt happy and settled anywhere, something always went wrong and we had to leave in a hurry, so now, if I let myself enjoy Finchbourne and — and everyone here, it frightens me."

"Don't be afraid any more, Char." Kit frowned. "Whatever happens now, remember that I will always . . . that we . . . that you have friends you can count on — for anything."

As he stumbled over the words, she met his gaze for a moment then she gave herself a little shake and looked up at him again, her eyes once more gleaming with amusement as she smiled; friendly Char once more rather than serious Charlotte.

"For the present let us be merry and think of cheerful things. Who knows, God may be merciful and let Uncle Henry fall off the church tower one day or shoot himself instead of one of his magpies, then Percy can become vicar in his stead."

"That would be a joyful day indeed," he laughed, accepting the change of subject. "My grandfather must have been in his dotage to allow Heavitree's appointment forty years ago."

An hour or so later Charlotte slipped away to tidy her hair, which was sadly tousled after all her dancing, not only with Kit Knightley but also with the bashful blacksmith and the bold stable lad, as well as with Barnard. Also, she shuddered, with Uncle Henry, who would not be gainsaid and whose ham-sized hands had ventured into liberties no gentleman, let alone a man of the cloth, should have taken, making it necessary for Charlotte to stamp viciously on his foot.

"You *must* tell me, Mrs Richmond." An insistent voice startled her and she turned with an apprehensive shudder to see the Indian gentleman at her shoulder. "You shall tell me, young lady. Tell me what has happened to everything he owned? I will not believe it has all been lost. That *cannot* be."

"I don't know what you are talking about," she protested, facing up to him. She felt very alone, and the hubbub from the assembly room seemed strangely distant. "Please, if you would only tell me, tell us, what you are seeking, but my brother-in-law showed you everything that was sent home. We truly have nothing to conceal. Please believe me."

At that moment Agnes appeared, her eyes starting from her flushed face. "Oh, there you are, Char. We must go home at once. Barnard has sent an urgent message."

Paying no further heed to the Indian, Charlotte seized Agnes's damp hand and the two girls ran across the village green and sped up the drive, Charlotte gasping questions to no avail. Agnes explained, panting, that the message had been terse in the extreme.

When they entered the drawing-room, anxious, tousled and out of breath, every face turned towards them, every mouth an "O" of hysterical excitement.

"Oh, Charlotte! Agnes!" Mrs Richmond wailed a greeting. "Oh, dear, dear Charlotte, such news, such news!"

"Yes indeed." That was Barnard's booming voice swelling the chorus while Lily contented herself with a silent glower from her chaise longue. It wasn't Lily's baby that was the problem then, thank God, Charlotte reflected, counting heads. No, they were all present and correct, nobody ill, nobody dead. What, in heaven's name, could be the matter?

Old Lady Frampton held out her hand to the girl in the doorway. "Come here to me, lass," she said, her voice roughened with emotion. "You come and sit by me so you can take it all in."

"Take what in?" Charlotte demanded. "What is it? What has happened? Is someone ill?"

"Far from it." Mrs Richmond's voice was actually unsteady though not from tears. "Far from it," she repeated in a ringing tone. "We have glorious news, dear Charlotte. News of the utmost importance to me and to yourself, even more than to the rest of the family. We have received a letter to tell us that dear Frampton, my dearest son and your husband, dear Charlotte, that dear Frampton is alive after all and is returning home shortly!"

CHAPTER
FOUR

Charlotte lay rigidly awake in her bed that night. *If I refuse to think about it,* she told herself fiercely, *it will go away, it won't have happened.*

Oh God! It was no use. She sat up and draped a shawl round her slim shoulders in a vain attempt to drive away the bitter chill that enveloped her and which had assailed her from the moment when Mrs Richmond trumpeted her appalling, catastrophic news.

He cannot be alive, it cannot be true. She repeated the words over and over, as a charm against evil, as a prayer, as a railing against the mockery of fate.

She had known she was being a fool. *For the first time in my life,* she agonized, *for the very first time, I am comfortable, I am respectable and I am settled. I'm even in a fair way to finding affection* — from Agnes and Lady Frampton and after a fashion from Barnard. Even Lily — oh God, poor Lily — even she had begun to be less implacably opposed to Charlotte once she was officially installed as the bearer of the heir to the sacred name of Richmond. Charlotte's mind shuddered away from a thought too terrible to contemplate and she continued to enumerate her friends at Finchbourne in an attempt to stave off nightmares. Mrs Richmond, she gabbled furiously, even Mrs Richmond seemed to have accepted her as an inoffensive member of the family. Once or twice she had even managed to win approval.

The village, too, and the surrounding gentry. I like them so much but I'm a fool, she thought bitterly, brushing the scalding tears from her eyes. Fool to be lulled into such a false contentment. She had no right to such a place in society. Born and bred a pariah, she should never have believed she could usurp the privileges of these people, of this lovely, ancient house and this increasingly beloved little town that felt so insidiously like home.

The evening had become a nightmare.

"Captured by the mutineers . . ."

"Wounded near to death . . ."

"Lost his memory, poor old Framp . . ."

"Wandering hither and yon not knowing who or what he was . . ."

The babble of voices each clamouring for her attention, to be the first to explain what had occurred, made her head throb with such pain that she could hardly take in what they said.

With a touch of that sympathy she had glimpsed once or twice, Barnard silenced the rest of them by the simple method of shouting them down.

"For pity's sake," he thundered. "The poor girl cannot make head or tail of all your babbling. Here, Charlotte, come and sit down beside Grandmama, that's right. Agnes? A glass of brandy, that's a good girl, and better make it a large one."

Charlotte let herself be put in a chair beside Lady Frampton, who reached out and took the suddenly chilled, slim brown hand in her own sausage fingers.

"That's better," approved Barnard and he sat down on a chair at Charlotte's other side. "Now, let me tell her. As we understand the matter, Charlotte, Frampton was not killed in that ambush, he was abducted by some of the damned mutineers. Either that or, having been left for dead, he was carried off to one of their villages. The letter is not clear on the subject but no doubt we shall find out soon enough."

"At any rate, Frampton seems to have sustained some injury to his head and he lost his memory. It appears he managed to escape his captors in some manner and wandered off, luckily in the direction of the coast. In some fashion he seems to have boarded a ship headed for home and is even now on his way. The letter was forwarded from Marseilles."

He patted her hand kindly as Charlotte sat pale and horrified, unable to move.

"Is he — is he completely recovered?"

When at last she could bring herself to speak, her voice was harsh and strained.

"Not entirely." Mrs Richmond could bear no longer not to be centre stage. "There is some lingering loss of memory, apparently, also some recurrent fever, and my poor, dear boy requires the services of the male companion whom he most fortuitously met on board the ship, and who will be accompanying him home to Finchbourne."

"A — a male companion?"

Involuntarily Charlotte glanced at Barnard Richmond, who caught her eye for a moment then looked uncomfortably down at his boots. So his brother *did* know about Frampton after all.

"It seems that this young man, Mr Lancelot Dawkins, was briefly employed in the Indian Civil Service." Mrs Richmond continued her explanation. "His health had suffered greatly in the unforgiving climate and he was most reluctantly returning home when he encountered dear Frampton on the ship and was able to be of service to him."

Stunned though she was by the news of Frampton's escape, Charlotte could not help wondering how Mrs Richmond, with her fanatical hatred of 'the abominations and perversions of degraded persons', would react to this male companion of Frampton's. Surely even his mother must come to recognize that there might be something other than mere manly fellowship between them? Especially, she reflected, if young Mr Dawkins resembled, in any fashion, the young man who had been Frampton's favourite in Meerut. Yes, she thought, even Mrs Richmond would have found something unusual in that creature's behaviour — a perfect candidate for her crusading zeal. Especially, she bit her lip, if he drenched himself in floral scent and painted his face as that other young man had done.

She came to herself to see Mrs Richmond apply the ever-present wisp of lace and lawn to her brimming eyes, and then continue with a happy smile.

"Ah me! You must all forgive the foolish tears of a mother who has been granted the dearest wish of her

116

poor old heart! As I was saying, Mr Lancelot Dawkins and my dearest boy struck up a friendship and Mr Dawkins, being so conveniently placed, is to accompany my boy home to Finchbourne and to act as his companion, his secretary, and in some sense, his nurse."

"Thank God for that." The words were out of Charlotte's mouth before she could stop them.

"Charlotte?"

"Thank God, I mean." She struggled to cover her indiscretion. "I mean, dear Mrs Richmond, that we must thank God for this deliverance."

Mrs Richmond accepted the explanation with a nod of satisfaction, no doubt reflecting that, at last, dear Charlotte appeared to be feeling just as she ought.

"Just fancy, dear Charlotte, you may even yet become the mother of the heir to Finchbourne!"

Her gloating was interrupted firstly by a swiftly muffled outcry from Lily and secondly by Charlotte herself as she rose abruptly from her chair and stumbled towards the door.

"Why? What is it, dear child?"

"I'm going to be sick." The words broke abruptly from Charlotte as she ran from the room, scarcely pausing to ward off an advance from Agnes. "No! Leave me alone, Agnes, please, I want to be on my own."

In the safety of her own room, Charlotte's nausea gradually subsided. No use being sick, she told herself, that won't make it any better. Oh God, please don't let him want anything of me when he returns. Let him stay an invalid, let him set up home with Mr Lancelot

Dawkins, anything. But *don't* let him anywhere near me. Let me continue to have this room, at least, as sanctuary, though all else is changed.

You've certainly got your just deserts, haven't you, Charlotte? an inner voice mocked. You married him for his name and his money and to get out of India.

What else was I to do, she retorted in angry response to that prick of conscience. A young unmarried woman in the middle of a war? And Frampton had only married her because his colonel offered him a stark choice: leave the army of your own free will, stay and be cashiered in disgrace, or marry to protect your own name and that of the regiment. It was a marriage of convenience for both of them.

It wasn't so convenient, though, was it, the voice mocked, not once the ring was on your finger and the major's crowns on his shoulder.

Charlotte shuddered at the recollection of that last night, before the regiment was ordered to march.

He had lounged into her room late at night, without knocking, as she brushed her hair before the looking glass.

"What's this, Mrs Richmond? No doting smile for your gallant husband off to the war?"

She had forced herself to respond with a wary smile. The brandy fumes had preceded him into the room; he was very drunk. He ranged about the room picking up a trinket here, a book there; only when he kicked off his boots and began to unbuckle his belt did she dare to make a protest.

118

"But . . . you said you wouldn't . . . that there was no question . . ."

"I know what I *said*," he threw at her as he swayed before her, clad only in his shirt and drawers.

"But — but I didn't think you . . . I thought you didn't like —"

"I know what I *like*," he mocked her, and she noticed with abhorrence the sudden brightening of his eyes as he appraised her angular figure. "But you, my dear new wife, you are more like a boy than a woman. Not a spare ounce of fat on you."

Now, months later, Charlotte lay back against the lace-trimmed linen pillows, staring round her dainty blue bedroom, sanctuary in the rambling old house in England, and realized that her whole body was tense and rigid as the memories assailed her.

"I'll kill him," she vowed through gritted teeth. "I'll kill him if he touches me again."

After the excitement of the previous night, the household awoke to a sense of anticlimax.

"You are looking very pale, dear Charlotte." Agnes was noisily solicitous as she hovered around the newly unmade widow. "You should have stayed in bed. Why don't you return to your room now, dearest. It will be no trouble to bring you some breakfast."

"No, please . . ."

"Stop fussing, Agnes." The welcome interruption came abruptly from Lady Frampton who was herself looking pale and anxious today. "Charlotte knows she

119

can stay in bed if she likes. Just let the girl be — she has troubles enough to bear and worse to come."

Charlotte raised her ravaged face to look in surprise at the old woman. Lady Frampton waddled over to her and patted her hand with clumsy kindness, wearing the ferocious expression which, as Charlotte had come to recognize, was a fruitless attempt to conceal a warm heart.

"There, there, my dear," was all the old lady said at first, then, when Charlotte, unexpectedly comforted, was struggling to swallow a cup of tea, Lady Frampton added a whispered aside.

"If it comes to it, my girl, I'll stand by you, never fear."

For Charlotte the next few days were an echo of that one, long hours of sleepless anxiety at night followed by having to suffer the incessant gloating of Mrs Richmond as she read and reread the fateful letter, exclaiming again and again at the intervention of providence and complaining yet more frequently about the negligence offered to her by Colonel Fitzgibbon in making no attempt to comfort her, either in her recent sorrow or now, in her triumphant joy.

As if in mockery the weather was now glorious and Charlotte spent as much time as possible out of doors, striding across the downs oblivious of the beauties of the countryside, or galloping across those same hills on the grey mare Barnard had offered her for her own use when he saw what an accomplished horsewoman she was. To Agnes's loudly proclaimed distress, Charlotte grew thinner, almost daily, and the mischief and healthy

120

glow that was her chief attraction disappeared, to be replaced by a gaunt apprehension that brought a ferocious scowl to Kit Knightley's usually pleasant face when he glimpsed her briefly in the village.

I'm not the only one who is afraid, Charlotte told herself as she knelt in anguished prayer, while Henry Heavitree thundered and ranted in the pulpit above. Barnard is riding about the estate with the face of a dying man, who knows that paradise will not be his after all. Lily is in a state of simmering rage and refuses to speak to me and Agnes is running off at intervals to sob about the curate. Even the Reverend Henry is apprehensive about Frampton's impending arrival. Indeed, the sermon ringing around the hallowed walls contained darkling references to the despoilers and barbarians who would soon be amongst the congregation, casting aside the cherished high church tradition of Finchbourne only to replace it with pusillanimous nonconformism.

That was a jibe at Frampton, a warning shot even before his arrival, that Henry would brook no interference from his nephew, whose low church opinions were anathema to the old monster. A reluctant chuckle almost escaped Charlotte, in spite of her despair. It would be a battle worth witnessing, she thought, and surely one that Henry would win hands down, so why did he wear such a look of apprehension these days?

That Lady Frampton was afraid of her grandson's homecoming was evident but it was some days before Charlotte discovered the reason.

"His Royal Highness is losing weight," Charlotte announced when she returned the amiable spaniel to his mistress's room one afternoon. "He and I have taken such long walks these last few days that we are both becoming shadows of our former selves."

Instead of the laughing reply she had come to expect of the old lady, there was a flat silence and, glancing up from the floor where she was sitting to rub down the dog, she saw difficult tears trickling down the wrinkled cheeks.

"Oh, Grandmama, dearest Gran, what is it?" The endearment was involuntary and the old woman summoned up a smile of gratification even in the midst of her distress as she reached out a hand to the girl.

"He don't like Prince Albert, dearie," came the broken whisper. "I don't know what he'll do . . ."

"Oh no!" The cry rang out sharp and shrill as Charlotte flung her arms round the stout old shoulders. "He wouldn't . . ." She scanned the other woman's face and gasped in disbelief. "You really are afraid that Frampton might . . . But Mrs Richmond would not allow it, surely?"

"Fanny?" It was the ghost of a smile. "Fanny will allow 'er returning 'ero anything he desires, me dear, and to be frank, I think she would leap at the chance of putting me out to grass. Besides, she don't really like dogs or indeed any h'animal apart from 'orses. She only tolerates Prince Albert as long as I keep 'im out of 'er way, but if Frampton says the word, she'll 'ave poor Albert shot!"

122

"We shall have to stand together," determined Charlotte, oddly heartened by the necessity of appearing strong in someone else's eyes. "There must be some way to outwit him. Perhaps we might run away to the colonies?"

"Per'aps pigs might fly, girl!" The old woman wiped her eyes as she snorted in amused disgust, but her colour was improved and her eyes brightened. "There now, if you 'aven't made me feel better. And you're right, if worst comes to worst, I've plenty of money, we can run away to h'Australia and set up 'ouse, you, me and Prince Albert; then the neighbours will talk and the scandal would just about kill Fanny, serve 'er right."

At noon the next day Lady Frampton cleared her throat in a portentous manner and addressed her daughter-in-law.

"I shall be going to Winchester today, Fanny," she announced. "So I shall need the carriage after luncheon. I 'ave some calls to make and I daresay Charlotte would like to accompany me, what do you say, my girl? That's right. Now, don't you commence to worry, Fanny, we'll be out for our dinner."

Charlotte recognized that a challenge had been laid down. Lady Frampton's complexion, always high, now resembled a marbled slab of well-hung beef, while Mrs Richmond flushed first with annoyance, then leaned back with a hand to her head and a sigh of resignation.

"Certainly, ma'am." Her plaintive, die-away voice was almost inaudible. "I must suppose that poor Charlotte — a young woman who has gone so suddenly from deepest mourning to such transports of emotion

123

as to render even the strongest character incapable of exertion — may find it in her heart to feel sufficiently charitable to humour the frivolous whims of an elderly and increasingly erratic relative. For myself, I plan to spend the early part of the afternoon in the church, thanking God for my deliverance from grief, and the latter hours laid upon my couch. Well for you, ma'am, and Charlotte too, that you have so much blunter sensibilities than I."

Within a surprisingly short time Charlotte and Lady Frampton were seated companionably in the carriage and bowling down the Manor drive.

"Phew!" Lady Frampton sighed gustily. "For a moment I thought I hadn't brought it off. Fanny can be very tricky you know, my dear. You were lucky she didn't decide you h'ought to be on your knees in the church beside her, and dancing h'attendance beside 'er couch. Even when she's off 'er 'ead with joy, she don't approve of anyone else 'aving any fun!"

In spite of the agonized worrying which had given her yet another sleepless night, manifest in her heavy, shadowed eyes, Charlotte managed an expectant grin at the old lady.

"Fun? Are we going to have fun?"

"Indeed we are." Lady Frampton nodded, while rummaging in her capacious black velvet reticule. "I can only support life with Fanny if I gets to h'escape regular and if that young devil's coming home . . . Well, never mind. Where did I put those teeth of mine? They're in here somewhere."

"Teeth, ma'am?" Anxiety fled for a moment as Charlotte stared with frank curiosity. As far as she could see Lady Frampton was in possession of a full complement of monumental teeth, firmly in her mouth, and certainly not in her handbag.

"What? What's that you say? Oh, not these, girl. These teeth are my everyday ones, good enough for the slops Fanny serves us during the day, though I usually changes them of an evening." She withdrew her hand from the bag with a crow of triumph. "See these 'ere? These are what I need for serious eating."

Under Charlotte's fascinated gaze, Lady Frampton, with a genteel apology, removed her glove and fiddled around in her mouth, removing the teeth she found there. With a slightly puckered smile she stowed them into her bag, from which she had drawn out a second pair. When these were in place Charlotte was the recipient of a flashing smile, revealing a set of even larger teeth, tombstone yellow in colour.

"Waterloo teeth, my dear," the old lady boasted proudly. "Best you can get." Alerted by Charlotte's puzzled expression, she explained. "They was my husband's teeth, dear, and I kept 'em in his memory. After 'e 'ad all 'is own teeth pulled out he bought these orf an army man of 'is acquaintance." She peered at Charlotte and laughed wheezily. "You still 'aven't an idea wot I'm saying, do you, dearie? After the Battle of Waterloo there was a lot of dead men, as I'm sure you've 'eard. Well, it was quite the rage in those days for dead men's teeth to be pulled and made up into sets like these. Yes, I see that shocks you, my girl, but let me

125

tell you, there's nothing like 'em when you wants to get outside of some proper vittles — to get your teeth into, so to speak."

Guffawing loudly at her own joke, Lady Frampton allowed Charlotte and the groom to manoeuvre her down the carriage steps and into the vulgar public house of her choice, close by the station. As they paused at the entrance so that the old lady could catch her breath Charlotte's attention was caught by a familiar figure hastening across the station approach.

"Please, Gran," she apologized swiftly. "I'll catch you up in a minute, I've just seen somebody I must speak to."

Casting to the winds the dignity and decorum required of a Richmond lady, she flew through the crowded station and on to the platform, ignoring the angry protest of the ticket inspector. Too late, the train was even now puffing out of the station, a white turbaned head barely visible, wreathed in a cloud of smoke and steam.

"I wonder if he has heard about Frampton?" she said aloud, then wiped some smuts from her face, dropped a penny into the ticket inspector's indignant hand and made her way back to the public house and Lady Frampton. Her companion was in high good humour, despite her fears for the future under Frampton's rule.

"I've been coming 'ere at least once a month," she explained, her voice muffled as she tucked into jellied eels and mash, specially made for her. "Fanny's got a shocking cook, no idea how to do anything but boil, and that for hours on end. Like I told you, I've been

126

used to good food and plenty of it and in the three years since I let Frampton and Barnard persuade me, against my better judgement, to close me London 'ouse when Fanny 'ad 'er h'accident and come down 'ere to look after 'er, I've suffered something cruel. I knew all along it wouldn't do, Fanny and me's never got on and she don't tolerate no interference, let alone lookin' after — but there you are, it's done now."

She wiped traces of glistening jelly from her whiskery old mouth and beckoned to the waiter to help her to some bloody beef. "See, Fanny just serves these fiddling modern courses, one at a time, but I like to see what I'm getting — something to whet my juices — and that's 'ow they do it 'ere. Just you take a plateful of that roast fowl, or try that beef-steak pie, my dear, you'll find the suet crust will melt in your mouth. And do you wash it down with some of that good porter, none of your finicking French wines what won't put you in good heart and good heart's what you'll be needing soon."

The letter came the next day.

"Tomorrow! My boy will be with me tomorrow!" Mrs Richmond was beside herself with triumph, so much so that she failed to observe the funereal demeanour of the rest of her family. "This letter is from the young man who accompanied him home on the ship, Mr Lancelot Dawkins. He writes that he has the honour — a nice touch of deference, I must say — to be in my boy's employ as secretary and companion and that Frampton wishes to have the bed in his

127

dressing-room made up for this Dawkins, in case of need during the night."

She addressed herself once more to the letter, and failed to notice the glance which passed between Barnard and Charlotte as the latter slumped with sudden relief.

"I am to ensure that Dr Perry is on hand to attend my poor boy on his arrival as the journey will occasion him the greatest fatigue so that he will require complete rest with no disturbance to his poor, troubled soul."

"Does Frampton, or rather, does this Mr Dawkins inform us, Mama, of the hour of their arrival?" asked Agnes.

"Why should he? This is Frampton's home. He is returned to us, the noblest of them all. The hour is immaterial."

"Immaterial to you, no doubt, Mama." The dry comment came from Barnard, who was looking disgusted. "But of great moment to Dr Perry. He is a busy man and cannot be expected to dance attendance all day upon Frampton's whim."

As soon as she could decently make her escape, Charlotte changed into her riding habit and ran to the stables. Instead of galloping across the countryside in aimless unhappiness, she set her horse towards the well-kept parkland of Knightley Hall, two miles away.

"My dear." Elaine Knightley looked up from her embroidery with a smile of delight as Charlotte was announced. "Come in, come in. Kit, fetch a chair, there's a dear."

128

Charlotte felt the strain slip away before the bustle of kindness as Kit hurried to set a comfortable chair beside his wife's sofa, and Elaine rang for tea and cake, then, after a thoughtful glance at her guest's face, she called for the Madeira too. At last, settled amongst the rose-coloured silk cushions, with a glass of wine in her hand and the concern manifest in the faces of her two friends, Charlotte relaxed.

"I believe this is the first time this week that I have been able to sit still without a tight tangle of nerves making me restless. Indeed, even if I were able to remain calm, the rest of the family would infect me with their fidgets. There have even been times when I confess I have failed to find the humour in my situation. I, Char, who invariably laughs at the wrong time and in the wrong place, even I have struggled to raise a smile at Mrs Richmond's hyperbole."

Setting down her glass for a moment, she gave an unexpected grin. "I thought Barnard would explode when his mother decided that Frampton's room must be completely refurbished — "*a fitting sanctum for England's hero*". Luckily, she was persuaded that Frampton might like to choose his own decorations, a suggestion she applauded because of her darling's exquisite taste."

"Though, to be sure, she has received one or two checks to her extravagant outbursts." Charlotte's eyes danced briefly. "Once or twice my revered mama-in-law has attributed divine intervention in what she persists in calling Frampton's resurrection from the dead and on the first occasion she uttered this blasphemy Uncle

Henry was so appalled he dropped his gun — we were in the churchyard at the time — and shot the blacksmith's grandmother's pet goat when the gun went off by mistake. It cost poor Barnard a good deal of money to set matters straight, particularly as the blacksmith would have preferred to lose his grandmother rather than the goat."

She smiled reminiscently and took a sip from her glass, then she looked squarely at both the Knightleys.

"He's coming tomorrow," she said dully. "I don't know what to do."

It was only a brief lapse, that moment of dread, then Charlotte stretched her lips in a smile and told them, making a game of it, of the anxieties she had discovered in the other members of the Finchbourne household.

Elaine Knightley listened to the girl who had become, in so short a space of time, so dear a friend and protégé and applauded the courage that made a joke of Henry Heavitree's fear that his nephew would forbid all incense and saints' days in favour of abstinence and puritanism. A sudden movement, almost of protest, from her husband made Elaine look at Kit in surprise. He was leaning back now, almost detached, but Elaine saw that he was biting his lip and that the knuckles on his tightly clenched hands were white, as though he were suppressing an overriding anger.

Just once he shot a glance through his eyelashes at the girl who was their guest, then went back to staring blankly at the window. Elaine felt a stab at her heart and knew that, for once, this was no physical ache. Has

130

it happened? she faltered inwardly. Is she the one? The fear that walked with her always, the fear of leaving Kit to sorrow and loneliness, was eclipsed by a sudden, burning jealousy.

She ventured another look at Kit and saw nothing but kindly concern on his face. Foolish, mawkish creature. She scolded herself for the unbridled imagination of an invalid but inwardly she felt like weeping. For it will come one day, I know it will; if not this one, then some other, and I shall have to pretend I have noticed nothing and protect him when he realizes what he is feeling.

Gallantly she raised her glass to her lips, concealing a tiny gasp as the real, physical pain struck again, and she resumed her constant crusade to protect Kit from recognizing the extent of her suffering.

Kit must have noticed her pallor after the sudden flush of colour and he hastened to pour her another glass of wine.

"Nonsense," he scolded her lovingly as she demurred. "You need your strength, my dear, if we are to make some suggestions to help Charlotte. My own feeling" — and he stood looking very kindly down at the younger woman — "my own feeling is that if, at any moment, you believe you can no longer support the situation at Finchbourne, then you must come here at once and Elaine will take you under her wing. Isn't that right, my dear?"

"Indeed it is, Kit, well said." Elaine smiled at him with approval and turned to Charlotte. "My dear child, I would say come now, at once, but it is against your own interests. It would cause talk and that would be to your disadvantage, were you to run away from your husband — or at least until your husband has alienated all our good friends and neighbours! Come and see me — us — as often as you please and remember that we are here as your bolt-hole."

Charlotte smiled tremulously and wiped away the suspicion of a tear. "I promise," she said and then, as Kit bade her farewell and left the room to speak to his steward, she shrugged and smiled at her hostess. "Enough of my problems. Let us change the subject, if you please."

"Certainly," agreed Elaine, settling herself against the cushions of the chaise longue and disposing a silk shawl over her knees. "Perhaps instead you would like to relieve my vulgar curiosity at last and tell me all about yourself?"

"*All*?" Charlotte raised her eyebrows at this outburst of unexpected interest. "Not quite *all*, I think."

"I shouldn't be shocked, you know." Elaine tilted her head and gave Charlotte her warmest, most encouraging smile.

"No, I know that. But even so . . ."

"Even so." Elaine nodded and changed tack, her face showing her relief that Charlotte was looking less drawn. "You know that Kit laughs at me because I read so many novels? Lying here, day after month after year, I have plenty of time to fill and reading foolish romances is one of my trusted methods of doing so. You seem to me to be the epitome of romance as portrayed in such volumes."

"Romance?" Charlotte raised a cynical eyebrow. "That's not the word I should use."

"What?" Elaine's tone was satirical. "No princess in disguise?"

"I'm afraid not."

"Not even a strawberry mark that will reveal you to be the missing heiress?"

"Not even that. I'm sorry."

"Surely you will allow that you are poor but honest?"

"*Poor,* certainly."

"Oh dear, oh dear." They exchanged amused grins and Elaine heaved a dramatic sigh. "I had hoped, at least, for a Cinderella story."

"Oh? Cinderella?" Charlotte's tone was harsh. "And as Prince Charming you had cast . . . Frampton?"

"Oh, my dear!" Elaine looked aghast. "Don't look like that. Oh, how dreadful, I've brought back the shadow to your face. Forgive me?"

"Of course." Charlotte heaved a long, difficult sigh and managed a smile. "Perhaps only Mrs Richmond could envisage Frampton as Prince Charming to some poor Cinderella, but not for me, I hope."

"No." Elaine looked suddenly bleak. "I had in mind a quite different Prince Charming for you, Charlotte."

"Really? An unknown prince who will ride to the rescue over the hill in his suit of shining armour?" Puzzled at the bitterness in her friend's voice, the younger girl laughed a little then her eyes softened as she recognized the signs of weary pain, and, kneeling beside the chaise longue, she clasped the pale hand in her own.

"Oh, I'm sorry, Elaine. I'm sorry that you have to suffer so . . . that you cannot . . ."

"Hush." The anger and sadness had vanished and Elaine's delicately lovely face was as kind as ever as she stroked the tumbled brown hair. "Come now, there's nothing more to say on that topic. Let us try another."

Charlotte flung herself back into her chair, casting about her for something, anything to divert Elaine from her suffering.

"I'll tell you, some of it, about my mother and Australia, and Will. Some of it, but not everything, not even to you."

"Ma was just on fourteen when she had me." She told the story baldly, with no embellishment, while Elaine listened with breathless attention. "She was brought up in an orphanage and put to work in the parson's house when she was twelve. The parson's son came home from school, Eton, I think, and saw her and that was it. He fell in love, so she said, and she thought he was wonderful."

"Poor child," Elaine whispered softly.

"Yes, poor child. I don't know if she loved him, but she certainly believed him when he said they should be married. To do him justice, so did he. You can imagine how his parents felt when they discovered the lovers. He was only seventeen, after all." Charlotte shook her head. "You can't blame his mother, I suppose; who knows, I might have done the same. The boy was shipped back to school and Ma was reported to the magistrate on a trumped-up charge of stealing a brooch. The sentence was transportation to the colonies."

She fiddled with her wedding ring, then glanced at Elaine. "Everything happened so hastily she didn't realize she was with child till she was on the transport ship. I think that at that moment, even Ma, the most determined of optimists, must have been seized with despair."

Charlotte turned to stare out of the window. "You can imagine," she said quietly. "You can just imagine how Mrs Richmond would take this news — that her cherished hero should be married to the bastard daughter of a transported thief." She dashed a hand across her eyes and spoke in a whisper. "And there's more, much worse, that I can't tell anyone, not even you."

She rose and took a distracted turn around the room, coming back to rest again beside her hostess. "And now she's had another letter," she told Elaine. "Mrs Richmond, I mean. It was from that companion of his, Dawkins, and he reports that Frampton says he's looking forward to seeing me again, and that he has news of some old friends of mine." Gnawing at her knuckle almost until it bled she raised anguished eyes to Elaine. "What shall I do? Suppose he knows about Ma? Or Will?"

CHAPTER
FIVE

At nine o'clock on yet another glorious morning in early summer the Richmond family were to be found at the trough, awaiting the arrival of the young master.

At eleven o'clock on that same morning Mrs Richmond, Agnes, Lily and Lady Frampton, together with a reluctant Charlotte, were on show in the morning-room, each lady, with the exception of the oldest present, apparently engaged upon some sewing. Mrs Richmond, indeed, set constant stitches into the scrap of fine lawn that was intended as a handkerchief for her returning hero but Charlotte, observing under her downcast lashes, saw that the needle was not actually threaded.

Lily was making a cover, in Berlin woolwork, for a gout stool for her dear papa, but today she stabbed viciously at the canvas in a manner reminiscent to Charlotte of a tale told her by an ex-convict years before. I wonder, she mused, if I should make a mammet of Frampton and stick pins in it? She watched Lily and wondered if Lily really saw the colourful canvas that she held so tightly. She is a country girl, Charlotte realized in sudden alarm. Perhaps her fancy was not so unlikely. That old woman in Adelaide had been transported for making a wax image of her neighbour, perhaps Lily also knew those old tales.

As with the other women, the piece Agnes was working on was typical of her. With her bull's eyes puffy and reddened and her long face cast into gloom, she was laboriously sewing at yet another small garment for yet another impending arrival down at the poorer end of the village. As Charlotte watched, Agnes paused for a moment and stared at the tiny nightgown. Pity wrung the younger girl's heart as she caught the expression on Agnes's face — poor Agnes, who only wanted a husband to look after and a baby to love, and who regarded the coming of her brother with unmitigated dread.

And what of me, Charlotte wondered as she worked her way efficiently through a heap of mending, her own and Agnes's, which she had commandeered in order to release Agnes for her charity work. I have spent a week of craven terror at the prospect of reunion with my lawful wedded spouse, and with good reason, so why am I today consumed with optimism? Surely it is a fallacious belief that no harm can come to me on so beautiful a day?

Her optimism might indeed be misplaced, she knew, but even so she hugged to herself the knowledge that at least one offer of sanctuary had been made to her. She would not take up the Knightleys' offer, she could not take advantage of their generosity by making difficulties with their neighbours, though the kindness warmed her heart. But what of Lady Frampton's situation? If Frampton threatened his grandmother's dog, would the old lady be earnest in her desire to leave Finchbourne or would she, in spite of her spirit and her own wealth, feel that she could not bear to alienate the only family left to her?

At half past twelve the Richmond ladies were joined at luncheon by Barnard who had visited every tenant in an effort to stay the general alarm. Mrs Richmond's temper was beginning to fray and she turned her wrath upon the absent Dr Perry.

"It is unforgivable of him not be here, in attendance," she fumed, tearing at a piece of bread. "What if my poor darling should faint upon his arrival, overcome by the emotion of his homecoming? It is not well done in the doctor, not well done at all. I have a good mind to dispense with his services, that would teach him a lesson."

"Indeed it would, Mama." Barnard gestured silence to the indignant Lily and Agnes, allowing a slight smile to reach his eyes as he exchanged glances with Charlotte. "He would be very well served. Of course, it would not be so convenient for us if we had to engage a doctor from Winchester — as indeed we should, there is none nearer — but it would certainly show Dr Perry the error of his ways."

At four o'clock the ladies were gathered yet again, though on this occasion in the drawing-room, where Agnes poured tea with nervous incompetence.

Charlotte accepted a cup, surreptitiously mopping up the sloppy saucer with her handkerchief, and wondered how they were to survive the rest of the day without breaking into open warfare. Lily had spent the day aiming her sharp little darts at Mrs Richmond, wondering at Frampton's escape, speculating upon his lengthy journey out of India, tittering at the gossip the whole episode must be occasioning in military circles both abroad and in London.

As Mrs Richmond responded angrily to this last, Charlotte engaged in some speculation of her own. Was it possible that Lily, of all people, had any suspicions regarding Frampton and his conduct? Not, to be sure, of Frampton's lack of interest in the ladies. Lily might be a country girl but her upbringing, Charlotte knew, would have been sheltered in the extreme, but might she have heard a hint of Frampton's financial concerns?

Barnard, although admirable and steady, was the last man to indulge in any thought beyond his immediate concerns, the estate and his household; could Silly Little Lily have received some intelligence from her Dear Papa? Charlotte had been privileged to meet this worthy and thought it highly unlikely that the Master of Martindale had a thought in his head beyond himself. No, Charlotte decided, if Lily had the slightest notion that Frampton might be under suspicion of making hay with the funds of the officers' mess, let alone of the even more contemptible matters she, Charlotte, had discussed with Kit Knightley, then Lily's pink gums and monumental teeth would have been bared in a constant grin of delight and her little piggy tongue would have wagged to such effect that the whole neighbourhood would now resound to the rumours.

They were still awaiting the arrival of the newly resurrected scion of the noble house of Richmond as

139

they sat down to their dinner. A hearty one, Charlotte noted with wry amusement. How appropriate, perhaps it would choke them all and thus relieve them of any further anguish.

With the arrival of her husband drawing ever closer — and surely, she thought, he must be almost upon them — Charlotte found her spirits unaccountably rising. To be sure, she mused, I am afraid of Frampton, particularly of his vicious tongue. But I have been brought up ever mindful of the need for an escape route, running away is what I do best. If the worst comes to the worst, I have that money safely tucked away in the bank in Southampton and I can just disappear. I could make a new beginning in London, Paris, New York, any one of those places must have openings for a governess who can produce the highest references. And some of those references might even be genuine. She found herself concealing a smile. Surely Elaine Knightley or Lady Frampton would oblige, not to mention the doctor's wife.

The smile faltered on her lips and the surge of optimism receded. Escape would be perfectly manageable so why am I so reluctant to consider such a course, she chided herself, knowing that the question needed no answer. Because I do not want to run. I have spent my entire life running away from everyone and everywhere and now I have found my place, this southern corner of England, this village with its ancient church, even this family.

Ludicrous as Mrs Richmond's ancestor worship might be, rootless Charlotte could sympathize with her, little as her mother-in-law would relish that sympathy. To put down roots, to live in the lands of one's ancestors, to sleep in a bed that once, a hundred, two hundred years ago, sheltered a man or woman of one's kin, to walk downstairs with one's hand on a bannister that had steadied one's forebears for generations. That feeling could never be Charlotte's, born fatherless to a frightened child, but living here she could pretend that she had a family, that she had a heritage, that she belonged.

It was not until the family had gathered uneasily in the drawingroom and were awaiting the tea tray that Frampton Richmond returned to the home of his fathers.

"Mr Frampton, ma'am, he's home!"

That was Hoxton as he threw open the door. Charlotte was aware, even as she stiffened in anticipation, that here was yet another member of the Finchbourne household who regarded Frampton's return to life as a mixed blessing. Behind Hoxton's mask of perfect service Charlotte was sure that she could detect an air of unease, but why? Mrs Richmond would as soon dismiss one of her children as lose Hoxton, the indispensable butler, no matter what Frampton might say, but why should Frampton do any such thing? What could it be that the man feared, for afraid he certainly was. Charlotte had lived too long as fear's companion to mistake the signs.

There was little time for conjecture as Frampton Richmond entered the room and all conversation stilled as the family stared with frank curiosity uppermost among the tumble of emotions each felt.

He looks . . . *smaller* . . . was Charlotte's first impression. He looks *ill*, was her second, and the thought was succeeded by a tiny involuntary shudder of relief. She had not realized how greatly she had feared his strength, that he might yet force himself upon her. Why, she breathed in relief, he looks as though a good strong wind would tip him off his feet. I am strong enough to handle him now.

As Frampton succumbed to his mother's raptures, Charlotte studied the man who had entered the room in her husband's wake. *Not* what I expected, she concluded, contriving to stare under her lashes, not at all as I imagined. The male companion she had envisaged had been one of a kind with Frampton's Indian favourite or those she had encountered in townships now and then, usually under the protection of some burly friend. I thought you would be another of those, she inwardly addressed Lancelot Dawkins as she watched him being presented to his hostess by a suddenly bashful Frampton. I expected a pretty boy and instead, what do we have here? A willowy youth, certainly, and very young too, which is no surprise since I saw Frampton's fancies in India, but this Dawkins could be apprentice to Machiavelli's Prince! Or to Old Nick? He's dark and sinister enough, in all conscience.

Every thought fled her mind now as Frampton, disengaging himself from his mother and brother, hostile Lily and clinging Agnes, made his way across the room towards his wife.

142

"Ah." He addressed her, with an odd little smile. "My sorrowing widow, I presume?"

"Frampton." She nodded coolly. "Won't you sit down? You must be exhausted after your journey." Her reserve broke a little. "Indeed, you don't look well. You should rest."

"Quite the little Miss Nightingale, is she not?"

Frampton beckoned to his companion.

"Here, Lance, come and make your bow to my lady wife. Charlotte, meet my dear friend, Lancelot Dawkins."

Frampton watched fondly as Lancelot Dawkins bent over her hand and received another cool nod and a polite greeting. Charlotte's studied indifference was suddenly shattered as, withdrawing her hand from the newcomer's grasp, she caught his eye. He was appraising her in a manner that was only too familiar yet even as she gave a tiny gasp he turned back to Frampton and resumed his role of admiring, even adoring, acolyte.

There was no time to puzzle over the episode. Frampton's arrival broke up the party, even Mrs Richmond ceasing in her paean of joy as she realized just how frail was her son's health.

Two days later Charlotte sat in her room awaiting the clangour of the dinner gong. With her hands clasped tightly in her lap she sat, fully dressed and awaiting the summons, reviewing the hours since Frampton Richmond set foot once more upon his own land. Only two days! Less than forty-eight hours and already the fears of so many people, family and estate workers alike, bade fair to be realized.

The frailty she had remarked in her husband had prevented him from asserting himself on the Friday evening, although his companion, the surprising Mr Dawkins, had been quite assertive enough for the pair of them with his constant harrying of Hoxton, the footmen and the maids, as they scurried to do his bidding, fetching in box after box, trunk after trunk, all apparently acquired en route, draping shawls and covers and hanging lamps as he directed.

It had fallen to Charlotte to soothe the harassed servants and, on Saturday, to mop up the tears occasioned by demands for delicacies, such as sherbert and curries, unknown to the cook, who, however, did her best, rising to the occasion with a cornflour shape, accompanied by her much-acclaimed raspberry jam.

"Indeed, Cook," she attempted to reassure the afflicted woman. "We must always remember that Major Richmond has lived in India for several years now and that he is really not at all well. Some recurring fever, I should guess. We must make every allowance for him. Come now, I think that shape looks delicious. Why not serve it up to the rest of us tonight?"

"That I will, Miss Char." Cook cheered up and dried her eyes. "And if, as I hear, they do like spicy food in those foreign parts, I'll do a nice sage and onion stuffing for the fowls too, and I'll make one of my caraway cakes, with an extra help of seeds. Though I must say, dress it up how you may, Mr Frampton always had a nasty way about him and it seems to me

144

that he's picked his friends according. You're too good for him, Miss Char, and that's all there is to it. However did you fetch up with him, if you don't think me impertinent for asking?"

"*I* don't," allowed Charlotte. "But you had better not let Mrs Richmond hear you say so, or let her hear you call me Miss Charlotte. As to why I married him? Let us just say that I was alone and penniless in a strange land in the middle of a war."

Agnes had disappeared after breakfast, pleading a long overdue visit to an old friend in Winchester. She had returned only in time to go straight to bed. Charlotte had tried to talk to her but Agnes put her off, with loving apology.

"It does no good, Char," she said in a dull tone. "I've spent most of the day in prayer in the cathedral and I've made up my mind. There is no arguing with Mama when she has Frampton to support her, so I shall tell Percy tomorrow that he is free to love another!" With a gulping sob and heaving bosom, Agnes shut herself into her bedroom and locked the door leaving her sister-in-law outside wondering whether to scream aloud in frustration or indulge in strong hysterics of her own.

Barnard had spent a second day out and about the land, coming home only in time for dinner, which was thankfully free of Frampton or his young friend. Lily continued to smoulder though she seemed less inclined now to blame Charlotte for the loss of her hopes for Barnard and even ventured a civil remark once or twice.

Charlotte herself was grateful to her husband for absenting himself for most of the day. Their only encounter occurred when Charlotte entered the drawing-room to hear Mrs Richmond in full, dramatic flight, telling her son all about her charity work. As the room rang with descriptions of the perversions and horrors she had encountered in her reading, Frampton stared at his mother with an inscrutable expression. He looked relieved at Charlotte's entrance and turned rapidly on his heel, muttering as he passed his wife: "She's mad, by God! Quite certifiably mad."

Old Lady Frampton kept to her room all day, sending for her meals on a tray and refusing to speak to anyone, even Charlotte, apart from a few brusque words uttered when Charlotte collected Prince Albert for a long tramp on the hills in the afternoon.

The fresh breeze up on the downs did much to clear Charlotte's head of the anxiety that seemed to assail her at every turn. The recollection of that moment of foresight in setting up a small secret hoard of money in the bank had given her something like hope and the picture in her mind's eye of the many moonlit escapes engineered by her stepfather reminded her that she was not trapped as she had feared.

"But I don't want to run away," she repeated aloud as she threw stick after stick for Prince Albert to retrieve. How tame Will Glover would have found this life of hers, how urgently he would have sought excitement, following some shimmering rainbow. But Ma would have understood, Charlotte thought, sobering suddenly. Yes, Molly would have entered wholeheartedly into her daughter's feelings. How she would have relished the bovine Richmonds and the appalling Henry Heavitree; how her eyes would have sparkled upon observing the love-lorn curate and his poor, plain sweetheart; and how she would have enjoyed the friendliness of village and gentry alike.

At that point in her deliberations, Charlotte espied a tall figure half a mile away on the further hill — Kit Knightley, accompanied by his retrievers. For a moment a longing swept over her, to cast her burdens into his capable hands, along with a desperate desire to discuss with him everything that had transpired since their last meeting, but in truth there was little to tell. And I cannot be rushing to Kit — to Kit and his *wife*, she reminded herself with a tiny pang — with every little problem. Turning on her heel, she whistled to the dog and headed homewards.

Just as she had recognized him in the clear light of the summer afternoon so Kit Knightley knew at once the slender woman hurrying away from him. He knew an instant's hot anger — why should she run from him — then his habitual good sense reasserted itself and he guessed at her emotions. Little enough he could do, in all conscience, he sighed, whistling up his own dogs as he too set off for home.

Mrs Richmond presided over a largely silent company at dinner on the Saturday night, the majority lost in thoughts too disturbing to utter. The lady of the house, however, had no complaint, indeed it was unlikely that she even noticed the general air of nervous anticipation.

"Aah!" she cried aloud as the cornflour shape made its appearance at dessert. "Well done, Cook. I see she has been trying to tempt my poor boy's appetite."

"Your poor boy, Mama," rejoined Barnard, "has rejected Cook's efforts to please him, in remarkably ill-chosen words. Unless," he added, spooning raspberry jam on to his plate, "unless he knew nothing of it and it was all the doing of that . . . of his companion."

His mother turned her astonished gaze upon him.

"Why, Barnard, my dear, you sound remarkably peevish. Do you not feel the utmost gratitude to Mr Dawkins for the care he takes of your poor brother? Indeed, I had a long, cosy talk with the young man this very morning and he has told me, in heartrending detail, of the suffering he has tried to alleviate. We owe him a debt of gratitude, not censure."

"If you say so, Mama," was the colourless reply as the animation faded from Barnard's face, which then assumed what Charlotte thought of as his "dumb ox" expression, something which had been more in evidence than usual since his brother's untimely return.

Lily, however, was not content to leave the matter.

"Did Mr Dawkins himself tell you how good he had been to Frampton, Mrs Richmond?" she asked sweetly. So sweetly that her mother-in-law eyed her with some suspicion, but her frown was met with a flash of gums and a head tilted in artless enquiry.

"Indeed he did." Mrs Richmond had evidently detected no note of sarcasm and made haste to elaborate upon her son's ailments, all of which had apparently been described in unsavoury detail by his constant companion.

"Serves you right, Lily," whispered Charlotte, taking advantage of an interruption by the butler. She was rewarded by a porcine smirk from across the table, quickly followed by a wary glance at Mrs Richmond.

That lady, however, was otherwise occupied in harrying the butler.

"Old Nurse informs me, Hoxton," she said in magisterial tones, "that the boot-boy has taken himself off home and it is not known when he will return. I am most displeased."

"I'm sorry, ma'am." Hoxton stood his ground. "It's young Tom, ma'am, my grandson. We had word that his mother, my daughter, that was widowed not long since, has been taken poorly and the boy is needed at home. I took it upon myself, ma'am, to let him go. I hope I did not do wrong."

Disarmed, Mrs Richmond could only nod, confirming the butler's course of action. Charlotte looked thoughtfully at the man, noting his heavy frown and the shadows under his eyes. Looking up suddenly she caught Barnard's eye as he wrenched his own gaze away from Hoxton; it seemed that the same thought had crossed both of their minds. Did Hoxton have grounds to fear something from Frampton, on his grandson's behalf?

That had been Saturday night.

On Sunday morning Frampton, apparently recovered from his intermittent fever, began to make his presence felt.

It began at breakfast when the head of the family appeared just after the rest of the household had taken their places at the massive mahogany table in the breakfast parlour, their jangled nerves soothed as they salivated at the vast quantities of bacon and eggs, pig's cheek, fish and bloody roast beef that temptingly overflowed the best Worcester plates set before them. (Following her outing with Lady Frampton, Charlotte had spent many patient hours coaxing Cook to try something other than boiling and the subsequent improvement in their meals had been met with approval from the family.)

Now Charlotte, as always, found herself lost in astounded admiration of the gargantuan appetites displayed by her Richmond in-laws. She herself ate sparingly at all times following another of Will Glover's many practical maxims: *"Cultivate a small appetite, Char, you never know when you might find yourself in a siege, or worse!"*

Well, she had found herself in just such circumstances only last year during the Mutiny, Charlotte reflected, and had seen for herself the force of Will's argument as the plumpest had died while she and the rest of Pharaoh's lean kine had survived famine.

"Shall you go to church today, Frampton dear?" fussed Agnes, casting a wary eye at her elder brother.

"Indeed I shall." Major Richmond frowned and blotted the sweat from his brow, although the morning was chill and overcast. "I have plans for the church, substantial plans. Uncle Henry will have to toe the line. I should have made great changes when I was last home

150

on leave but it was not so long after Mama's accident so I let it be for her sake."

He took a sip of his coffee.

"Faugh! This is disgusting, take it away, Hoxton, and bring me some new. Where was I? Ah, yes. Henry has always had the most regrettable tendency to follow the most Romish of practices, with his incense and saints' days and so forth — such nonsense. I'll stand it no longer. He will return to simple forms of worship or he will retire — the choice is his."

Unwisely, Agnes protested.

"But, Frampton, everyone in the village loves the service. I know Uncle Henry can be a little difficult, but —"

"What? Still hankering after that puny curate, I suppose? Don't think I cannot see what is behind your protest, sister. You may as well have it straight. I will not, under any circumstances, allow you to marry that puling commoner. No indeed, I have my own plans for your marriage, which will be infinitely more suitable."

With one accord the family's heads swivelled towards the willowy, saturnine youth at Frampton's right hand and a collective shudder shook them.

"That's right." Frampton had observed the direction of their stares and nodded, a genial smile failing to mask the determination on his face. "My friend, Lancelot Dawkins, will be a fine match for you, Agnes. To be sure you are a year or so his senior but that is no matter. Lance can match you pretty well in breeding — his aunt is Lady Tenterden and his uncle the Earl of Marlbury, so even Mama will be satisfied." Frampton

151

smiled fondly at his companion. "Setting that aside, I think you will agree that Lance is in every way ten times the man the curate is, Agnes, and I congratulate you heartily."

As Agnes paled in horror and the rest of the family looked on aghast, Lancelot Dawkins half rose in his seat and gave a graceful bow in Agnes's direction.

"Frampton has pre-empted me, Miss Agnes," he said with a smile. "It was only on Friday evening that we met, after all, though to be sure I told him myself, that very night, how very much taken I found myself by your charms. I hope to make myself acceptable to you in every way, if you will allow me."

Charlotte stared at the young man with narrowed eyes. That he wished to please Frampton was evident, and understandable, but to go to the length of marrying the unwilling Agnes? Perhaps, she thought, giving a tiny shrug, perhaps he wishes to hedge his bets — a wealthy paramour and a wife with a comfortable income of her own, which would be hers upon a marriage approved by her mother and brother.

The rest of the family maintained that stunned silence until it was broken by the arrival of Mrs Richmond, rising early for once in honour of her son. Barnard put a restraining hand on his wife's arm; Charlotte cast a warning glance at old Lady Frampton and reached under the table to aim a good, hard kick at Agnes who had half risen to reply to her brother's monstrous proposition.

"Ow! What? Why, Charlotte, what . . .?"

Charlotte scowled and shook her head, putting a finger to her lips as she looked at Mrs Richmond and mouthed the word "Later". Agnes subsided into a misery so heartfelt that even Lily became conscious of it.

"Oh, Frampton." She hurried into the conversation in, for once, a well-meant effort to distract attention from her spinster sister-in-law. "Old Nurse has been telling me about a visitor in the village. Did you hear of the mysterious Indian gentleman who was here recently? He was most anxious to talk about you and Nurse says he has returned and is staying at the Three Pigeons. How delighted he will be to find you alive and well!"

"What?" The colour darkened in Frampton's face as he turned angrily towards Lily. "What's that you say?"

As Lily repeated, with malice, her words, Frampton made a gesture of contempt.

"I'll have no stranger in my house," he declared, looking furiously round the table. "Do you hear me? If the fellow dares to accost any one of you, turn on your heel. And you, Hoxton, you will deny the fellow if he tries to get in here. I won't have it, I say. *I will not have it*!"

As soon as breakfast was finished, Charlotte took Agnes by the arm and dragged her, unresisting, upstairs.

"Come with me," she said firmly. "Never mind your mama, or Frampton, or anyone. As far as they are concerned we are getting ready for church."

"Now." She closed her bedroom door behind her and thrust Agnes into a comfortable upholstered chair. "First things first. Why is Frampton so out of tune with the rest of you about church? Mrs Richmond likes the High Church service, she has told me so, several times. What makes Frampton different?"

Agnes looked pained at what she clearly considered an irrelevance but the protest died on her lips and she sighed. "Frampton used to enjoy the service as much as the rest of us. Then near the end of the leave before his last he became very friendly with a curate at a parish in Southampton. This young man held decidedly Low Church views and Frampton came under his spell, almost lived in his pocket. It was all most unpleasant. Frampton was very vehement in his condemnation of Uncle Henry and what he called his popish ways, but luckily his leave was up then and everything settled down. And as he said just now, his last leave was not so very long after dear Mama's accident and he could not bring himself to distress her so."

"But he feels able to distress her now?" Charlotte felt a pang of reluctant sympathy for Frampton's mother, rejoicing at her great good fortune, only to face an uproar that must shake the eminent foundations of the sacred Richmond family.

"What am I to do, Charlotte?" Agnes was too wrapped up in her own drama to care about Uncle Henry and the rites of the Anglican church. "He can't make me marry that young man, can he? He can't be twenty yet and such a creature, I'd rather die!"

154

"Oh, don't be so melodramatic," Charlotte snapped. "Of course he can't. Pull yourself together, Agnes, and let us think."

She paced round the room considering and rejecting plan after plan.

"I know," she proclaimed suddenly. "Percy must go to the bishop and ask for a living somewhere else. The bishop is of the same High Church persuasion, he will sympathize with Percy and will make no difficulty. Then all you have to do is be strong and wait until Percy is settled, then you can marry him and everything will be all right. You're quite correct — Frampton cannot *force* you to marry Dawkins."

The plan seemed to her to have as many holes in it as a colander but Agnes was comforted so Charlotte continued. "You must seize your chance and tell Percy today and he must go into Winchester tomorrow, first thing in the morning, and see the bishop, even if he has to sit outside the door all day." She cast a look at the damply distressed creature huddled in her armchair and sighed. "For pity's sake, Agnes, have some backbone. There must be plenty of parishes crying out for a hardworking man like Percy, not to mention an even harder-working curate's wife, as you will prove."

There was no time for further discussion. The church clock could be heard striking the hour and the two girls hastened to join the family party.

At the church door Charlotte contrived to push Agnes towards her hovering swain, shielding them from Frampton's gaze by drawing his attention to the display

155

of pink and yellow tulips which adorned the nearest grave.

"Do you not admire it, Frampton?" she enquired in a bright, artificial voice. "It must strike so fresh upon you after so long in India. I find the colours of England so delightful and so must you."

"Hmm? What? Oh yes, very fine." He stared at her in surprise but made no attempt to resist as she urged him onwards into the cool darkness of the porch. To her relief she spotted Agnes hurrying after them with the curate following at a discreet distance. If Percy Benson had been amazed at Agnes's proposition he betrayed no sign of it, rather displaying a thoughtful face while Agnes seemed much calmer.

Charlotte, meanwhile, was conscious of a moment of sudden joy, hastily suppressed, when she caught sight of Kit Knightley making his way towards their party.

"Richmond!" He nodded to Frampton and shook his hand. "I heard you were restored to life. Your mother must be delighted."

They exchanged a few commonplaces, Frampton appearing surprised but pleased at this attention, then after a cool nod in acknowledgement of Lancelot Dawkins and a friendly handclasp to Barnard, Kit was bowing slightly over Charlotte's own hand.

"Mrs Richmond." His greeting was polite, her curtsey demure. "Still managing to see the funny side, Char, in spite of all?" This last was in a lowered tone as Frampton stopped to speak to an acquaintance.

"Sometimes." There was the ghost of her merry twinkle in the hazel eyes and he pressed her hand again.

156

"Good girl," was all he said, then, as he turned away, he added, "Come and see Elaine — she says that even if she is in bed, she will have them admit you."

Charlotte was a little comforted. The service took its normal course, if possible, even greater wafts of incense so that Charlotte's head began to swim while Henry Heavitree bellowed from the pulpit above her, making great mention of miserable sinners who would despoil his church — and this, as Charlotte well knew, without yet having confronted Frampton. He then launched into a condemnation of the parable of the prodigal son.

"And what, in God's name, was Jesus thinking of?" he thundered, causing several of his hardened parishioners to start awake. "Why the devil *should* the poor bastard of a father celebrate the arrival of a bloody wastrel? Eh, can you tell me that? Fatted calf, God's nightgown, I'd give him fatted calf! I'd shove it down his throat, the bastard, till he choked on it. Send him back with a flea in his ear, that's what they should have done, and by God, I can tell you, that if I had been the good son, the one who stayed at home and did all the damned work, I'd have peppered his breeches with more than shot, the bloody Bulgarian, that I would!"

Charlotte's downcast lashes flew up at this diatribe and instinctively she shot a glance across the aisle to where Kit Knightley was struggling to retain his composure. As she watched him bite his lips he caught her eye and was lost, and, as at their first meeting, he sought to disguise his laughter as a coughing fit. I do have friends, Charlotte consoled herself, whatever else befalls me. She firmly set aside that sudden leap of

157

delight at the sight of Kit and thought instead of her friend, Kit's wife.

The vicar's confrontation with Frampton could no longer be put off. At the church door Henry loomed above his nephew, baring yellow fangs in a snarl of rancour.

"Well, nephew Frampton? Back from the dead, I see. There is no understanding of the ways of Providence. Why should you be saved, by God, and many a good man lost?"

"Why, Uncle . . ."

As Frampton began to expostulate, Lancelot Dawkins stepped swiftly into the fray, drawling: "Major Richmond is indebted to you, sir, for your good wishes upon his miraculous restoration."

This interruption, while it gained Dawkins a look of gratitude from a suddenly weary Frampton, inspired the vicar to greater heights of affront.

"What's that? Hey? You young puppy, do you address me? What are you if not Frampton's catamite? Do you dare soil the air around us with your viper's tongue?"

"Really, sir?" The viper's tongue was suddenly in evidence as Lancelot Dawkins smiled at Henry Heavitree. "I advise you to keep a civil tongue of your own in your head, sir, as I speak for Major Richmond on *all* subjects. I assure you, sir, that you may believe me, for I quote my friend's words exactly on this — you will cease to contaminate the air of this holy edifice with your smells and your saints and your statues, and you will dress in a decent black suit of clothes as befits a man of your calling. Major Richmond is determined that you will desist from making a mockery of God's word by dressing in a popish gown."

He let this intelligence sink in and cut in smoothly as Henry opened his mouth to protest.

"Pray, sir, do not dispute this command."

Taking advantage of the sudden silence that fell upon the group at the church door, Lancelot Dawkins looked about him, cast a glance at Frampton, who nodded with that same weary look on his face, and raised a hand.

"While I have your attention," Dawkins continued, "I should warn Major Richmond's tenants to expect drastic changes in the near future. The major is appalled to discover how lax management of the estate has become of late, with tenants pampered and promised improvements to their cottages that are quite beyond their station. Major Richmond wishes me to inform you all that what was good enough for his father and grandfather is good enough for him and that all pretensions will be discouraged — forcibly."

As a sullen murmur began, Lancelot Dawkins raised his hand again.

"Rents, will, of course, be reviewed in the near future. The estate has been run most uneconomically and this *will* be rectified."

This time it was Lily's turn to restrain Barnard as he caught the tail of this pronouncement and rounded angrily on his brother.

"*Frampton!* You cannot —"

"Barnard, take me home at *once!* I feel faint." Lily would not be gainsaid and Barnard reluctantly took her arm and led her home, the dark colour in his face reflecting his anger.

Charlotte and Agnes followed suit in silence. There was too much to say and no answer as yet apparent. They dawdled round the village in order to let Frampton reach the house ahead of them, no sense in provoking a confrontation.

"Go and do some sewing, Agnes," Charlotte suggested as they entered the house at last. "As for me, I think I'll take Prince Albert for a long tramp."

A rapid tap at the door and Charlotte let herself into old Lady Frampton's room.

"Gran! What is it?"

Lady Frampton was half lying in her chair, her handkerchief to her face.

"He's done it, me dear. What I feared all along."

"What? Not Prince Albert? He hasn't . . . He can't . . ."

"Oh yes 'e can." The old lady roused herself and blew her nose resoundingly. "I'm to 'and the dog over to that Dawkins tomorrow, 'e says, and then I'm to get meself packed as 'e intends to put me out to grass in some 'ouse in London that's owned by that Dawkins's h'aunt."

"He can't do that!" Charlotte was incensed. "I'll go to Mrs Richmond — she won't let him."

"Ah, but she will, me dear." The old lady was sorrowful but definite. "I spoke to 'er meself, straightaway, but she's all fired up to please 'er boy, as she calls 'im, so she won't h'interfere."

160

Charlotte sat down on a stool at Lady Frampton's feet, idly fondling the silky spaniel ears as Prince Albert nuzzled her hopefully.

"First thing tomorrow morning," she announced with resolution. "I'll take Prince Albert over to Knightley Hall — Kit and Elaine will look after him for us until we can think of something. Please, Gran, don't cry anymore, everything will turn out for the best, see if it doesn't."

Having fired warning shots across the entire village, the estate workers, the vicar, his brother, his sister and his grandmother, Frampton reserved his most terrifying bolt for his wife, delivered as she encountered him at the open glass doors of the drawing-room.

"Ah, Charlotte." He addressed her amiably. "Admiring the garden? It is very pleasant, is it not? Something new in your experience, I have no doubt?"

"As you say." She eyed him warily and was not reassured by his smile.

"Come, let us sit in the arbour. I want to talk to you and I do not want to be overheard. I had forgotten that the world and his wife eavesdrop on everything in this house."

Silently she let him precede her to the charming arbour on the boundary of the rose garden. Equally silently she accepted his offer of a seat, where she tried to concentrate on the tendrils of the honeysuckle winding its way up the trellised arbour, the scent from the lilacs to the side, shading from purest white to deepest royal purple, and the sounds of the garden,

161

bees, birds and the distant sound of sawing from the stable yard.

"We have had very little opportunity of conversation since my return, have we, Mrs Richmond?"

"You have had much to do," she returned quietly and was aware of the sour twist of his smile.

"Oh yes," he answered. "You must be wondering what your portion of my reforms will be."

"I don't deny it." She strove to remain calm, holding her hands lightly in her lap, hiding the nails that dug into her flesh.

"You are a cool customer," he acknowledged. "I admire that. I chose well when I took you for my bride."

"I was not aware that you — or I — had a choice," she was goaded into saying.

"Perhaps not, but a sensible woman is far easier to deal with than some of the hysterical females I have encountered on my travels. For instance . . ." He smiled again and she felt a trickle of fear run down her spine. "There was a lady on board the ship who dwelt glowingly upon your charms and your skill in nursing; she had come across you in your flight overland from those mutinous dogs. Most impressed she was, apparently, by your helpfulness to so many other women in difficulties. I tell you, I was quite basking in your reflected glory."

"Is there a point to this narrative, Frampton?" Charlotte was angry with herself for rising to his bait but the tension was becoming unbearable.

162

"Oh yes, my dear, indeed there is. Later in the conversation, this dear lady, after she had indulged herself in one of her all too many bouts of reminiscent weeping and wailing, told how many of the poor ladies had found that they had been taken advantage of and had lost little trinkets and garments and so forth — only one or two objects from each lady, nothing greedy, nothing to inspire an immediate hue and cry. We agreed that the natives were shocking and I joined her in hoping that my dear, noble young wife had not suffered a similar misfortune."

He quirked an eyebrow as she sat in taut silence.

"No? How fortunate. But I did not think *you* would have done, not with your upbringing to sustain you."

Had it come, the moment Charlotte had been dreading? Was she to be exposed? She strove to school her expression into one of cool indifference, while her heartbeat sounded so loud inside her head she was sure he must hear it.

"What do you mean?"

"Mean? Why, my dear, I'll tell you. I discovered from someone, a person you will be glad to hear is now dead, that your precious stepfather, the sainted Will Glover, was nothing more than a common criminal, a convict who had escaped from Botany Bay and travelled the length and breadth of Australia posing as a clergyman. A nice little arrangement he made for himself, I was told. Settle in some remote area, build up a trusting congregation and then, when they had collected enough to build a church, a summons would arrive from Adelaide, or it might be Melbourne, or even

Sydney, and the Reverend William Glover would have to set off to see his dying father, or mother, or his brother, as it might be. What more natural than that his devoted wife and daughter should accompany him? As for the building fund for the church, why that accompanied him as well, leaving his parishioners older and wiser and considerably poorer."

Charlotte forced herself to stay in her seat, fighting an impulse to leap to her feet, to make an unladylike fist and punch her tormentor in his sneering mouth. And then what? Flight? No, she told herself, he has some scheme or other, he must have, otherwise he would have announced this as soon as he arrived. She felt as though her face had frozen into that expression of chilly calm and her back ached from being held stiff as a ramrod, but her pride in not letting go sustained her.

He poked his head down at her.

"What? Not a word to say? Dear me, perhaps I should tell you some more of my story. Now where was I? Ah yes, that was your stepfather. Your mother now . . . What was that, my dear? Did you wish to say something? How very wise, do not interrupt me now, pray, I am in fine voice. Yes, your mama . . . Unfortunately my informant could not furnish me with any history for your dear mother, but she was *most* forthcoming when it came to your exalted godmother."

"Lady Margaret Fenton. What a ring that name has, does it not? Nothing about it to suggest the drab she became. As I heard it the lady's exasperated brother, the earl, paid good money to ship her to the colonies,

164

and a retainer to stay there, rather than have her embarrass him at every turn. Very fond of young gentlemen, I believe, was Lady Meg, *very* fond."

He gave a snort of laughter and clapped his hands on his knees as Charlotte sat white-faced and shivering in spite of the warmth of the sun.

"I can't say *I* find it in my heart to blame her, not *I*, certainly. However, I digress. The final straw, I believe, came about when Lady Meg announced herself with child by one of her many, many, *many* amours and when her brother suggested marrying her off she almost sent him off in an apoplexy by informing him that the father of her child was a fine strapping footman from Jamaica whom she had seduced in a ducal household and therefore a trifle difficult to foist even upon the most unsuspecting dotard. What became of that child, I wonder? Did your godmama ever confide in you? I have no information as to how she picked up your mother and yourself but I was told, as an incontrovertible fact, that Lady Meg met her death from a seizure while pleasuring — on the dining-room table, too! — a distinguished foreign guest (a very distinguished foreign guest!) of the governor of New South Wales and that the whole affair almost caused a diplomatic incident."

He sat back, waiting for a response.

"Why are you telling me this?" Charlotte spoke through dry lips.

"Isn't it obvious? I want you to do as you are told and if you do not I shall, with great regret, be forced to reveal the shocking truth about my bride and how grievously I have been deceived." He shifted his position and added, "At present, no-one but myself knows about this, not even my dear Lance. He can be, alas, a trifle indiscreet at times. I might be persuaded to hold my tongue, Charlotte, upon terms."

"What do you want of me?"

"No need to grit your teeth, my dear." He laughed and patted her hand, laughing again as she snatched it away. "Oh no, you are quite safe from my attentions now; as you are very well aware, my tastes run in quite another direction. However, my beloved Lance is altogether a more complex character."

"What?" She was outraged. "But I thought you wanted to marry him off to Agnes?"

"I do, my dear, I do indeed. I can think of no better brother-in-law and of course I shall always welcome them in my home. In fact, I shall *insist* that they live with me. No, Charlotte, think for a moment. My mother has already lost no time in harping on at me about an heir for Finchbourne." He looked aggrieved as Charlotte shrank away in horror. "For pity's sake, girl, be practical. *I* need an heir, *Lance* is willing, *you* have no choice."

"I won't do it!" She spat the words at him.

"You will, if you wish to continue living within a hundred miles of here." He spoke decidedly, the pleasant air gone and in its place an implacable determination. "I have heard your praises sung by almost everyone since I arrived, Charlotte. I know how much you have made this place your home. Do you think I do not understand you? I've been watching you, my dear, when you were unaware. You love this place and all the people in it and there is very little that you would not do if it allowed you to remain here."

Even in the midst of her distress, Charlotte was amazed at the perception Frampton displayed. That he, of all people, should recognize her desperate need for the security and love afforded her by Finchbourne and its inhabitants, tore at her heart.

"There, there." Frampton patted her shoulder again in a parody of husbandly affection. "You are overcome, and no wonder. I shall not press you, you may rest assured, but I promise you, Charlotte, you *will* do as I tell you. Between us you and I and Lance will furnish my mama with the heir she so desires!"

CHAPTER
SIX

Dinner was a sombre affair. At one point Charlotte observed Agnes cast a harried glance around the table, open her mouth to utter one of her usual inanities, catch her mother's glacial eye and perform her celebrated, if involuntary, impersonation of a rabbit, eyes staring, nose twitching and teeth nibbling at her bottom lip as she subsided meekly into her chair.

Barnard attacked his thick slice of beefsteak with an air of frowning concentration, shrugging off Lily's interruptions. He and Frampton had come in together from the stable yard but there was nothing friendly or fraternal about their attitude. Now and again Barnard raised his eyes from his dinner and stared thoughtfully at his elder brother from under furrowed brows but Frampton ignored him, chatting all the while, in an inconsequent manner, with his mother and Lancelot Dawkins.

Charlotte picked at her food, shrunk in on herself so that she was at the farthest possible distance from Dawkins, who sat next to her, so that no part of her body could conceivably be in contact with his. Her mirror had shown her a face pinched and wan with misery but tonight even her most heroic efforts failed, and she made no effort to conceal her state of mind.

Uncle Henry, who was dining with them, tore into his bloody beef with yellowing tombstone incisors, glaring all the while at his nephew with an expression of disbelief and mounting anger. Frampton's (or Dawkins') announcement at the church door had all but robbed his uncle of the power of speech — no mean feat, Charlotte reflected, dragging herself out of her introspection. Frampton had later, after shaking his wife's foundations, taken off to Winchester accompanied by the obsequious Dawkins, thereby robbing his uncle of a legitimate prey. Tormenting the hapless curate had, for once, failed to satisfy the vicar, so Charlotte had gathered from Agnes's hurried aside, and only a concerted blast at the rapidly decreasing colony of magpies in the churchyard elms prevented him from an apoplexy.

Agnes was apparently not the only diner to notice the brooding atmosphere in the room. Charlotte observed that Lily had withdrawn from her self-absorption and was smiling with bright malice at her inlaws. With little difficulty Charlotte read Lily's thoughts; her sainted papa's code of conduct at Martindale required women to be spritely and sweet, so Lily had apparently determined that she would be both, in spite of her fury at Frampton's atrocious treatment of his brother. She leaned forward to address her mother-in-law.

"My goodness, we are all so gloomy today, are we not? Mama Richmond, how is your back today? You are looking very well."

She ignored the martyred sigh with which this deliberate provocation was received and turned her fire upon Frampton.

"How was dear Lady Walbury today, Frampton? I saw her talking to you in the village this afternoon as I drove home from my visit to my friends. Poor creature, she seemed much agitated, I thought. Such a waste of a sweet bunch of early pinks she was carrying, the way she was shredding the petals. Still, hers is such a sad, sad story."

"Lily!" Agnes hurtled into the breach in horror as a frozen silence filled the room. "Won't you have another glass of wine, dear? And perhaps you, Charlotte dear? In fact, let us all have some more wine in — in celebration." Her voice tailed off in the ensuing silence.

"Oh do hush, Agnes, do!" There was an edge to Mrs Richmond's voice and Agnes subsided, bright patches of colour on her cheeks, eyes downcast in mortification. She brightened a little when Charlotte gave her a small, tight smile, immediately extinguished when Lancelot Dawkins edged nearer, smiling also.

"Frampton?" Mrs Richmond's tone was surprisingly chilly as she addressed her Lazarus. "I did not know that Lady Walbury had returned from London. What did she want with you? The woman is mad and I wish you to have nothing to do with her."

"The woman was an exceeding nuisance," put in Lancelot Dawkins in his irritatingly languid voice. "Poor Frampton was so much agitated by the encounter that he had to lie down upon his bed for quite half an hour, his pulse racing. He is not well

170

enough for such scenes, indeed he is not. Why is the woman not locked away in some suitable asylum?"

For once the Richmonds were a united herd as they glared with disdain at the upstart Dawkins.

"That is not your concern, Mr Dawkins." Barnard spoke with a decision that elicited a rare nod of approval from his mother and admiration from his other female relatives, despite their own preoccupations, old Lady Frampton going so far as to say, "Well spoken, lad, 'ear, 'ear!"

"Lady Walbury is an elderly woman and a much respected resident of these parts," Barnard continued. "And everyone is more than willing to make allowances for her eccentricities of speech and manner. We all, unhappily, know the cause from which they sprang. Pray let us hear no more about it."

He returned his attention to his plate, ignoring his brother who seemed about to speak, then thought better of it, throwing down his spoon and slouching back in his chair.

"My dear Frampton," was Lancelot Dawkins's next foray into the conversation. "You really do not look well, my dear fellow. You should retire early tonight."

"Yes, you do look ill, Frampton," agreed Mrs Richmond, peering at her heir in concern before turning to the butler, who had brought her the evening post. "Perhaps you should take more rest, dear, you are very flushed. Here, let me see if there are any letters for you. No, no, one for Barnard; one for you, Lily, from your papa; one for me."

Making no apology to the assembled company, she proceeded to open her own letter.

"Why, good gracious me! Frampton, my dear boy, you will be interested to hear this, most interested indeed. Your very own commanding officer, Colonel Fitzgibbon, writes that he will be in Winchester on business for a day or so — no, let me see, for the better part of a week, he says — and intends to call upon us tomorrow having heard of your return. What a very pretty attention to be sure. I wonder . . ." She paused and brightened. "I wonder if I could interest him in my charity works? The military must furnish him with so many *dreadful* . . . What . . .? Why, Frampton, dear boy, whatever is the matter?"

"No, Mama!" Frampton was on his feet, his chair overturned behind him. "He must not come here. I will not . . . I cannot see him. You must send at once to tell him to keep away. I — I cannot . . ."

To their consternation he took a step back, clasped a hand to his head with a groan and collapsed in a dead faint, his face suddenly drained of the blood which had suffused it.

Barnard was beside him in an instant.

"Out of my way," he bellowed as he thrust Lancelot Dawkins aside as Frampton's supposed nurse dabbed ineffectually at Frampton's brow with his own elegant silk handkerchief. "Here, Hoxton." He gestured to the butler. "Send someone to prepare Major Richmond's room then come back and help me with him."

He ripped open his brother's coat. "Let him have some air. By heavens, he is burning up with fever and shaking like a leaf besides. He must be got to bed without delay."

Charlotte rose quietly and left the room. At Frampton's door she met the head housemaid, who was trying to have hysterics because she had missed all the excitement and felt it to be her due.

"That's enough," Charlotte said decidedly. "Stop that noise at once or I'll throw a bucket of cold water over you. Let me check Mr Frampton's room. Here, get rid of all these cushions and kickshaws and open the windows at once. A sick man needs fresh air, not this stifling atmosphere. And what's this? Incense burners? Good God, I thought Frampton preached austerity!"

She turned at the sound of footsteps on the stairs.

"Is that you, Barnard? Lay him down on his bed for a moment and I will help you. Unless you would care to do so, Mr Dawkins? You are, after all, allegedly employed as nurse-companion to my husband?"

Lancelot Dawkins was too preoccupied in making dashes about the room bewailing her depredations on the Ottoman elegance of his arrangements, to heed her tone.

"Oh, how could you!" He sounded, for the first time in their acquaintance, like the very young stripling he was, his voice raised in complaint, shorn of its drawling veneer. "Look at this velvet cushion, this silk coverlet; they're worth a fortune and thrown aside as if they were common calico. I told Frampton the moment I met you that you were beneath him."

"I take that as meaning that you do not intend to be of any practical assistance, Mr Dawkins," was

Charlotte's only response, delivered in her driest tone, as she and Barnard rapidly stripped the invalid of his evening dress.

"What's this? Oh, thank you, Hoxton, just what we need, tepid water. Could you ask cook to send up some barley water, please? Lots of fluids, I think, don't you, Barnard?"

Barnard nodded as they sponged Frampton's burning, sweating body, wringing out cloths and laying them on his flushed forehead as he shook and muttered incoherently.

Lancelot Dawkins then tried to recoup his position as he retreated to the bedroom door.

"This is not the same fever that I have nursed Frampton through," he told them, shaking his head. "It is something new, and to me, it looks very much more serious."

"Then you must leave us, Mr Dawkins," Charlotte told him, feigning concern. "I have no doubt that you have already caught the infection from Frampton so I will ask Hoxton to have a room prepared for you in the attics, that the rest of the household need not suffer. I think you should lie down at once, you may be in grave danger. I wonder if it could be cholera?"

Barnard waited until they were alone, the reluctant Dawkins, stripped of his sophistication and now plainly a frightened adolescent, firmly under Hoxton's magisterial hand.

"What do you actually think it is, Charlotte? *Not* cholera really, I think?"

174

"I think it must be malaria or some similar sort of fever." She shook her head slightly and answered in her usual matter-of-fact manner. She took an invalid feeder from the butler who had passed Dawkins to the footman, and tried to induce Frampton to take some liquid. "I've seen these chills and tremors before, in Australia, and in India. The only thing we can do is what we are, in fact, doing; plenty of fluids and keep him sponged down, taking care not to let him become chilled."

For some time they were fully occupied with their work, addressing only brief commands to each other. After what seemed an age Charlotte straightened up for a moment, her hand in the small of her back.

"Oof! How I ache. You know, Barnard, if it is malaria, he should have quinine, so perhaps we should send again for Dr Perry."

"Whatever you require, dear Charlotte." Barnard's tone was warm with approval as he wiped the sweat from his eyes and watched his sister-in-law as she deftly tucked her husband's sheets about him. "Mrs Perry promised to send the doctor here the moment he returns from his business meeting in Southampton, but I think you may have done the trick without him. Frampton seems a little quieter now, don't you agree?"

She nodded and went to look out of the window into the summer darkness, taking in great lungfuls of the scented air wafting up from the lilacs in the bed below.

"Oh, that's so much better. How lovely this dear place is, you can have no idea."

Barnard wiped his hands on a towel and set it down before he joined her, gazing up at the hills behind the house.

"You are a remarkable woman, Charlotte," he said quietly and put a comforting arm about her shoulders. "Instead of fighting for his life you might rather have been hoping for a different outcome."

She turned her head and stared at him, their eyes meeting for a long moment in the shadowy silence before she shrugged and turned aside.

"I know, I'm a fool to myself, am I not? But I think you are exaggerating, you know, Barnard. I don't think he was — or is — in any danger of dying." Her lashes drooped and she rallied for a moment. "But perhaps we should not tell that to the unspeakable Dawkins; with luck he might take fright and leave!"

"Hmm!" Barnard set her gently into a chair. "That's a capital notion. Here, sit down and rest a while. I'll call for a cup of tea — I know you'd like one. And a brandy for myself, I think. Or would you prefer spirits yourself?"

She shook her head with a weary smile.

"A cup of tea would be perfect, thank you. And Barnard, I think you should go and reassure Mrs Richmond and find Lily — she will be missing you. I can manage Frampton quite well now. I think the fever will probably return but just for the moment he is sleeping." She shooed him towards the bedroom door. "Go along. If I need help I'll send for you, don't fret, but Lily needs you more, especially at this delicate stage of her condition. And don't forget my cup of tea!"

176

He left the room in haste to do her bidding. Charlotte sighed with relief. What bliss to be alone for a few minutes. She stared down at her husband, tossing and turning on the bed before her. Why *am* I doing this? she queried. Barnard is quite right, she reflected, if Frampton were to die of this fever it would solve all our problems. She sighed and turned to the open window again. Foolish even to embark upon such thoughts, she shrugged, and as to why I'm nursing him — why not? *Somebody* has to and nobody else seems capable of doing so.

The night wore on endlessly. Frampton slept intermittently and awoke to bouts of fever and delirium while Charlotte and Old Nurse took turns with Barnard to sponge him down and administer the quinine Dr Perry had left with them.

"To be frank with you," the doctor had confessed, "I have no idea if this is malaria or not but I suppose the quinine will do no harm and may do some good. I'll grant it looks like malaria but you cannot always tell." He looked kindly at Charlotte. "Managing all right, are you, lass? Why can't that secretary-companion creature of Frampton's do this for him? I'd have thought the last thing you wanted to do was to nurse the man."

"That's just what Barnard said," she told him with a tired laugh. "What a hotbed of gossip this village is, to be sure. Does everyone know how matters stand between Frampton and me?"

He took her pulse while looking at her in thoughtful silence then, restoring her hand to her with a reassuring pat, he nodded.

"Well, that's village life for you, I'm afraid. In any case, Barnard's not so stupid as he looks and he can be a good friend once he makes up his mind to do so. A pity he had to go and ally himself to that monstrous little female though perhaps if she succeeds in whelping she may become a little less self-centred."

He clearly saw that she was still concerned and raised a quizzical eyebrow. "Well, what is it? You're too sensible to worry about a fever."

"No, of course not." She leaned out of the window to take a deep breath of fresh air then turned back to him. "It's just . . . Lady Walbury's daughter, the one who drowned herself. Was she really with child by Frampton?" At the doctor's look of slight bewilderment, she made a hasty gesture of apology. "It's not idle curiosity, I'm trying to understand him."

"I see." He took her hand and patted it again with fatherly kindness, warming her chilled heart. "Put your mind at rest, my dear. Emily Walbury was never pregnant. The poor lass was dying from a dropsical complaint, which is what gave rise to the rumour. Pain and fear led her to do away with herself, nothing to do with your husband." He shook his head in pity. "As for her mother, poor soul, well — grief takes us all in many different ways."

"You would tell me if there were any risk of infection, wouldn't you, Dr Perry?" She smiled her thanks and changed the subject.

He reassured her again, this time with a kindly arm round her shoulders.

178

"I would say there should be no risk of infection either to yourself or Barnard. Yes, I realize you are thinking of Lily but I would tell you if I thought her in any danger. Mind you, I have no objection to telling that young Dawkins that I fear for Frampton's life!"

At two in the morning Old Nurse bustled her off to bed, scolding in her soft country accents.

"As if I couldn't look after Master Frampton that I nursed that time the dog bite on his backside went poisonous and serve him right for tormenting the poor creature. Oh dear, he does look bad, whatever the doctor says. Still, off you go, my dearie, there's a good girl, you need your rest, as do we all, to bear this life of sorrows."

Sent packing by these heartening words, Charlotte lay wakeful for a time, going over the last few hours. That Frampton was really ill was irrefutable, even if his collapse had occurred at a remarkably convenient moment for him.

Why had he been arguing in the street with Lady Walbury? Lily was not the only witness to the encounter, Frampton's grandmother had also been on the spot, emerging from the draper's side entrance (opened illicitly on the Sabbath just to oblige an excellent customer), whither she had taken herself in search of distraction and a length of red flannel for her rheumatism. Lady Walbury had, it appeared (Charlotte had learned from Old Nurse), made repeated efforts to speak to Frampton in the short time since his return. All of these attempts had been foiled by Lancelot Dawkins or by Frampton himself.

179

And what was all that to-do about Colonel Fitzgibbon? Charlotte pondered Frampton's almost hysterical response to the news of the colonel's proposed visit. His agitation might indeed have been sparked by the onset of the fever but it had seemed rather different. Rather like an outburst of terror, but why should Frampton, a grown man and a major in Her Majesty's army to boot, be afraid to meet his commanding officer?

At half past nine the next morning Charlotte opened reluctant eyes and looked at the clock on her mantelpiece. "Oh, heavens!" she exclaimed aloud as she leapt out of bed and splashed cold water on her face. Oh well, she thought as she pulled on her clothes, I suppose Frampton is no worse or Old Nurse would have called me. And there is one blessing, at least I shan't have to endure family breakfast this morning.

A timid knock at the door heralded Agnes accompanied by the upstairs maid carrying a tray.

"Dearest Charlotte! You *are* awake, after all. Here is some breakfast for you. We have all had ours already."

"Frampton?" Charlotte nodded her thanks for the breakfast and looked anxiously at her sister-in-law.

"Up and down, is what Nurse says." Agnes thumped her shoulder affectionately, not noticing how Charlotte recoiled under the blow. "The fever comes and goes and Nurse thinks it will go on for a day or so."

"That's just what I thought would happen." Charlotte was drinking her tea with thirsty enjoyment. "Fevers like that always look very distressing to relatives but are usually over and done with quite quickly and with little harm done. I imagine Frampton picked it up somewhere in India or on his mysterious travels home."

She ate some of the toast Agnes had brought and drank another cup of tea.

"Tell me, Agnes, will Percy go to see the bishop?"

Agnes purpled in embarrassment and nodded mutely.

"Well done." Charlotte congratulated her heartily and Agnes was encouraged to speak.

"Indeed, Percy felt you must have been divinely inspired when I told him what you said," she gushed. "He managed to slip word to me a short time ago that he was even now on his way to the bishop's palace and would do as you advised — refuse to leave until he has spoken to His Lordship!"

"Well done, Percy," Charlotte said again, rejoicing at the improvement in Agnes's spirits. "You must hold firm to that and remember that Frampton cannot force a grown woman into a marriage she does not want." She recalled another of her husband's victims. "How is Lady Frampton this morning? I must try to have a word with her."

"Oh, Grandmama is in fine fettle." Agnes smiled. "She was muttering something about Judgement Day but she was looking very pleased."

Charlotte sighed with relief. Lady Frampton's problem, like her own, could be postponed while the heir to Finchbourne lay ill. Another thought struck her. "What about Dawkins?"

Agnes gurgled with sudden delight.

"Dr Perry has been so naughty! He told Mama that Mr Dawkins must have infected poor Frampton with this illness and that he must be kept in strict isolation, then he told Mr Dawkins that he was in grave danger and must keep to his bed. I do not know everything that has happened but Old Nurse has been muttering something about castor oil so I thought it best to pretend ignorance."

"Oh, excellent Dr Perry!" Charlotte laughed aloud. "I gather that Mrs Richmond has withdrawn all favour from the dreadful Dawkins as a consequence?"

"Yes, indeed, he is quite out of favour and Mama is scheming how she can rid Frampton of him, which would be wonderful, would it not?"

"Indeed it would." Charlotte's agreement was heartfelt. "Now, off you go about your duties and to await Percy, while I relieve Old Nurse. She is elderly, after all, and must be quite exhausted."

The morning passed in peaceful tedium. Frampton tossed and turned and muttered, then slept for short periods. Nurse had fussed around the invalid for a good forty minutes before relinquishing command of the sick room to Charlotte.

"I don't like to leave you to do it, my dear," she repeated over and over. "It's not fitting for such a young lady but somehow my old bones don't seem to stand up so well these days. Besides, I must look in on my poor Miss Fanny and give her some words of cheer about her boy. She'll be that anxious about him, he was always her favourite, in spite of him being such a little heller, her and her nonsense about them old knights and all. Still, there's no sense going over what she gets in her head, but then Master Barnard was always worth ten of him."

At that juncture Barnard himself put his head around the door and laughed aloud.

"What's that?" Then as he was roundly hushed, "Oh, very well, but he's asleep, ain't he? So I'm worth ten of Frampton, am I? Well, I wish you would tell Mama and Lily so, they've done nothing but scold me all morning."

With great good nature he took the old nurse by the shoulders and gently marched her out of the room. "Off you go, Nurse. Mama is champing at the bit awaiting your report on my brother, then make sure you take some rest yourself.

"How is he today?"

He came into the room and quietly closed the door, his manner suddenly sober.

Charlotte shrugged.

"It is as Nurse and I and Dr Perry all said," she answered him. "It's some kind of intermittent fever and it will almost certainly go on for a day or two more. I don't think he is in any danger, as I said yesterday."

"When do you estimate he will be well enough for me to have a serious discussion with him, Charlotte?"

"A serious discussion? I don't know. How can I say? A day or two, at least, even if the fever breaks tonight. It is this business of halting your reforms, I take it?"

"Aye!" His short bark of laughter held no mirth and was closer to despair. "Has he not propounded his views on farming to you, Charlotte? No? Well, he has done so to me and in no uncertain fashion."

He threw himself down on a chair near the door and Charlotte, after checking on the sleeping Frampton, took another chair close by.

"Tell me."

"Simply that I am to be relieved of my 'duties' as steward and manager of Finchbourne and the farm and all my reforms are to be put back as they were." He looked up from contemplating his hands, his face ravaged. "All the repairs for the tenants' cottages cancelled, all the new system of crop rotation I had planned, everything to revert to the way it was. You heard him yourself. What was good enough for our grandfather's day is good enough for Frampton. Even young Ned is to be cast out from his position as under-bailiff and put back to work as a labourer. Frampton considers him to be dangerously above himself, assuming airs above his station as a result of my foolish promotion of him."

He pounded his right fist into the palm of his other hand.

"I tell you, Charlotte, I could happily see him dead of this fever. I mean that and it's something I never thought to say. He has no thought for the tenants or the villagers, no thought for Lily and me, no thought even for you."

He looked across the room with guilty haste, but Frampton was sleeping soundly, his mouth open and dribbling slightly.

184

Charlotte shook her head at Barnard's last remark with a faint, wry smile, then a thought struck her.

"But Barnard, surely he cannot put any of this into practice? Finchbourne is your mother's property still. Frampton will not be able to do any of these things while she is yet living."

"He believes otherwise," Barnard replied, still with that note of flat despair in his voice. "He has always been able to twist Mama round his fingers and he sees no reason why he should not continue to do so. And neither do I. She will be persuaded by him, she always is."

"Even when it touches upon the welfare of the tenants? I think you must be mistaken on this, Barnard." She spoke with quiet conviction. "Mrs Richmond is much influenced by Frampton, it is true, but I believe that even greater is her love for Finchbourne and the good name of the family. If Frampton tries to bring disrepute on either of those I think he will find her much more resistant than he expects."

He refused to be comforted and stood for a while glowering at his sleeping brother before trailing dejectedly out of the room.

While Frampton snored, Charlotte carried on with her sewing, refusing to consider her own precarious situation, rather preferring to wonder about the rest of the family. Poor Barnard, she thought, matters will come to a head between them when Frampton is better and then what will happen? I suppose the answer would be for him and Lily to move away. Perhaps Lily's Dear

Papa might buy them a place or they could even move back to the sacred Martindale, though I doubt Lily's stepmother would approve that course. But Barnard loves Finchbourne passionately, he feels himself part of the place in a way that Frampton can never have done. What will become of Barnard if he has to leave? For he may be right, in spite of what I told him. Mrs Richmond may very well allow Frampton to take charge of the place and make a mockery of all Barnard's well-intentioned schemes. Or, she grimaced, he may have another steward and manager in mind.

Later, she made out the almost-silent whirring of wheels along the landing and Mrs Richmond propelled herself into the doorway, where she halted, unable to manoeuvre the chair through the narrow old entrance.

"Ah, my poor boy, my Lazarus saved from the grave only to be reft from me once more. How can my poor heart bear such pain?"

"Pray do not distress yourself so, Mrs Richmond. Frampton is a little better today," whispered Charlotte, interrupting the heartfelt moans of the grieving mother.

"A little better?" Mrs Richmond was taken aback but made a rapid recovery. "Ah, the optimism of youth, dear Charlotte. You, of course, have not had to perform the many sad offices that I have been forced to undertake; my poor dear late father and mother, my dear departed husband, three of my precious little ones — who came between Barnard and Agnes — taken from me so soon after birth. You would not speak so, had you suffered as I have done."

"Perhaps not," Charlotte interrupted the throbbing plaint. "But," she continued drily, "within the last year, I have watched my mother and stepfather die, knowing there could be no hope. I cannot feel that Frampton is in such a bad case, and Dr Perry and Nurse agree with me."

"Nurse? What can Nurse know of these new fevers, pray? And as for Dr Perry, he is a worthy enough man, no doubt, but he is not skilled in eastern diseases. I am seriously disappointed in that Dawkins creature. Dr Perry tells me that the infection undoubtedly emanated from him. How he had the temerity to foist himself upon my dear deluded boy is beyond me. He has not a particle of proper feeling that I can detect, nor has he offered a hand's turn to relieve you of the nursing, I hear. I begin to have grave doubts as to the truth of these so-called relations of his in high society. I believe he may be nothing but an imposter!"

Charlotte encouraged her mother-in-law's thoughts to continue in this direction and saw her depart with considerable relief, even though she was then obliged to endure an onslaught from Lily, an experience she had previously been spared because Lily was forbidden entrance to the invalid's room, on account of her delicate condition.

It had become Charlotte's custom to take a brief respite from attendance in the sickroom by walking briskly up and down the twisting landings of the old house. As she emerged from Frampton's room Lily, who had obviously been lurking outside, accosted her.

"How is he?"

187

Charlotte smothered an involuntary grin as she observed Lily's nose wrinkled in distaste at the sickroom atmosphere as the door opened, while she arched her neck to stare inside.

"As well as can be expected," she replied soberly and was startled to see the piggy features contort with sudden rage.

"I wish he would die of his fever!" hissed Lily, baring her gums with great ferocity. "Have you heard what he has told my poor Barnard?"

"Yes." Charlotte spoke with hurried sympathy, while attempting to hush the furious young woman. "And I sympathize most heartily with you and Barnard. It is a horribly ungrateful notion, after all Barnard has done, and it's monstrously unfair on the tenants. But you must not allow yourself to be distressed, Lily, it's so bad for you in your condition. We must hope that Mrs Richmond will not allow it."

"I still hope he dies." Lily was too angry to listen to forlorn hopes. "It would solve all our problems if he died."

It was with relief that Charlotte saw Lily take herself off as the maid looked in with a light luncheon for herself and a bowl of sustaining broth for the invalid. As the maid left the room, Charlotte realized that Frampton was shaking his head in a daze.

"Awake, Frampton? That's better. Here, let me help you to some soup — you must get your strength back."

"Where — where is it?" came the muttered reply as Frampton first searched under his pillows then struggled to climb out of bed. "What have you done with it?"

"You must calm yourself, Frampton," she remonstrated, pulling him down on to the bed. "Nobody has taken anything. Do not concern yourself."

He consented to take a little of the broth and seemed more himself, though continuing to fret about something.

"What is it, Frampton?" she asked at last, afraid he was working himself up into another bout of fever.

"My — my money." He hesitated on the word and cast a sly look at her. "Yes, that's it, my money."

"Money?" She stared at him. "My dear Frampton, I was under the impression that you had none! How *did* you manage to make the journey home? I thought you had gambled away all of your own money and what remained of the regiments' funds that went missing? Surely young Dawkins did not pay for you?"

"Aah." The sly look became more pronounced and the feverish glitter was back in Frampton's eyes. "You would like to know, would you not? But you shall not take it from me, no-one shall." He gave an odd little laugh and said, sounding almost lucid: "I've hidden it, you know, where no one will ever find it."

The lull during the fever came to an abrupt end and the sick man's temperature rose while he sank into further delirium, though not before he had succeeded in clambering out of bed while Charlotte was absent from the room for a space, summoned to answer a query from Old Nurse. When she returned Frampton

189

was in the act of climbing back into bed, looking discomfited when he realized she was watching him.

When Lady Frampton lumbered heavily into the room half an hour later, the fevered mutterings had resumed along with copious sweating and tossing.

"What's that? A slight respite? Well, I suppose the good Lord knows what he is about, though I must say I can't see it myself. Still, I looked in to tell you I 'ave been putting on my thinking cap and whatever 'appens I shan't let you be 'armed, so you can take that 'arassed look off your face. No 'arm shall come to you with me." She wheezed her way into the room and lowered her bulk on to the sofa. "Now what was it I . . .? Why, yes, of course. I just had the shock of my life, Char. If you'll believe me there was a *man*, a foreign body, standing on our landing just now, large as life!"

Charlotte's gasp of astonishment gave entire satisfaction.

"You may well say 'Oh!' I near 'ad a seizure meself. 'What are you doing there, my good fellow?' I asked him and would you believe he just bowed and shook 'is 'ead and took himself off down the stairs. Aye, walked through the front door as if 'e was a Christian! What do you make of that, eh?"

Charlotte lifted a bemused face and the old lady nodded with great good humour.

"It must be that Indian gentleman that was so mysterious. Lily said he was back in the village," Charlotte said slowly. "He wanted to know about Frampton's personal effects, didn't he? He certainly pestered Barnard about it and he stopped me more

190

than once, insisting that Frampton had stolen something of value." She frowned, wondering what it could be. "Frampton became very agitated, didn't he, when he heard the man was here again? I don't understand it, Gran, I really don't."

"Nor I, me dear," came the reply. "If you ask me that young rip 'as put up the backs of more folks than 'e could count. There's most likely 'undreds would like to 'ave a little talk with 'im."

She gave Charlotte one of her shrewd but kindly glances, wagging her finger in mock disapproval.

"You look pasty and peaky, my gal, and it won't do. You just take yourself off for a blow of fresh h'air. I've seen plenty of fevers in my time. Why, I mind once when my dear 'usband caught some such fever once after he took 'imself down to the docks to see after one of 'is cargoes. Lord above, 'e was took so bad I thought 'e'd gone; picked it up from the ship it turned out. Nobody thought to tell 'im there was fever aboard. Nasty dirty heathen foreigners the lot of them, Frenchies they were."

She arranged her bulk more comfortably and patted Charlotte on the arm.

"Go on, child, Frampton will do very well. You go and stretch your legs." She looked up with a comical expression of dismay. "What would Fanny say if she 'eard me mention your legs, eh? And 'er so prim and proper!"

"Perhaps you should refer to my nether limbs, Gran," giggled Charlotte as she bent to hug the old lady.

"Per'aps I shouldn't mention 'em at all, young lady," wheezed Lady Frampton in high good humour. "Off you go and enjoy your freedom for a space."

Freedom? If only it were, thought Charlotte with longing as she sped along the landing towards her room in the Queen Anne wing, pausing briefly at the top of the stairs at the sounds of welcome and bustle. It must be Colonel Fitzgibbon, she thought, come to see Mrs Richmond and her son, the hero. Frowning, she recalled her anxious conversations with Kit Knightley, not long ago in terms of actual days but a world away in a time when Frampton was safely dead. The suspicions she and Kit had entertained had no place now, surely? If there had been any foundation for them, why, Frampton was in no state to rejoin his regiment. Surely they would allow him to retire into obscurity so that any irregularities might be quietly buried.

It was all so nebulous. In her room Charlotte quickly set her straw bonnet on her head and caught up a light shawl then she made her way down the back stairs. As fervently as Frampton himself, the army must be intent upon avoiding scandal, if scandal there were to be told.

This is nonsense, pull yourself together, Char, she scolded herself briskly. You have a respite from the sickroom, so do as Lady Frampton bade you and go for a blow in the fresh air. God only knows you need a clear head if you are to muddle through all of this.

The hills, dotted with sheep and lambs, beckoned enticingly but Charlotte kept to the lower slopes. Some delicacy of feeling made her avoid any possibility of meeting Kit Knightley up there in what he had named as his "special" place. Her desperate fear for the future, coupled with her growing awareness that she felt for him something more than friendship, might cause her rigid control to slip. If he goes there for sanctuary, she told herself, I cannot be always intruding upon him with my troubles, nor must he ever know how I feel. She squared her shoulders, frowning. He is my friend, *only* a friend, and I must do as I have always done — solve my problems myself.

She considered her options. Was Frampton in earnest when he vowed he would spread rumours of her less than snow-white past? Would it matter if he did? Perhaps not, but can I trust him, was the answer to the first question, and a resounding yes to the second. It was important to Frampton to conciliate his mother as she held the purse strings and what Mrs Richmond desired above all was an heir to the sacred name of Richmond. That poor Lily was already with child with just such an heir was no longer sufficient for the lady of the manor, the heir must now come through Frampton. Charlotte could see only too plainly why Frampton's devilish though ingenious solution made perfect sense to him, because it made perfect sense to Charlotte also.

So why do I not simply comply with his wishes? she asked herself. Had things run otherwise, if he had not gone missing in that fashion, I might very well have gone along with his plan. To be sure I cannot like Lancelot Dawkins but he is handsome enough and personable, at least on first acquaintance; yes, I might very well have followed Frampton's suggestion, and needed no coercion.

So what is different now? For I cannot do it. She frowned fiercely and bit her lip. Because I have come to know these people? Because I cannot betray Barnard and Lily in such a manner, the answer came at once. I cannot simply stand back and let Frampton ruin their lives while I cravenly yield to his blackmail, for that is what it is. But what am I to do? Lady Frampton's hints were merely flags to fly, to keep up her own spirits. Nothing would come of them, so what was Charlotte to do?

The answer dropped suddenly, clearly, shockingly, into her head.

I shall have to kill him!

CHAPTER
SEVEN

"Charlotte! Charlotte! Come quickly!" Agnes was running down the path towards the gate into the fields, waving a frantic handkerchief.

Charlotte quickened her pace, her heart pounding.

"What is it, Agnes? What's wrong?"

"It's Uncle Henry," gasped Agnes, clinging to the gatepost while she caught her breath. "He's had some sort of seizure and I don't know what to do."

"Where is he?" Charlotte panted as they broke into a run. "At the vicarage?"

"No, no, he's in the drawing-room at home. He had been up to see Frampton and came downstairs looking so strange, then he gave a loud groan and collapsed in a heap in the doorway, just as Lily and I were taking a cup of tea."

She halted again, clutching her side.

"Oh, oh, a stitch! You go on, Char, I'll catch up. Oh, his poor old face, it's all twisted to one side . . ."

Predictably the house was in uproar. Agnes must have fled straight to look for Charlotte without even checking to see if Henry Heavitree was still alive, Charlotte thought, as she was brought up short at the drawing-room door. For even now people were swarming from all over the house.

"Let me see him," Charlotte commanded, flopping down on to her knees beside the stricken behemoth. "He is still alive, but it looks bad. Has the doctor been sent for? Here, Hoxton, is the vicar's usual bedchamber ready? Good, then have him conveyed there at once. Has Mrs Richmond been informed? And how is Major Richmond? I must go and check up on him."

"No need." It was Mrs Richmond, in the arms of the stalwart footman, her wheeled chair following her downstairs, carried by a brawny housemaid. "Frampton is asleep. What is the matter with my brother?" She gestured imperiously to her chair and once settled into it, wheeled herself across the polished oak boards. "Oh, woe is me! What? Another blow for a poor widow to bear? What have I done that the good Lord should smite me so?"

Charlotte blinked, even as she prepared to follow the procession bearing the vicar upstairs. Mrs Richmond was looking very pale, the habitual complacency fled from her long, arrogant face. Was she so fond of her brother? Charlotte wondered, but thought that her mother-in-law had looked distrait even before she caught sight of Henry's bulk stretched out on the floor. The clamour must have alarmed her. As Charlotte cast a distracted glance backward, Fanny Richmond caught her eye and frowned.

"Take Agnes with you, Charlotte," she commanded. "Lily can stay with me. Go and sit down quietly, Lily and take some deep breaths. Hysterics will do you no good. Hoxton, send for the doctor. Do what you can to help Mrs Frampton and send in some more tea for Mrs Barnard and myself."

Henry Heavitree breathed stertorously on his bed, his face twisted, as Agnes had said, the whole of his right side flopping limp and helpless. As Charlotte settled him against the lace and linen of his pillows, she realized his eyes were open and that he was glaring at her, his intelligence unimpaired.

"What is it, sir?" she asked, bending over him in pity, forgetting for a moment that he was a monster, recalling only that he was a very sick man. "The doctor will be here directly and we are doing all we can to make you comfortable."

"Fah — fa — gah!" The words were unintelligible and the eyes blazed with a spark of red fire as the misshapen mouth made a further effort. "Faugh — ugh!" Saliva drooled down the uppermost of Henry's several chins and he groaned as Charlotte took up a napkin to wipe him.

"Perhaps he is saying Mama's name," suggested Agnes and she hung over him dripping tears in a manner calculated to send him into a further spasm. "They do love each other so dearly. Did you want to speak to Mama, Uncle Henry? Did you want to see your dear sister?"

For a moment Charlotte thought another spark flickered then she was distracted by the entrance of the butler, looking grave.

"I brought hot water, ma'am," he told her. "But there's word from the village that Dr Perry is gone to

197

Portsmouth this morning and will not return until tomorrow noon at the earliest."

"Oh dear." Charlotte put a hand to her brow and pursed her lips. "Well, we shall have to do the best we can. Thank you, Hoxton. Have you had tea sent in to Mrs Richmond and Mrs Barnard? Oh good, they will both be suffering from the shock of it all. Perhaps you could send up some to Lady Frampton also? You have? The perfect butler! What should we do without you?"

Hoxton looked extremely gratified by this commendation and bowed his way out of the room, promising to send in more tea for herself and Agnes.

"And something for the vicar," she called out to him as he left. "I suppose brandy would be what he would like most, and it can hardly do him any harm, poor man."

Another garbled gobbling issued from the vicar's flaccid lips. Agnes leaped feet first into the breach.

"Dear Uncle Henry," she gushed, "I am sure you need the comfort of the Lord's word. I will send for Percy, I — I mean Mr Benson, directly."

"Graagh! Glub! Blaargh!"

"I think that means no," Charlotte interposed swiftly as the vicar's eyes bulged dangerously and spittle sprayed his devoted niece. "Never fear, sir, you shall be safe from being prayed over. Now, try to rest, it will do you so much good."

Henry Heavitree subsided into angry despair, apparently falling into a doze, so Charlotte and Agnes retreated to a small table and chairs set in the window overlooking the church.

"Sit down, Agnes." Charlotte waved to a chair. "What a commotion. I cannot admire your Uncle Henry but it is shocking to see so powerful a force of nature struck down like this, rather as if a hurricane had been stopped in its tracks in front of one. What can have brought it on, I wonder?" She saw that Agnes was looking very weary. "Sit quietly, Agnes, tea will be here soon. Now, tell me, what was Henry doing just before his attack, do you know? You said he had been to see Frampton? Oh heavens, Frampton, I should go to him."

"No, Char." Agnes pulled herself together and spoke firmly. "You heard Mama tell us that Frampton was sleeping. Take a few minutes peace for yourself, do. Let me see, were you here when Colonel Fitzgibbon was closeted in the drawing-room with Mama? Oh no, I spotted you running across the garden and pretended I had not seen you when she asked me. Oh, Charlotte, it was so strange. Colonel Fitzgibbon asked first to see Frampton and was quite insistent. It was only when Mama wheeled herself into the hall and practically ordered him into the drawing-room that he desisted, but Mama would not have Frampton disturbed at any cost."

"I could see that Mama was most displeased, but she ordered Hoxton to send in the Madeira and then, when I was about to join them, the colonel spoke up angrily. Very grave, he was, but most definite: he had pressing matters to discuss, if not with Frampton then with Mama and he was afraid he must ask for complete

199

privacy. Mama was even more chilly but he would have it no other way."

"How — how very strange," Charlotte faltered. Did the colonel's demeanour have anything to do with the suspicions she had voiced to Kit Knightley? He seemed to have behaved very oddly if all he was doing was paying a visit to an ailing fellow officer.

"Yes, indeed." Agnes was agog, bulging brown eyes glistening with emotion. "I did not see him leave but when I went into the drawing-room (I saw the door was open and ventured in), Mama was sitting in her chair staring at the wall. She did not hear me when I spoke and it was several moments before she realized I was there, then she spoke very shortly and ordered that she be taken upstairs. Charlotte, I was quite shocked to see her face. She looked quite unlike dear Mama."

"How do you mean, Agnes?"

"I can't explain." Agnes plucked at her sleeve. "She looked as though she had sustained a deadly blow. I know that is fanciful but that is how she seemed and she brushed me aside as if I had been a fly."

The arrival of the tea-tray interrupted this interesting conversation and Charlotte sipped thoughtfully while Agnes embarked on a flight about Percy and his hoped-for appointment with the bishop.

"The bishop will offer Percy the archdiocese of Canterbury," Charlotte joked, jumping to her feet, refreshed by the tea. "I'm sure you would make a wonderful archbishop's wife. Now, I must return to my first invalid and see how he does."

At the head of the main stairs she encountered Old Nurse, full of gloom, prophesying that Mrs Richmond too would succumb to the same affliction as her brother.

"That's just the way her poor father went and her mother too," she announced, her soft country voice ringing with thinly-veiled relish. "Lucky she did not see Mr Henry collapse, laid upon her bed as she was, poor dear, after seeing that redcoat."

It was with a feeling of relief that Charlotte closed the door of Frampton's bedroom behind her. There is too much excitement in this house, she told herself with a wry smile. How I long for the gentle tedium of those first days that I spent here.

A time when you thought Frampton was dead, reminded her rogue inner voice. What are you going to do about him? You were very full of determination out on the foothills, Char, were you not? But can you do it? Can you really kill him?

Firmly repressing that inner voice, Charlotte crossed the room towards the ancient oak bed with its carved posts and heavy tapestry canopy, relieved to see that Frampton appeared to be sleeping soundly, the coverlet pulled up over his hunched shoulder. She let out a sigh of relief: let him rest undisturbed and let me have a peaceful interlude.

She picked up her sewing and sat down on a comfortable chair in the wide bay window, stretching luxuriously in the warmth that beat down on her. Much as I love England, she mused, it has to be admitted that I miss the sun; if only it would stay like this all the time.

As she sewed she tried in vain to ignore the idea clamouring for attention. Could she, would she, kill Frampton? And if she would, if she could, how might the deed be accomplished? It was at this point in her deliberations that she shivered uneasily, struck by something odd about the silence of the sickroom.

The silence, that was it. There was no noise at all; only the faintest sound of her needle piercing the lawn petticoat she was stitching, only the sound of her own breathing. Her *own* breathing . . .

"Frampton?"

She cast aside the folds of lawn and leapt to her feet, running to her husband's bedside. He lay there looking quiet and peaceful — too peaceful. Instead of the hurried, uncertain gasps brought on by his fever there was silence, and not the near silence of a healthy slumber, just silence.

Frampton Richmond was not breathing at all.

The blood drained from Charlotte's face as she stared down at the lifeless body of her husband and she surprised herself by dropping to her knees beside the bed.

"Oh, thank you, Lord," she prayed earnestly. "Thank you for taking the decision out of my hands, thank you for letting him die so gently in his sleep. I hated him for what he planned to do but I doubt if I could really have harmed him. Thank you for this, Lord."

Unhurriedly she began to straighten out the body of the man with whom she had struck so strange a bargain. Perhaps only his mother could have loved him but he should be accorded every mark of devotion that

202

she could muster. Her own humanity demanded it, rather than his.

A knock at the door interrupted her train of thought.

Heavens. She pressed her lips firmly together. The house is in upset enough, this need not be made public straight away. She sped to the door and opened it a crack.

"If you please, Mrs Frampton." It was Hoxton. "Miss Agnes sent to say will a tray be sufficient for you for dinner tonight? Cook is having to cope with the scullery maid who is having the vapours in the kitchen because her grandfer was struck down just the same way as his reverence, and what with that, and looking after the Vicar, the house is at sixes and sevens. I regret that dinner will be much delayed."

"Of course." Charlotte was relieved. "I'll spend the night in the major's dressing-room, so a light meal will suit me excellently."

"How is he, Miss — Mrs Frampton, ma'am?"

"Not well, Hoxton," she said deliberately. "I'm not optimistic about him at all."

Was it relief she read in the butler's craggy face? She could not tell, nor did she really care, her own relief was all-enveloping. Just as she was about to close the door, Agnes galumphed along the landing.

"Oh, Charlotte!" She was looking important. "We're all going to bed early, after dinner, everyone's exhausted, but I just wanted to let you know that I will sit up with Uncle Henry tonight. Old Nurse is taken up with Lily."

"Lily? There's nothing wrong, I hope?"

"Oh no, Nurse and Mama both say there is not, it's just that Lily felt rather faint."

"I'm not surprised." Charlotte gave a tired sigh. "Well, bed is the best place for her, and you are an angel to look after Uncle Henry. What about your mama? Can she manage without Nurse?"

"Oh yes, Barnard will keep an eye on Lily while Nurse is helping Mama to bed and I shall be in dear Uncle's room, just across the landing from her, and not far from you too, of course. Do not hesitate to call on me, dear Char."

Indeed I will not, Charlotte laughed to herself, in spite of the awkwardness of her situation. If I require a patient excited into a fit, medicine poured into an ear rather than down the throat, a gouty toe heavily trodden on, then to be sure I will call upon you, dear Agnes. A thought struck her — neither she nor Agnes had remembered Lady Frampton in all this — so she locked Frampton's door behind her, thrusting the key into her pocket, and crept stealthily along the broad landing. I do *not* want to be interrogated about Frampton's health at this moment, she thought.

"Gran? I just looked in to say good night and to see how you are? But I need not ask. You are looking in excellent spirits."

"And feeling better too, me dear."

The old lady had regained her high colour and the twinkle was back in her eyes.

"I wanted to say again that whatever 'appens I'll not let young Frampton beat me down, nor you neither, Char," she announced. "I 'ear that young feller that 'e

204

brought 'ome is quite out of favour with Fanny so maybe everything will turn out for the best. In any case, I've thought up a plan, so don't you commence to worry."

"Oh, Gran." Charlotte knelt beside the bluff old woman and hugged as much of the vast bulk as she could encircle with her slim arms. "I wish you were really my grandmother. We could have had such fun in Australia, you and I and Ma and Will. Do you know how much I love you?"

"Get on with you!" Lady Frampton gave her a little push but her eyes were brighter than ever. "If it comes to talking about loving . . . well, I reckon you know 'ow I feel, me girl. Now, be off with you and get to bed early tonight. You need your rest."

Charlotte was just letting herself back into Frampton's room when her belated supper arrived. She took it from the footman with a smile and nodded to him to leave.

"I'll put the tray on the table outside," she told him. "I don't want Major Richmond disturbed again tonight."

The presence of the dead Frampton did not in any way impair her appetite. Indeed, she considered, tucking in to soup, a plate of cold meat and bread and butter and a custard, I feel hungrier tonight than for what seems like weeks. She looked across at the still figure in the bed and sighed. I'm sorry, Frampton, she thought, a man should have a better epitaph than that his wife should regain her appetite upon his death.

Her supper finished, she slipped the tray on to the table outside the door and turned the key in the lock once more, then she returned, reluctantly, to the man in the bed. The footman had also presented her with a copper can of hot water so she poured a little into a basin and prepared to wash her dead husband.

As she wiped his face she hesitated, struck by something odd. She bent to look more closely and delicately reached a finger to Frampton's nose. Yes, there was something there, a strand of black thread, and another, and another, this time, surprisingly, in bright rose pink. She satisfied herself that there was nothing more to be found then she sat back on her chair, catching her breath as she stared at the fragments between her fingers.

Almost involuntarily her head swivelled towards the sofa beside the fireplace. On it lay her mother's shawl, the black silk patterned with large pink cabbage roses, one of her few mementoes of Molly Glover. She had caught it up in her own bedroom the evening before when the air had begun to strike chill and she must have left it here in Frampton's room when she made her escape earlier today.

Stiffly she rose and picked up the shawl. Pink silk in the roses, pink silk strands in her hand. A perfect match. And here, as she examined the shawl by the light of a candle, was a place where the threads were torn. A long shudder ran through her entire body, a shudder of horror mingled with relief and a dreadful gratitude. All very well to convince myself I could kill him, she thought dully, recovering her wits, but it's a very different matter to find that someone else has actually done it for me.

A sudden wave of exhaustion overtook her and she sat down hastily in the nearest chair, thinking longingly of her bed. I cannot put it off any longer, she told herself, I must call somebody. Instead, abandoning the idea of bed, she steeled herself to continue the task of laying out her unlamented husband's body, working methodically and calmly as was her custom.

"What on earth?" Released from its indelicate and unlikely hiding place something surprising had come to light, something that immediately brought to mind Frampton's fevered mumblings as he searched frantically under his pillow.

"*Really*, Frampton!"

Charlotte took the object between a reluctant forefinger and thumb and immersed it in water, drying it thoroughly on a soft linen towel.

It was a large, very beautiful, heart-shaped ruby.

CHAPTER
EIGHT

I must call Barnard, she thought. He must be told about this. Even as she made the decision she realized that her hand, of its own volition, was determinedly tucking the ruby into her pocket and covering it with a handkerchief. A moment later she swept back the covers on Frampton's bed and made a meticulous search of every inch of it, then, setting aside her revulsion, she further searched the dead man's body.

Nothing. She straightened the bed and sat down for a moment's reflection. Was this what Frampton had been so frantically seeking? There must be more, she thought. He cannot have survived without money, but where did this come from? Not the officers' mess, that's for certain, but is this what the Indian gentleman was after? I can understand why Frampton would hide it, but really, in such a place! Rapidly she quartered the room, rifling through the drawers, poking under the bed and in the wardrobe, running a hand under the feather mattress. Still nothing.

As she crawled backwards out from under the big old bed she spotted something odd on the floor. It looked for all the world like the scattered petals of some flower. But Frampton refused to have flowers in his room, she thought distractedly. Where had they come from? She was still not sufficiently familiar with English flowers to recognize a few isolated pink petals but . . . wait. There was something about pink flowers. Who? That was it, Lily had mentioned something about pinks — a singularly unoriginal name for a flower — when she spoke about Lady Walbury!

Charlotte rocked back on her heels and stared again at the wilted pink scraps. Lady Walbury? She could not possibly have slipped into Frampton's room, murdered him, shredded a few flowers and made her escape quite unnoticed. Could she?

It was nonsense. Charlotte tucked away the problem to the back of her mind along with the rest and returned to even more pressing matters. If Frampton has been concealing money in this room, she determined, I am going to find it, yes and keep it too, unless I find someone else with a more legitimate claim upon it.

Immediately in front of her was the fireplace, empty in such glorious weather as they had enjoyed of late, and there on the hearth was a slight sprinkle of soot. She reached a tentative arm up the chimney and encountered a ledge; upon the ledge was something hard and square.

A box, a square wooden box. She had seen similar boxes in India, intricately carved in rosewood and inlaid, as this was, with ivory or mother-of-pearl.

Breathing hard, she dusted off the soot and opened the lid to disclose a heap of banknotes, a scattering of precious stones — emeralds, pearls and sapphires — and some gold sovereigns, almost £700 in all.

"Good gracious, Frampton." She chewed her lower lip and stared at the hoard before her eyes. "What on earth did you *do*? Where did this come from?"

Her long training stood her in good stead. Swiftly she thrust the contents of the wooden box into the pocket which hung under her skirt from her waistband. A few moments later the box was safely despatched back to its hiding place in the chimney and the hearth swept clean. She gazed down once more at her late, unlamented husband.

"Well, well, Frampton." She spoke in a satirical voice that masked her anxiety. "Here you are, dead *again*, I see! I wonder what is to become of me now?"

There was no time for contemplation. A last glance round the room to make sure that there was nothing else unusual — no further distressed floral tributes, no diamonds draped around the marble clock on the mantel, no sooty footprints on the floor — and she slipped out of the room, locking the door behind her. In the Queen Anne wing she hesitated at the door of Lily and Barnard's bedroom. No, Old Nurse was sure to be ensconced by Lily's bedside, ready to dispense tales of disaster and gore that had befallen every expectant mother of her acquaintance.

For the first time Charlotte was struck by the similarities between Nurse's enjoyment of her woes and portents of doom and Mrs Richmond's throbbing appropriation of any passing drama. Small wonder, I suppose, she thought, grinning faintly. Nurse brought her up, after all.

No sense in rousing Lily or Nurse. She guessed that Barnard would have retreated to the spartan simplicity of his dressing-room, stifled by the aura of fecund femininity. She rapped her knuckles gently but firmly on his door and waited. Sure enough she heard movements within almost at once.

"Charlotte?" Barnard thrust a tousled head round the door and gawped at her. "Wha . . .?"

"Please come," she whispered, her finger to her lips. She turned back the way she had come, leaving him no choice but to catch up his dressing gown and follow her, stealthily closing his door behind him.

"I'm sorry, Barnard." She drew him into Frampton's room and shut that door behind him too. "It's bad news. I know you had your differences but he was still your brother."

She led him to the still figure in the bed.

He gasped, turned to her in shock then bent to take a closer look. As he straightened his back, she saw that his face was pale and his eyes suddenly shadowed. He looked at her again.

"I don't know what to say," he stammered. "As you say, he was my brother, but he . . ."

He sat down heavily on a nearby chair and thrust a hand through his dark curls.

"When did this happen?"

"I don't know." She told him the truth, then disguised it with a further half-truth. "Your mother said he was asleep about the time Uncle Henry had his seizure, that was around teatime. Then I was quite a while working with Agnes to settle your uncle — we had our own tea in his room — and when I came back here I thought I should not disturb Frampton's rest."

She brushed a weary hand across her brow.

"Agnes sent me up a tray in here because of all the upset in the house and I was going to bed in the dressing-room. I know it's quite early still. What time is it now? I thought I should fetch you at once, but I did not want to raise the alarm. It could do no good, after all."

He glanced at the clock.

"It's not eleven yet," he said, rubbing his eyes and looking suddenly exhausted. "I don't know how my mother will . . ." He sighed, then he looked at her with that frank honesty that was his chief attraction. "I wish I could say that I'm sorry this has happened," he confessed, then threw out his hands in a gesture of resignation. "But how can I? It makes everything so much — easier."

Apart from Mrs Richmond, who was reported to be prostrate upon her bed and no wonder, the entire family gathered at breakfast the next morning. The air of relief was palpable, so too was the air of desperate guilt brought about by this very easing of their troubles.

Agnes, dressed once more in her most unbecoming black, presided over the tea and coffee cups, working her way so rapidly through a succession of dainty, black-bordered handkerchiefs that Charlotte eventually

212

leaned across the table and thrust a large linen table napkin at her.

"For goodness' sake, Agnes, mop yourself up with this!"

As Agnes looked set to indulge in another extravagant outburst Charlotte relieved her own feelings by aiming a kick under the table. The gasp and wince that greeted this action halted Agnes in mid-wail and Charlotte took the opportunity to hiss at her:

"Agnes, hush, you're upsetting Lily, and Grandmama too. You must control your feelings, there's too much to be done."

"Quite right, Charlotte." Barnard spoke with quiet authority. He was looking pale and stern but the tension that had hunched his broad shoulders for days was gone entirely. With no pretence as to great grief, he held himself with an air of grave competence, and looked, Charlotte considered, the worthy squire he was born to be.

Lily, too, was pale after her fright of the day before but a night's rest, undisturbed by any of Old Nurse's worst forebodings, had done much to restore her balance. She, like Charlotte herself, was making no pretence of sorrow, though unlike Charlotte, Lily was hard put to conceal her actual delight in Frampton's death.

I wonder. Charlotte watched her revived sister-in-law truffling away at a plateful of pork chops. (How appropriate she thought, looking at the serene but undeniably piggy, pink face across the table.) Did she do it? Could she have done it? Agnes said that she and

Lily were having tea when Uncle Henry collapsed; no, Mrs Richmond said Frampton was asleep then. Just when was Lily taken ill? she wondered. Was she ill at all? Perhaps she slipped into Frampton's room when Agnes and Charlotte were otherwise occupied and — what? Smothered him with Molly Glover's shawl?

It was absurd.

With narrowed eyes, Charlotte considered the rest of the family. Lady Frampton? She had certainly feared and disliked Frampton but the excitement of thinking up ideas for her own and Charlotte's escape had put new life into her. The old lady had talked of an adventurous solution, of setting up house with Charlotte. A pipe dream or would she really have done it? Why should she kill him? As far as the old lady had been aware, the adventure, if it had come off, would have offered the added spice of seriously annoying Mrs Richmond, something Lady Frampton would have relished. Not knowing anything of Frampton's attempt to blackmail Charlotte by blackening her name, his grandmother would have seen no obstacle in their path, least of all the grandson she had come so heartily to dislike.

Barnard? Nonsense. Her mind instantly refuted the notion. Bluff, upright, God-fearing, law-abiding Barnard would never have done such a thing. Charlotte could, with difficulty, picture him killing someone in a fight, an angry brawl, or even, were they still legal in England, a duel. But to smother a man as he lay helpless in his bed? Never.

214

A loud sniff followed by a hearty blow drew her attention back to Agnes and a reluctant little smile touched her lips. Oh no, not Agnes. If Agnes had murdered her brother his pillow would have been wringing wet with her tears where she had wailed and wept over him at the course she was forced to take and he would have been drowned instead. It was quite, quite ludicrous. Besides, Charlotte recollected, she and Agnes had been together in Uncle Henry's room all the time. Agnes had no opportunity at all.

A sudden idea flashed into her mind.

"Uncle Henry!" she exclaimed out loud.

"Oh, Charlotte, dearest," mooed Agnes. "How like you to be so concerned in the midst of everything. Our poor uncle is just the same, unable to speak or move, but I'm glad to report that he took a little beef tea earlier this morning."

What? Beef? That great bull of a man, eating beef? With Lily, piggy little Lily, eating pork, too — are they *all* cannibals? Charlotte shook her head slightly. I must remain calm and sensible, she warned herself. *I* cannot indulge in hysterics. Her thoughts returned to Henry Heavitree. Why had he collapsed with that seizure? Agnes had said that her uncle looked strange as he came downstairs after looking in on Frampton; had he done more than look? But was it, after all, so strange? A man in his sixties, heavily built and given to gratifying his every whim with regard to food and wine, not to mention his less genteel pursuits — might not a shock bring on just such an apoplectic turn? And what more shocking than to find oneself murdering one's own nephew?

Charlotte came back to her surroundings to hear the butler announce, in sepulchral tones, that the curate was at the door.

"Oh, oh, Percy!"

"That's enough, Agnes." Barnard hushed her and waved her back into her seat. "Ask Mr Benson to join us, Hoxton, and bring some more coffee."

Percy Benson scuttled in to the room, halted at the sight of Agnes and blushed crimson, then looked at the other women and shifted his feet nervously.

"Ah, Benson." Barnard took pity on him and gestured to the chair that the butler was pulling out. "Join us for breakfast, won't you? My mother is, of course, laid down upon her bed but the rest of the ladies felt strong enough to come downstairs, though they will not, of course, be going outside until after the funeral — which, by the way, we must discuss later this morning. Dr Perry has already called, so there is no great rush for your services, I'm afraid, except in a pastoral role."

Charlotte had been present at that early morning consultation after Barnard had roused the butler to send for their medical man.

"What can I say?" Dr Perry straightened up and gazed at them, his bushy eyebrows meeting in a frown above his long nose. "A trifle surprising, but as I said, we know very little about these eastern fevers. It has to be said that it is a blessing in disguise, but you need not fear; I shall not mention that outside this room!"

216

No, Dr Perry was clearly under no illusion about Frampton. And what a fortunate circumstance, reflected Charlotte, that the butler had seen, with his own eyes, the doctor's carriage the previous evening. Dr Perry's unexpectedly early return from Portsmouth had certainly made everything much easier for the family. He had gone with Barnard to break the news to the one person in the world who would sincerely mourn the dead man and Charlotte, hovering in the background, had been relieved to see her mother-in-law soundly dosed with a sedative once the first outpouring of grief was on the wane.

Now Percy Benson sat beside the woman he loved, at the table of the man who had despised him, and ate his way steadily through a plate of thick ham, marbled with white fat, raising his eyes now and then in mute adoration as he gazed at Agnes.

Barnard set down his knife and fork and caught Charlotte's eye, then he nodded to the curate.

"You'll excuse me, Benson. Agnes will take you up to my brother's room when you are ready. Gran, Lily, you should rest; yesterday was difficult for you both and the next few days will be very full. Charlotte, may I have a word?"

Outside the door he looked at her in entreaty.

"We've quite forgotten Lancelot Dawkins," he said and when she exclaimed in agreement he added, "I think I may forget myself if I have to see him. Do you think . . .?"

"Heavens, I'd forgotten him too. Of course." She smiled faintly. "You're quite right, a brawl would be most unseemly. I'll arrange for Hoxton to send him packing but it will give me great pleasure to announce the fact myself."

And ask him a few pointed questions, she resolved. Dawkins! Barnard had spoken nothing less than the truth — they had all forgotten him. She considered Frampton's young travelling companion in the light of her secret knowledge. Left alone and unregarded in isolation in the attic, might not Dawkins have tiptoed down the stairs and smothered Frampton? The man who had presumably paid his passage home and who gave every appearance of doting upon him? No, it did not make sense. Dawkins was the only person Charlotte could think of who did not benefit by Frampton's death — apart, of course, from his grieving mother.

She marched into the spartan attic room and flung open the low window, taking a tray of breakfast from the footman who had accompanied her, and setting it on a table. "Mr Dawkins, do forgive me, but I have to tell you some sad news. Awake? Good. As I said, there has been a sad occurrence. You will be sorry to hear that Frampton succumbed to the fever during the night."

She watched the young man's face keenly, searching for signs of sorrow. There were none. Shock, panic and a sudden calculation all flitted across his dark, young face, but not a single sign of regret at the death of one who had loved him.

"Dr Perry believes that you have escaped the worst of the disease," she reassured him briskly. "Now, Hoxton is arranging for you to be taken to the station,

218

so pack up your belongings as soon as you are up. Here is your breakfast." She indicated the tray. "Mr Richmond, Mr Barnard Richmond, that is, has authorized me to tell you that he will pay your wages for the next two months, but that you must not apply to him for a reference."

He sat up in bed and glared at her, disappointment written clear upon his face.

"I *told* Frampton you were no lady," he said pettishly. "Look at you, standing there bold as brass in a gentleman's bedroom. Have you no shame?"

"Take your breakfast," she said kindly. "Don't let it get cold. No, of course I have no shame, but then, neither are you a gentleman. Let us not mince words, I shall be heartily glad to see you go and so will everyone in this house, but there are one or two questions I believe you can answer for me."

"Why should I?" He sounded more than ever like a sulky boy rather than the smooth creature in attendance on the late master of the house.

"Why should you not? All I want to know is where Frampton got the money to pay for his journey home. And what, if anything, you know about the circumstances of his escape from the ambush that killed his men."

He gave her a disdainful stare and took another mouthful. After a moment or two, during which she could see that he was weighing up the advantages and disadvantages of co-operating with her, he made up his mind.

"He never told me anything about the ambush," he told her with a sniff. "I kept asking, because I thought it must have been exciting, but it made him start to rage at me, so I stopped. When I met up with him he had been hanging around the port for an age, I gathered, in disguise. I think he was waiting for somebody, but in the end he gave up, took me into his employ and we started for England."

A spiteful smirk flashed across his saturnine features and Charlotte felt her hand itch to slap him.

"Who was it?" she asked. "That he waited for? Did he ever tell you?"

"No, but he wept every night on the voyage home," the young man said with a shrug.

"What about the money?"

"He never told me that either, but he used to disappear now and then, and come back with cash. I think he had some jewels that he was selling, but he was very secretive. I was never allowed to see them."

Charlotte scrutinized his face again. As far as she could make out, he was speaking the truth. Indeed, why should he lie? For a moment she toyed with the notion that the boy might have taken some of Frampton's supposed jewels for himself, but she discarded it. If you had found Frampton's hoard, she addressed him inwardly, I think you would have taken the whole, and would not be here now, for me to dismiss.

Not unkindly she bade him hurry up with his breakfast and be ready to leave, then she slipped downstairs to have a word with the butler, whom she discovered giving orders to a skinny lad who looked familiar.

"Mr Dawkins is almost ready to leave, Hoxton," she announced. "Did Mr Richmond give you the packet with his wages? Good. Make sure that he is seen on to the train and that it departs with him aboard." She hesitated. "That boy just now, wasn't that the boot-boy, Tom? Your grandson? I hope this means his mother is well?"

"Er, yes, ma'am, thank you, that she is."

Hoxton gave her one of his stately bows and went upon his dignified way. Charlotte looked in at the breakfast parlour where Agnes was languishing around the curate, who had moved on from the ham to the beef.

"Agnes, Mr Benson." She nodded and paused on the threshold. "What did the bishop say, Mr Benson, when you saw him?"

The curate choked as a crumb of beef went down the wrong way and Charlotte waited patiently while Agnes applied various remedies, such as banging him forcefully on the back, slopping a glass of water at his face and finally indulging herself in a small fit of the vapours. However interesting this performance promised to be, Charlotte reflected that she herself had little time to spare and that Percy was turning blue so she entered the room with a resigned air, took the unfortunate young man in a firm grasp from behind and dealt him a vigorous blow in the chest. With a wheezing whoop the offending morsel shot across the snowy expanse of the breakfast table.

221

Charlotte waited for the vapours to cease and when Percy, too, had gathered his wits about him, she returned to her interrogation.

"Well?"

"Percy did not feel he could interrupt His Lordship." Agnes rushed in on the defensive. "His Lordship was extremely occupied."

Charlotte sighed and bit her tongue. It was nothing more than she had expected.

"Oh well." She shrugged as she left the room. "I don't suppose it matters any more."

Exasperated by the spineless behaviour exhibited by Agnes's suitor and frustrated by the knowledge that the sight of a distraught young widow enjoying a good, healthy tramp across the hills would scandalize the neighbourhood, she climbed the stairs with a determined step that came perilously near a stamp.

In her room she pulled herself together. How quickly I have become accustomed, she thought ruefully. Yesterday I faced the prospect of Frampton's blackmailing scheme and gave serious thought to committing murder, while today I am irritated by Percy Benson's inadequacies. What a change to my priorities.

She stood at her window for a few minutes and watched the groom bring the pony and trap round from the stables. That must be for young Dawkins, she thought. Hoxton clearly didn't consider him worthy of the carriage. She was shaken by a sudden, unexpected fellow feeling for Lancelot Dawkins. If Hoxton knew anything about me, she grimaced, I wouldn't even merit the pony trap, I'd be out on my ear before I knew

222

it. The impulse stayed with her and she ran across the room and thrust her hand into the secret compartment at the bottom of her stepfather's old valise, then she hastened downstairs and flung open the front door.

"Just a moment, Mr Dawkins," she called out, breathlessly. "May I have a word with you?"

He swung himself down from the trap and she nodded to the groom to wait, then indicated to Dawkins to walk a little way with her.

"I just thought . . ." She was finding it difficult to understand that moment of sympathy and she stumbled over the words. "I — Frampton was so fond of you and whatever else, I felt he would have wanted to . . . Here . . ."

She thrust some banknotes and some gold into his hand.

"There's fifty pounds there," she told him abruptly and watched as he slowly realized what she had done. For a moment he stared at the money in his hand then he raised his dark eyes to her in genuine astonishment.

"Blimey!" he said, all pretensions to gentility stripped from him by surprise. "What's this for?"

"I told you." She fidgeted uncomfortably. "Frampton was . . . well, I expect you know that I can't be sad that he has died, but you're young, you can make a new start." She looked at him curiously. "Did you know what he planned, for me?"

The dark eyes lit up with a sardonic gleam and one shoulder lifted in a jaunty shrug, a street arab from head to toe, the foppish young gentleman quite vanished.

"Of course I did," he grinned. "That's all he kept on about, how his mother *would* go on at him about having an heir. I waited till I saw what you looked like and I suggested a way out of his troubles."

"And Agnes?" Charlotte was too intrigued to be angry at this impertinence. "Surely you wouldn't have married poor Agnes?"

"Ah well, we'll never know now, will we?" He nodded coolly and turned back towards the waiting pony trap. "I'll tell you one thing" — there was an imp of mischief in his eyes — "I'll be glad to stop being Lancelot Dawkins. He was a clerk I came across at Bombay: he'd just died, poor bugger, so I didn't think he'd mind me pinching his papers, *or* his baggage, *or* his name."

"What do you mean?"

"Oh, come *on*." He moved closer so that the groom could not overhear them. "You're a chancer, same as me, I knew that soon as I saw you. I was in the army, just arrived in India, but when the bloodshed started I made myself scarce. It was a stroke of luck bumping into Frampton like I did."

Charlotte found herself quite unable to be shocked and at once understood her curious feeling of sympathy. He was a liar, a cheat, he was devious and manipulative; they were, as he had said, two of a kind, though she had, she hoped, changed her ways. Impelled by a sudden curiosity she asked: "What's your real name, then? I won't tell."

"Don't care if you do," he said as he stepped lightly up into the trap. "Jem Barlow, at your service," he said with a mocking flourish.

224

"Make good use of the money, Jem Barlow," she told him as the groom clucked to his horses. "Maybe you should go on the stage. You fooled us all. Perhaps you were born to act."

It seemed tactless, to say the least, to return through the front door with a broad smile on her face so she walked round to the rear of the house where she encountered the boot-boy, Tom.

"Good morning, Tom," she said kindly. "I'm glad to hear your mother is feeling better now. I hope she can manage without you?"

"Oh yes, miss — ma'am," he mumbled shyly. "My brother will come back home now and Grandfer, that's Mr Hoxton, miss, he says he reckons Mr Barnard'll give him his old job back."

"Your brother? When did he leave Finchbourne? And why?"

"Oh, miss." The boy turned scarlet and hopped from foot to foot. "It was when Mr Frampton was home last time, miss. I dunno why, miss."

She sent him on his way and returned to the morning-room to find Barnard and Lily making a list of people who must, on no account, be omitted from the mourners invited to the funeral which, she learned, was to be held the day after next.

"Yes, I watched him leave," she replied when Barnard asked about Dawkins, then she frowned. "Barnard? Do you know anything about Hoxton's grandson? The elder brother of Tom the boot-boy?"

Barnard frowned in turn. "As I recall, Frampton told me he had been sullen and disobedient. Why?"

225

"Just that Tom tells me his brother is hoping to return to Finchbourne after two years' absence, to his old job."

He raised his head at that and their eyes met, then he sighed and his shoulders slumped. "I — I see. Very well, I'll speak to Hoxton."

At that moment the butler announced Kit Knightley, who edged past him with a nod of thanks.

"Barnard, old fellow," he greeted his friend. "And Charlotte." He turned his head to where Lily was now hastily arranging herself in a languid pose upon the chaise longue in the bay window. "Mrs Barnard, I beg your pardon. I have just been informed of the news. I can scarcely believe it."

As Barnard began to explain the circumstances of his brother's death, Charlotte retired discreetly and went to sit beside Lily, who was gleefully explaining how she would redecorate the room if only her mother-in-law would permit. Charlotte listened with half an ear, throwing in a word of restraint now and then as Lily enthused over a scheme of gothic furniture and gilded trimmings or a Pre-Raphaelite drapery; all the while she watched Kit Knightley under her eyelashes. It seemed to her that he looked like a man who had been released from a strain and she wondered anxiously about Elaine. That she had felt again the same surge of relief and happiness on his arrival was something to be repressed, now and for ever. He is Elaine's husband, she reminded herself, and Elaine is my friend — my friend.

His visit was a brief one and she walked to the front door with him, her unruly emotions now firmly under control.

"I met Dr Perry in the village," he told her. "He sees the hand of Providence in this and so, I must admit, do I."

"Ye-es." She bit her lip but said no more and he looked down at her in inquiry.

"I understand that Colonel Fitzgibbon called at Finchbourne yesterday?" he said suggestively.

"I believe so," she answered briefly. "I did not, myself, see him, but Agnes has told me of his visit."

"Did he see Richmond? Frampton Richmond, I mean?"

"Apparently not." She felt a curious reluctance to discuss Frampton with Kit Knightley. Frampton was gone, this time for good. Let him lie, she thought, there is no use in poking and prying. Let him lie.

It was obvious that Kit was a little hurt by her reticence, as he bowed gravely over her hand in farewell. She felt a pang, but there was no time for regret or reflection as she was once again summoned by Agnes to Henry Heavitree's bedside.

"What is it this time?" she panted as she hastened up the shallow oak treads of the main stair. "Is he worse?"

"I can't tell." Agnes huffed and puffed alongside long-legged, rangy Charlotte. "I found him on the floor, though how he managed to get out of bed, I can't imagine."

It took the combined efforts of Charlotte, Agnes, Old Nurse and the footman to manoeuvre Henry's vast bulk back into his bed.

"There's always a silver lining, my dearie." Nurse patted the invalid on the arm. "Look there, my dear, if he hasn't got back some of his strength." She spoke loudly over the incomprehensible groaning and flying spittle, then when Henry let out an even louder roar as they hoisted him up against his pillows, she took a closer look. "Oh dear, I spoke too soon, poor lamb. He's gone and broke his leg, poor dear, and the good one at that, the left one, not the poor twisted one at all."

When the doctor had been called yet again to the stricken household and Charlotte was the last person remaining in Henry's room, she bent over him curiously.

"What were you doing out of bed, Uncle Henry?"

His eyes flickered at her and for a moment she thought she saw something like fear, then he turned his head with difficulty and stared with angry concentration at his wardrobe.

"Is there something in there that you would like?" She thought he made an attempt to nod so she went to investigate and found a brandy bottle hidden in a hat box.

"Is this what you were looking for, sir?"

He gobbled again so she poured him a drink and held it to his lips. He managed to down several copious draughts and she mopped his face with brisk kindness. However, the gobbling began again, accompanied by that same urgent turning towards the vast mahogany cavern of a wardrobe. Charlotte investigated further

228

and in the deepest recess of the gloomy depths she found what Henry Heavitree had been seeking.

His gun.

CHAPTER
NINE

On the morning of Frampton Richmond's funeral, his mother emerged from her bedchamber to preside over the breakfast table, a proceeding so unusual as to send Agnes into a frenzy of agitation.

"Oh, *mama!*" she mooed, knocking Mrs Richmond's black lace cap askew as she pounced on her mother and embraced her moistly. "How brave you are. What an example to us all. But should you not be laid upon your bed? After all, you do not usually descend until after breakfast. What if you should exhaust yourself? Where should we all be?"

Never had Charlotte heard Mrs Richmond's "Oh hush, Agnes, do!" with more sympathy. Little as she found herself able to warm to her mother-in-law, Charlotte was nonetheless grateful to Mrs Richmond for providing her with a home and it must be unbearable to be so mauled and sobbed over. Quietly, she removed Agnes and steered her back towards her own chair, then reached over, with a smile of apology, and straightened the offending cap, before drawing Agnes's attention to the empty cup in front of Lily.

Her efforts won her a faint, bleak smile of gratitude from Mrs Richmond, who then accepted a plate of ham and eggs from Hoxton and set to with a will. Nobody spoke for ten minutes, Charlotte because she preferred silence in the morning and the rest of the herd because eating was too important an activity to sully with words. At last there was a slight easing of waistbands and a general air of relaxing, though not too pronounced in view of the day's programme.

"We will wear mourning today," Mrs Richmond announced suddenly in a harsh voice. "That is only proper, but afterwards, from tomorrow onward, I do not wish to see you in black; colours are, of course, not appropriate, but half-mourning will satisfy the conventions and purples and lavenders will do very well. You may inform the neighbourhood as you wish, but we have mourned my son already. Now we must look forward to the birth of the heir!" She set down her cup and prepared to wheel herself from the table.

"Mama? Are you sure about this?"

"You are Richmond of Finchbourne, Barnard, it is for *you* to set the standard. That is my final word on the subject," she warned, and left the room.

"*Well!*" Lily's eyes sparkled. She opened her mouth for further discussion but was interrupted by Lady Frampton.

"Fanny may say all she wishes," the old lady said stoutly, "but I 'ave worn black nigh on forty years since my 'usband died and black is what I shall go on wearing."

"I'm sure my mother didn't mean you, Grandmama," Barnard said with an affectionate smile. "She is thinking of Lily and the baby. You recall what she said not long ago, before Frampton . . . Well, she wanted us to look forward, not back, and I think she is very courageous. I applaud her."

Agnes having dissolved yet again in tears, it was left to Charlotte to smile at him and say, "As do we all, dear Barnard, though I must agree with Gran as I simply have nothing else to wear but black, apart from the dress Mrs Knightley so kindly sent me. I never did manage to see about some new clothes."

Frampton's coffin, mercifully closed, had been lying in state in the hall at Finchbourne since the night before and Charlotte could not suppress a shudder of relief as she watched from an upstairs window as the cortege wound its way down the short drive, along the dusty village street and up the church path to the porch. As the last of the gentlemen disappeared into the cool darkness of the church, Charlotte's shoulders sagged with relief as she shed the intolerable burden that had weighed her down for the past weeks. Whatever the future brings, she reassured herself, it cannot be as dreadful as the time since Frampton's return. And what of the future? That ever-present inner voice became insistent. *Are you going to stay here for ever?*

No immediate answer sprang to mind; for the moment she knew her assistance was invaluable. She cheered Lady Frampton up and walked her dog, coaxed Lily out of her sulks, had begun to discuss the farm, in a very tentative fashion, with Barnard, who had quietly resumed his old duties without let or hindrance from his mother, reinstating his under-bailiff

232

and setting out the improvements he hoped to make. Mrs Richmond, although she might not be aware of the circumstance, was also indebted to Charlotte, if only because she kept Agnes from buzzing like a bluebottle around her mother and driving her to distraction. And lastly, Charlotte knew that nobody else was so successful in managing Uncle Henry's angry bouts of caged malevolence.

When she had refused to hand him his gun on the morning when Frampton's death became public knowledge, she had stood by unmoved as he surpassed himself with invective and blasphemy, all mercifully incomprehensible.

"Why do you want the gun, Uncle Henry?" she had asked him calmly. "Do you want to shoot someone?" From the answering "gaarhs" and "blaarghs" she deduced that the response was in the negative. "Well then, are you afraid of someone?"

This question brought about a cacophony of mangled speech, apparently of denial, and she eyed him with frowning intensity as she wiped the spittle from his chins.

"I don't believe you. Now why should you be afraid?" she said slowly and gave him a thoughtful stare. "Did you — do something to Frampton? Or did you, perhaps, see someone else do something, someone who should not have been there?"

Henry's eyes met hers for a moment, intelligence clearly present, then with obvious deliberation he closed his eyelids and held them tightly shut.

It was all exceedingly puzzling.

* * *

After the funeral, during which the Richmond ladies reposed in mournful attitudes in the drawing-room reading their Bibles, Barnard returned to the house accompanied by a very few gentlemen, mostly elderly friends of his mother. Mrs Richmond graciously consented to see them and a subdued but genteel wake took place with Agnes awkwardly dispensing tea from her seat at the ancient oak gate-leg table while she tried not to eavesdrop on Percy Benson, who was deep in conversation with Barnard and Kit Knightley. Her patience was rewarded eventually when the rest of the company had departed.

"Forgive me for staying so long." Kit bowed over his hostess's hand. "We have just been deciding that in view of the vicar's serious indisposition and subject to the Bishop's approval, the living here at Finchbourne should be offered to Benson. He has served faithfully as curate and has acquitted himself well in these last difficult days."

"The living is in your gift, Mr Knightley." The bereaved mother applied a scrap of black-bordered lace to her eyes and shuddered. Somewhat daunted by this performance he said his farewells and turned back to Barnard, who was talking to Charlotte, while Percy Benson and Agnes hung round them looking bashful.

"But . . ." Charlotte was speaking urgently to Barnard, and including Agnes and Percy in the discussion. "If the living is in Mr Knightley's gift, why were you so afraid of Frampton? From what I understand now he would have had no jurisdiction over the running of the church, the order of service or anything. Surely you must have known that?"

Agnes and Percy Benson hung meek heads as Barnard weighed in.

"Well, of course we knew that, did we not? Agnes? Benson?" He stared at them in exasperation. "For heaven's sake, Agnes, do you mean you did *not* know?"

"How — how should I, Barnard, dear? There has never been a new vicar in our lifetime and dear Frampton was so very vehement on the subject."

"Uncle Henry was worried though, Barnard," Charlotte put in.

"Ah, yes." Barnard's bluff, ruddy face puckered in some embarrassment. "I should not mention this to you girls but, well, we know what Uncle Henry was. The ladies, you know . . ."

His voice tailed away in a sheepish mumble but Charlotte thought she understood.

"You mean that Frampton might well have forced Henry to retire?" She pressed him, to no avail. "By blackmailing him? But Frampton had only been back in the country for five minutes. It must have been an old scandal, surely?"

"Ah . . ." Barnard harrumphed and rolled his prominent brown eyes in an agony of embarrassment but Charlotte stood her ground, so her bovine brother-in-law followed the habit of a lifetime and capitulated to the will of a strong-minded woman. "The husband in that particular case is, I understand, both prominent *and* belligerent, besides being high up in the church. There are stories about him of horse-whippings

235

for no reason other than an implied slight and in this instance I believe there to be ample reason for conjugal suspicion. I suppose a word dropped in his ear might have . . ."

Barnard was plainly relieved, at this juncture, to be summoned to his mother's side while Agnes and her sheepish admirer retreated to the bay window under the benevolent supervision of Lady Frampton. It was left to Charlotte to speed Kit Knightley upon his way which she did by walking out to the stables with him.

"I hope that Mrs Knightley is not too unwell?" she enquired politely at the garden gate. "I hope to call upon her as soon as I am able. At the moment it is all a little difficult."

"Char," he broke in upon her polite chatter. "What is it? What is wrong? No, don't shake your head and look so prim. I know you better. Was Frampton's death so distressing? Did he suffer badly?"

"No," she told him quietly. "He . . . died in his sleep."

"Then what is it?" he insisted. "They have you dancing in attendance upon that old reprobate, Henry Heavitree? But that cannot account for your manner."

She raised her hands, palm upwards, in a graceful gesture of compliance and looked at him with her frank gaze. "No, it's something else. I — I can't talk about it just at the moment but I promise I will call for your help if it becomes necessary. I cannot say more than that at present, so please don't press me."

He was far from satisfied but the firmness of her closed lips clearly told him that further insistence would serve no useful purpose so he shook hands again and she could feel his eyes on her as she walked back to the house.

What could I have told him? Charlotte hugged her secret to herself. That I believe Frampton was murdered? For what? Seven hundred pounds, a scattering of jewels and a wonderful ruby that nobody else knew about? And by whom? If he was not smothered for the ruby — and if that was the motive the murderer proved singularly unlucky — then why? Because he threatened the vicar with an old scandal? Because the curate wanted to marry Frampton's sister and knew how implacably Frampton opposed the match? Or was it the brother whom he would cut off from the place most dear to his heart?

This is nonsense, she told herself, not for the first time. I might as well add to that list an elderly grand-mother afraid for the safety of her dog, or a distraught widowed neighbour bent on revenge for a perceived offence, or even a young wife intent upon outwitting her blackmailing spouse! No, I cannot set this rigmarole in front of Kit Knightley and say, "Here is my problem, what should I do?"

When the family assembled for tea in the drawing-room, there was a distinct lightening of the funereal gloom in spite of a sudden downpour outside. Lady Frampton sat in the bay window, a small table at her side, laden with cakes and scones, the fat spaniel, Prince Albert, all unaware of his eleventh-hour reprieve, sprawled snoring at her feet.

Agnes trailed around the room blundering into other small tables all littered with bibelots, her plain face wreathed in smiles which she hastily masked when she thought her mother might be looking. Barnard sat at his ease by the fire, which had been lit to alleviate the delights of an English afternoon in early summer, every inch the contented squire, Lily prattling at his side, while Charlotte simply sat drinking her tea and revelling in the peace of mind which her renewed widowhood had brought her.

"Did Colonel Fitzgibbon retrieve his gloves?" Lily enquired suddenly.

"When?" Barnard asked, not unnaturally.

"Oh, on Sunday evening," she replied, staring thoughtfully at the curtains half drawn against the murk of the afternoon. "I met him," she announced brightly as they stared at her. "It was just before Uncle Henry had his attack. I was in the hall on my way to this room to have tea with Agnes when I saw the colonel running down the stairs. He seemed a trifle startled to see me but, of course, when he explained that he thought he must have left his gloves behind, I quite understood. He said he did not wish to discompose Mrs Richmond any further, which I thought most considerate of him."

"But Lily," Charlotte urged. "Just think, why should the colonel look for his gloves upstairs? Surely he had spent the period of his visit down here?"

Lily pouted and Mrs Richmond opened her mouth to speak but was interrupted by the loud, cheerful voice of her own mother-in-law.

"I declare I don't know what this 'ouse is coming to," she said with a chuckle. "Did I not tell you, Charlotte, that I saw with my own eyes that Indian fellow on the stair? Large as life, too."

"That's not all." Lily hastened to impart further intelligence. "My maid tells me that she saw poor Lady Walbury on Sunday evening, in our very garden. It makes my blood run cold. The poor soul is mad, I know, but who is to say we shall not all wake up murdered in our own beds?"

Charlotte shuddered but pressed Lily for further details, trying to obtain a clear idea of when the gaunt scarecrow figure of Lady Walbury had been at large in the garden of Finchbourne Manor and also at what time Lily had encountered the surprising Colonel Fitzgibbon.

"That is enough." Mrs Richmond spoke in that new, harsh tone. "There is to be no further discussion of such things. My son Frampton is dead and a chapter of our glorious family history is closed. The time has come to turn to a new page. Barnard, it is your sacred duty, and Lily's," this last accompanied by a disdainful sniff. "Yours will be the awesome task of bringing ever more plaudits and honour upon the Richmonds of Finchbourne."

She ended her peroration with a flourish of trumpets and wheeled herself smartly away, pausing only to throw a final comment over her shoulder.

"Do not forget," she added. "I will have no more mourning. Lady Frampton, I naturally except you, but you, Charlotte, will need some new clothes. My dressmaker will attend upon you tomorrow morning for a fitting. It is all in hand. When you have some new dresses," she suggested in a sudden change of mood, "you will cease to concern yourself with this nonsense. You and Lily, and Agnes too, are not young girls to give way to the vapours about strangers in the house."

The injustice of this accusation stung Charlotte but Mrs Richmond was gone before she could remonstrate. And what would be the use, she thought, as she busied herself in her room and in checking on the vicar. Mrs Richmond was quite right: it was better left alone.

Late that night something happened which reinforced this sentiment. It had become Charlotte's custom, before retiring, to pay one last visit to Henry Heavitree's bedroom in case there was any change in his condition. She had finally persuaded him to accept the ministrations of Old Nurse who was now, full of self-importance, installed in Henry's dressing-room, making occasional forays to check up on the young maid who was her temporary substitute in attendance upon Mrs Richmond, but Charlotte preferred to make a final check for herself. Tonight she found nothing to alarm her. The room resounded with a duet for snorers, Henry's basso profondo almost overtopped by Old Nurse's baritone offerings.

With a slight smile, Charlotte closed the door quietly behind her, shielded the candle which was unaccountably flickering, and set her foot on the top stair of the half-flight which led to the main stair, dividing the Tudor part of the house from the Queen Anne wing

240

and her own sanctuary. To her horror her foot slipped on encountering something soft on the polished oak. She had barely time to realize what was happening when she found herself falling and it was only by an enormous effort that she wrenched herself round to grab at the newel post of the main staircase. Her headlong flight was halted and she clung, panting and sweating, to the carved wooden post.

When at last the shaking ceased, Charlotte dragged herself up to the top stair again and sat there, her breath coming in sobbing gusts, a burning pain in her shoulder. For what seemed like an hour she did not move, then, when she thought she could manage to rise she pulled herself up on to her feet and made a quick inspection of her injuries. Her shoulder was inordinately painful but not, she thought, dislocated, while her ankle, though sore and swelling rapidly, did not feel broken. The candlestick with its extinguished candle lay near her feet and as she bent to pick it up, and to probe the swelling ankle, she caught sight of something on the half-landing.

It was her mother's black silk shawl, the one Charlotte believed had been employed to smother Frampton. The blackness of the silk was near invisible in the shadows of the upper hall but there was just enough light to make out the rose colour of the embroidery.

Painfully, Charlotte crawled down a couple of stairs and reached out a hand for the shawl. It had been part of her life since her childhood, Molly Glover's one aspiration to gracious living, the one belonging that was never pawned. Soft, silken and familiar to the touch,

Charlotte knew the shawl could be padded small, the brightness of the flowers concealed in its folds. It could have been laid in an inconspicuous corner on a dark oak staircase, just where a young woman might not notice it and slip on the polished treads — a young woman who was known to be in the habit of making a late-night visit to check upon an elderly invalid and whose path would take her in this very direction. A young woman who had been asking awkward questions.

After a few moments during which her mind appeared completely empty, as though all cerebral function had ceased, Charlotte pulled herself together. I must get to my room, she determined, aware that while the practical Charlotte was inclined to make a further search for any more traps, the inner Charlotte, hitherto the cynical commentator, was even now struggling not to indulge in a hearty bout of tears.

The least movement jarred every bone in her body but she called on her innate determination and hauled herself upright again. After painfully climbing up the opposite half-flight to the Queen Anne wing, she hesitated, but although the noise of her tumble had sounded like the Last Trump in her own ears, it had evidently not roused the household. For a moment or so longer she wavered, then abandoned everything else apart from the effort of reaching her own bed where she somehow scrambled under the covers and fell at once into an exhausted slumber.

Next morning Charlotte began to wonder at the conclusions she had drawn. There might be any number of reasons why her shawl had found its way to the top of the stairs, she argued with herself as she tentatively tried her weight on her injured foot. No, certainly not broken, and by some mercy, not even sprained, all she could discern was the purple discolouration of a bruise accompanied by a slight swelling. How very ungratifying, she grimaced, all that fright and discomfort, and only this to show for it. Her shoulder, however, more than made up for the lack of visible injury, as she discovered while putting on her thin black merino dress.

"Ouch, that hurts. Now how am I to account for a painful shoulder?"

A thought, blinding in its simplicity, struck her. She would tell the truth. It would have the charm of novelty. She gave a rueful smile, which faded as she picked up the black silk shawl from the floor beside her bed. Taking care not to make any sudden, awkward movement, she flung the shawl across her shoulders. That should allay Mrs Richmond's irritations about mourning for an hour or two, she decided, admiring the effect in her looking-glass, while shying away from the knowledge of those broken threads amongst the silk.

As she limped into the breakfast parlour, it was inevitable that Agnes should be the first to observe her halting steps, and with a loud cry of apprehension the daughter of the house leapt to her feet, causing only minor damage to the cutlery and crockery but sending her coffee cup flying into her neighbour's lap. Luckily her brother was seated next to her and, inured by long custom, Barnard merely let fly a muffled oath and accepted the ministrations of the butler in mopping up the deluge.

"Oh, Barn, I'm so sorry! But Charlotte, dear Charlotte, what is amiss? My dear, your poor foot? You are limping. Oh dear, what can have happened? Have you spoken to Old Nurse? Where is the arnica? You must sit down at once, dearest, and let me do what I can for you."

"Thank you, Agnes," came the prosaic response as Charlotte took the chair Barnard was now setting out for her. "There is no occasion for alarm. It is merely that I tripped on my shawl somehow, on the staircase, and wrenched my shoulder and ankle. Pray do not concern yourself, my dear, I shall certainly live."

As she made the final pronouncement with some defiance Charlotte's gaze swept rapidly round the table to try to read the effect of her words. Lady Frampton, when her attention was distracted from her laden platter, looked concerned and addressed a couple of kind platitudes to her. Lily stared at her with undisguised interest tinged with anxiety.

"You slipped? Oh, Barnard!" She turned to her spouse. "If those stairs are dangerous I shall have to be carried down them. There must be no risk to me at this delicate time."

Barnard responded with suitable anxiety and Lily subsided complacently, attempting an appearance of fragility which was strongly at war with her air of lumping, rosy good health, while Agnes continued to bewail the incident and had to be forcibly dissuaded from fetching her smelling salts to brandish under Charlotte's protesting nose.

As an exercise in determining guilt, Charlotte had to concede it was a complete failure. Her observations had included the butler and footman and she could detect nothing unusual about their expressions. But I don't really suspect any of them of trying to send me tumbling down the stairs, she thought, any more than I seriously believe that Gran, or Barnard, or Lily, or Agnes actually smothered Frampton. I think I have led too adventurous a life, she concluded. Whatever I may have encountered in colonial parts I must remember that it is not likely that an allegedly respectable major would be murdered in his own bed in a quiet English country town.

But Frampton was *not* a respectable major and he *was* murdered, the inner voice clamoured insistently in her head. You found those threads of silk in his nostrils, and the threads matched the broken ones on the shawl.

It isn't easy to suffocate a grown man, Charlotte argued with herself, and barely needed to listen to the answer. But Frampton was ill, drained by the current attack, and already enfeebled and debilitated by months of fever. Lancelot Dawkins said so, and besides, it was perfectly obvious the first time he walked into the drawing-room. She had thought it herself; a puff of wind would have blown him over.

Charlotte frowned at her recollection. Surely Frampton would have tried to resist? He had been asleep but she could not believe he would not have woken and at least made some attempt to save himself.

At this point Charlotte became aware that her assembled relatives-in-law were staring at her.

"Charlotte?" That was Agnes, of course. "Char, dear, are you quite well?"

"What? Oh yes, I'm so sorry, I was just thinking. What's that? Coffee would be very nice, thank you."

The butler, Hoxton, bent obsequiously towards Agnes. "What would you wish to be done about Prince Rupert's chair, Miss Agnes?"

"Prince Rupert's chair?" Charlotte emerged again from her reverie to stare with lively curiosity at Agnes. "What on earth is that?"

"My dear Charlotte," interposed Lily. "Can it be that nobody has shown you the sacred chair upon which Prince Rupert of the Rhine is believed to have taken his rest? Agnes has been failing in her duties!"

"Oh, do hush, Lily." Agnes sounded uncannily like her mother. "It's that very old oak chair that lives on the landing, Charlotte, and as Lily says the family legend is that Prince Rupert, who, as you will of course remember, was nephew to King Charles I and cousin to King Charles II, left it behind after a visit during the Civil War."

"He was a damned brilliant cavalry general," announced Barnard unexpectedly, looking up from his plate. "Played havoc with old Ironside. Had a big poodle dog, called Boy."

"That's as may be, Barnard," reproved Agnes. "The thing is, Charlotte, that someone seems to have left a window open last night, at the end of the Tudor landing, and the rain blew in and has spoilt the cushion on Prince Rupert's chair and thoroughly soaked the chair itself. You had better give orders, Hoxton, that they must try to dry the cushion, and be certain to give the chair a good polish when the wood is quite dry."

"Certainly, Miss Agnes." Hoxton expressed suitable gratitude at being given this intelligent advice.

"The landing window?" Charlotte was startled and then very thoughtful as she remembered the flickering of her candle when she emerged from Uncle Henry's room. The flame had remained quite steady as she entered the room. Could it be that while she tended Uncle Henry somebody had opened that window — a narrow casement with leaded lights, as she recalled — the same somebody who had already positioned a folded black silk shawl in a shadowy corner of a well-polished staircase, to await the careless tread of a young woman who might be thought to know too much?

"Before I forget, Charlotte," Barnard broke in. "I understand that Mama wishes to talk to you this morning, after breakfast, about Frampton's will."

"His will?" All conjecture about the manner of her husband's untimely but welcome death fled. "I don't understand."

"My dear Charlotte." Lily assumed a world-weary tone and looked delighted at the opportunity to enlighten the other girl's apparent ignorance. "Frampton was your husband, and it is a husband's duty to provide for his wife — or widow."

"Thank you, Lily." Barnard's curt words implied a reproof. "You need not concern yourself, my dear. But

Lily is right, Char," he continued with a slight smile. "I think you need not appear so surprised at a perfectly normal circumstance."

She was shocked because there had been nothing "perfectly normal" about the circumstances of her marriage or her widowhood (on either occasion). This initial response was followed immediately by speculation about Frampton's will. Had he indeed made provision for her? And if so, when had he done this? There had been precious little opportunity since his return home. She contained her curiosity while she ate her breakfast then excused herself and headed upstairs to see Mrs Richmond.

"Ah, Charlotte." Mrs Richmond, out of bed and draped in even more black veiling than usual, greeted her daughter-in-law with a surprising brisk cordiality. "Sit down. Barnard has explained, I have no doubt, that Frampton naturally made provision for you in his will, but I felt I should impart the details to you."

"Thank you, ma'am." Charlotte's posture and bearing were demurely grateful. "*When* did Frampton make this will, might I inquire?"

Mrs Richmond cast a frowning look at her then addressed her gaze to the document in her hand.

"It was on the day of your marriage," she said and directed another stern glance as Charlotte gave a slight gasp. "You might well express surprise," she conceded with a martyred sigh. "Frampton had no idea, I believe, that this will still existed. It came into my hands through Colonel Fitzgibbon."

"Ma'am?" Charlotte was unable to contain the exclamation but bit firmly on her lips to prevent further speech.

"I received word yesterday morning that the colonel was unable to be present at the sad obsequies owing to an unfortunate indisposition, and this morning the post brought another letter containing Frampton's will. As you may be aware, my son's former commanding officer, whom I gather you met in India, went to his Maker as a result of injuries received during the Mutiny when a grenade rolled into the hospital tent where he was having a minor wound dressed. That brave and gallant gentleman ran to pick up the missile, without a thought for his own safety, and ran with it to some wasteground, no doubt intending to throw it out of harm's way. Alas . . ." Her voice throbbed with emotion and she touched a handkerchief to her eyes, which were, Charlotte noted with interest, as dry as Charlotte's own. "Alas, his aim was untrue and he blew up himself along with half a dozen chickens, a mule, two goats, a pariah dog and a punkah wallah."

Charlotte bent, at this point, to retrieve the handkerchief which had slipped from Mrs Richmond's grasp.

"Thank you, my dear. Colonel Fitzgibbon assumed command and brought back to England with him many relevant papers, including this last will and testament. As Frampton had only his pay and an allowance from myself, he had no great riches to leave you, but if you will examine this sheet of figures I believe you will agree that you will have a competence upon which you can live quite comfortably, here with us all."

Bemused, Charlotte approached the bed and held out her hand for the document which she scanned with increasing astonishment. Frampton to have done such a thing? Casting back to that period of confusion, all she could remember was her desolation at Will Glover's untimely death and her increasing panic as to her situation, alone, unmarried and penniless in the middle of an uprising. Small wonder that she had grasped at the bargain proposed to her by Frampton Richmond, himself desperate to salvage his career from a disgrace that meant dismissal with ignominy, together with the prospect of imprisonment if it became public knowledge.

Had it been Frampton, though, who initiated the proposal that was to be their common salvation? Through the haze of grief and fragmented memory, she recalled that the colonel, Mrs Richmond's "brave gentleman", whose aim was so sadly inexact, had been much to the fore. Had he suggested to Frampton that he marry the lonely waif cast upon his hands? And in doing so might he not have insisted upon drawing up a will to make some provision for her? It was too much to take in all at once but even as she dropped a polite curtsey to Mrs Richmond and quietly left the room, a swelling chorus of gratitude rang in her ears and whether the gratitude was owed to Frampton himself or to that soldier whose name she could not recall, it made no difference at present. I can stay here, she exulted as she made her way back to her own room. I can help Barnard around the farm, and Lily with the baby; I can

250

push for Agnes to marry her foolish little curate and I can act as lady-in-waiting to Lady Frampton.

The warm feeling of security remained with her as she set about her daily tasks and although the insistent inner voice called to mind, several times, her uneasy suspicions, she was, for the most part, able to put aside the conundrum that teased her.

An early encounter was with Lady Frampton.

"Well now, me dear," the old woman nodded comfortably. "We've nothing to fear now, 'ave we? Not with Frampton gone — well, there, I've no wish to speak ill of the dead."

"Of course, Gran." Charlotte squeezed the fat old hand. "We shall do very well now, I believe. Have you heard that I am a widow of substance?" She sketched out the terms of Frampton's brief will.

"An 'undred a year? That ain't enough to live on," protested Lady Frampton. "I'll give you an allowance meself, I should've thought of it earlier. You h'ought to 'ave a decent screw, you being the eldest son's widow, so you h'ought."

"No, Gran!" Charlotte's protest was vehement. "You are a dear creature, and I love you, but you must not. If I can live here with all of you I shall be very comfortable indeed with the money from Frampton as pocket money."

Her revulsion of feeling surprised her. All very well to take Frampton's money — it was part of their bargain and she had completed her side and earned it. But she couldn't take money from Frampton's grandmother, not without telling the truth about herself, and the old lady would be happier if she did not know. Apart from anything else, Charlotte acknowledged with a grin, Lady Frampton would feel the secret an intolerable burden next time Mrs Richmond tried her beyond measure. How could she stand by, knowing what she did, and not use that knowledge to shoot darting malice at the lady of the manor and her pride in her lineage? How could she bear to refrain from informing Mrs Richmond that her daughter-in-law was the bastard child of a convicted felon, goddaughter of a nymphomaniac (but a nymphomaniac of *impeccable* ancestry, was Charlotte's sardonic reminder to herself), stepdaughter of a thief and with a history of dubious honesty on her own account. No, it wasn't in human nature that Lady Frampton would retain such a juicy plum, so better that she should never know.

A summons sent her hurrying to the sewing-room where Mrs Richmond's dressmaker was ensconced with patterns and bolts of cloth, while Agnes and Lily hovered, both clearly determined to interfere as much as possible.

"Half-mourning, Mrs Richmond says, I understand?" the seamstress intoned in a suitably subdued voice as she measured Charlotte with an expert eye and held up samples of muslin and silk to Charlotte's cheek. "Oh dear, what a brown complexion you have. To be sure, madam, I don't see how we can put you in white or lavender!"

"Nor I," Charlotte agreed. "I'd look a fright." She reached across the table to a soft tawny silk. "What about this? It might look better."

The tawny silk was deemed acceptable, if trimmed with dark ribbon, as was a cream muslin with black trimmings and a greyish poplin that shaded almost to brown. The dressmaker sighed and raised her eyes to heaven when Charlotte refused to consider a wide crinoline or other modish accessories.

"I'm living a retired life in a country village," she protested. "Only make me neat and respectable and I shall be quite content. Do what you like, as long as you satisfy Mrs Richmond's requirements, but the only thing I can think of that I really need is a new straw hat. Oh yes, and some stout boots for walking on the hills."

The rest of the morning was taken up with domestic tasks, which included sewing for yet more needy infants, Agnes having widened the scope of her charitable activities to include the poorhouse in town, now that the Finchbourne bazaar was safely over for twelve months and each baby in the village had been provided with enough small garments to clothe a set of triplets. When this palled there was always Uncle Henry to attend, though the waves of rage that emanated from his room made for uncomfortable visiting.

In the afternoon Charlotte noticed that Agnes was moping by the window in the drawing-room. It was not difficult to diagnose her ailment so Charlotte took pity on her.

"When can we go out, Agnes?" she enquired. "I know we were not supposed to be seen in public before Frampton's funeral, and that we were not, on any account, to be present at the funeral itself, but may we not go into the village now? I am running out of sewing thread and would welcome a visit to the drapers."

"Oh!" Agnes gave a guilty start. "Should you really? Then of course we must go, and while we are out, perhaps we might look in at the vicarage to collect some more of Uncle Henry's belongings."

"And we could take a proprietorial look over the vicarage, could we not?" asked Charlotte cynically, as they walked decorously across the village green. "Perhaps with a view to seeing it as a home for you and Mr Percy Benson?"

"Really, Charlotte." Agnes managed an outraged pout that was almost worthy of her mother. "The very idea!"

Following the rapturous Agnes round the vicarage Charlotte felt depressed. The house was exactly the kind of gloomy mausoleum that she would have expected Henry Heavitree to inhabit and his housekeeper just the downtrodden slavey to suit his little ways.

"What a lot of bedrooms," she said in commiseration to Agnes, thinking of the vast acreage of linen it would take to provide sheets for so many beds.

"Oh yes," sighed Agnes, blissfully, her face mottled with an unbecoming purple blush.

Oh, for heaven's sake. Charlotte did not speak the words aloud, however. It would be cruel to wipe that smile off the other woman's face as she stood, obviously contemplating each bedroom crammed to the picture rail with little Percy Bensons.

Charlotte dragged Agnes away after they had inspected the house from attic to cellar and parcelled up some of Uncle Henry's best night-shirts to be sent over to the Manor.

"Let's go to the church," she suggested. "Is that allowed? Is a widow allowed to visit her husband's grave or is that forbidden?"

"Oh, Charlotte," mooed Agnes, clasping her in a damply emotional embrace which jarred Charlotte's injured shoulder so painfully that she had to clamp her teeth together over her tongue to stop herself from crying out. "Oh, my poor dear, I had almost forgotten your dreadful sorrow, in my own selfish happiness. Of course you may see his dear grave."

The sexton's cottage nestled beside the church and they had to run the gauntlet of the old man himself as they passed his wicket gate.

"Y'ere, Miss Agnes, Miss Char." He gave them a toothless grin and touched his forelock. "Be ye goin' up to see Mr Framp's grave, then?"

"Yes, we be, I mean — yes, we are," Charlotte hastily corrected herself, deciding it was pointless to correct him — the whole village happily called her Miss Char. "Did you dig it? I hope it was deep. I mean, that was very good of you. Here . . ." She delved in her pocket and dropped a coin into the outstretched hand, which had mysteriously appeared under her nose. As she turned towards the lych gate, she noticed a splash of colour by the sexton's front path.

"Those flowers are very fine," she commented. "What are they? I keep finding new flowers that I've never seen before."

255

"They'm my early pinks, Miss Char," he told her proudly. "Y'ere, you take a little bunch, and you, Miss Agnes. All the ladies like 'em. Why, only a few days ago that poor Lady Walbury, she stopped and noticed 'em and I give her a bunch too. Well, poor creature, she don't get much pleasure, do she, always a-mopping and a-mowing about the place, and cursing Mr Frampton uphill and down dale, as she do."

In the churchyard, Charlotte waved the hovering Agnes away.

"Go and find Percy," she said abruptly. "I'm here as chaperone so nobody can object. Only, please leave me alone, Agnes, I need to think."

It was a fatal thing to say and it took much patient diplomacy to disentangle Agnes from about her shoulders and to despatch her towards the church. At last Charlotte was left in peace beside her husband's grave.

"Well, Frampton," she addressed its occupant aloud. "I confess I shall not rest until there is a very large, very heavy tombstone laid on top of you, to ensure that you stay where you belong."

She glanced at the small bunch of flowers that the sexton had pressed upon her and stared dispassionately at the grave again.

"I wish you could tell me," she said. "But if you could, you wouldn't be six feet underground, so I shall have to find out for myself, in spite of Mrs Richmond's strictures."

Careless of her old black merino, she knelt down at the graveside and curled herself into a sitting position.

"There, that's more comfortable," she said, and looked at her flowers once again.

Pinks, yes, that was the name of the flower apparently, and pinks were what poor, mad Lady Walbury had been carrying on Sunday. Pinks, too, were what Charlotte had found on the floor of Frampton's room, after his death.

She recalled her deliberations at the breakfast table. Why did not Frampton wake up and struggle when someone smothered him? She had already determined that it would not take much strength to press her shawl down over his nose and mouth, his physical condition being so enfeebled. But surely he would have called out?

Perhaps he did, the thought came to her suddenly. Would anyone have heard it with all the fuss and commotion about Henry's collapse? Mrs Richmond was in her room and Old Nurse, however hale and hearty, was nearly eighty years old, after all, and just a trifle deaf. But if he did not cry out, why did he not? A possible reason flashed into her mind: he might have been drugged.

An irresistible picture followed the thought, a picture of Lady Frampton's dressing table, littered with nostrums and lotions, and potions all of which were apparently invaluable for her rheumatism and the other ailments she bore so gallantly. Rapidly following upon this image came the sight of Mrs Richmond's bedside table, with those pathetic little marble hands, accompanied by enough medicines to stock an apothecary's shop. On the heels of that notion there rose a vision of Agnes in the still room incompetently ministering to a young maidservant with a scalded finger.

Oh dear, she thought, there must be enough drugs in the house to do away with an army and there must certainly be something like morphia or laudanum amongst them. Then why not simply dose him so soundly that he would never wake up? Because they — whoever *they* might be — could not trust me not to notice and raise the alarm and revive him. Any drug that was administered must be sufficient to send Frampton into a deep sleep, deep enough so that he would not wake and struggle when the shawl was pressed down on him.

But why the shawl? And why had the shawl been the instrument intended to bring about Charlotte's own downfall?

CHAPTER
TEN

I should be quite able to tolerate the discovery that
Frampton was murdered by Colonel Fitzgibbon, she
realized, but for what? Bringing, or threatening to
bring, disgrace upon the regiment? If it turns out that
poor mad Lady Walbury somehow managed to put an
end to him, that too would cause me no crisis of
conscience, nor would the appearance in the case of the
mysterious Indian gentleman whom Gran observed so
surprisingly on the landing on Sunday. But not one of
those people had an opportunity, at least so far as she
knew, of drugging Frampton, if indeed he was drugged.
And not one of them could possibly have padded up
her shawl, hidden it in the corner of the staircase and
opened the landing window in order to cause her
candle to flicker, so that the landing was even darker
than usual.

And if those outside people could not have killed
Frampton, it means that someone in the house had.
Someone who belonged to the family, someone,
perhaps, whom she loved. Someone who was trying to
kill her too.

"Charlotte?" It was Kit Knightley. He halted in his
stride up the path towards the west door and stared at

her in undisguised astonishment. "Is there something wrong? My dear girl, what on earth are you doing?"

She scrambled to her feet, colouring vividly, as he sprang across the turf, shorn close by the sheep that Henry Heavitree had allowed to roam.

"What is it, Char?" He stopped his headlong rush as he scanned her face. "You're not unwell?" He suddenly noticed that she was standing beside Frampton Richmond's grave and raised frowning eyes to her. "You cannot expect me to believe that you are grieving for that — that unspeakable . . ." He struggled for words and eventually came out with ". . . *creature!*"

"Of *course* I'm not grieving for him," she protested hotly. "I came here to make sure he was safely underground and I'm trying to make sense of everything that has happened."

They stood facing each other across the new grave, each with heightened colour and angry heat in their eyes. For an instant Charlotte had a feeling of standing at the edge of a precipice. Kit Knightley was the first to recollect himself. He stepped backwards a pace or two and spoke in a quieter tone.

"I beg your pardon, I should not have spoken so." She acknowledged his apology with a slight nod as he cast a keen glance at her. "What do you mean, you are trying to make sense of everything? What sort of thing? What is *wrong*, Char? Please let me help. Surely, if I may speak bluntly, surely Frampton's death solves all your problems at a stroke?"

"I don't *know* what's wrong!" Her outburst shocked her as much as it evidently surprised Kit Knightley. "I can't tell you what I don't know — and what I *think* would sound nonsensical if I spoke it aloud. You will have to contain yourself in patience until I can do as I said, make sense of it."

She raised her hands in that odd, half-supplicating gesture of hers and shot him a smile of apology that illuminated the angular planes of her face with an elfin charm.

"Please, Mr Knightley — *Kit*! I need to gather my thoughts together and when I have assembled them into some sort of sense, I promise that I will come to you. Then you can laugh at me for my foolish fancies."

He frowned and gave a little shake of his head but she led the way towards the church porch.

"How is your wife? I had hoped to be free to call upon her today but the house is still in such an upset that it has not proved possible. I trust she is keeping well?"

He returned a polite answer, still frowning slightly, and they entered the church to find Agnes and the new vicar-designate engaged in serious discussion.

"M-Mr Knightley, sir!" Percy Benson approached them, ducking his head in bashful diffidence. "M-Mrs Frampton. Might I crave a moment of your time? I should like some advice." On being assured of their attention, he fidgeted and writhed with embarrassment for several moments then rushed into his request. "It's about Agnes — Miss Richmond," he gasped and Agnes coloured violently and simpered. "I should like to apply to Mrs Richmond for permission to marry Agnes but I do not want to upset her so close upon her bereavement. What would you advise?"

What a muff he is, Charlotte thought as the happy pair waited with baited breath upon Kit's answer.

"Is Barnard in favour of the match?" enquired Kit, endeavouring to remain solemn. Upon being assured that was the case, he shrugged slightly. "Well, there you are, Benson, you should apply formally to Barnard for his sister's hand, and let him announce the fact to his mother. His shoulders are broad so he can weather the storm, if storm there be, though I doubt it. After the drama and emotional draining of Frampton's return and second death, Mrs Richmond seems disposed to let Barnard order things, so perhaps there is hope."

Charlotte concealed a smile as she watched Kit Knightley suffer the gratitude of the happy pair until he could bear it no longer and rolled mutely imploring eyes at her.

"Come now, Agnes," she spoke briskly, calling Agnes to attention. "Naturally you and Percy are grateful to Mr Knightley but that's no reason for you to weep over him, nor should you, Percy, delay in speaking to Barnard. I believe he is in his library at this moment. You should apply to him this very afternoon and let him be the judge of when it will be politic to approach Mrs Richmond. You go too, Agnes. I will be home shortly."

As she and Mr Knightley followed the almost betrothed pair as they stumbled shyly to the door, Charlotte nodded gaily to her companion.

"Thank you for infusing some common sense into them. I think you have solved their problem."

He stared down at her, his face devoid of all trace of its usual irreverent good humour. "I wish to God I could solve my own problem as easily," he said and, with a curt nod, he stalked out of the church.

A slight chill struck her but soon she was deep in contemplation of the mystery which exercised her every waking moment. A few discreet questions of the servants brought no enlightenment and her preoccupation went unnoticed until dinner when Lily kindly informed her that Mrs Richmond had addressed her twice without success.

"What is the matter, Charlotte? Is anything amiss?"

"No, of course not, thank you, ma'am. I'm so sorry, I was lost in thought."

"I am sure it is very understandable," her mother-in-law said, though her tone belied her words so that Charlotte sat up and forced herself to join in the conversation. A few moments later she was glad that she had done so.

"Mama." Barnard spoke up in his ponderous tones. "I am glad that we are all here as I have something to tell you all. I have had an application from our new vicar-elect, the Reverend Percy Benson, who assures me that he loves Agnes and wishes her to be his wife." Above the hubbub, his announcement occasioned Barnard raised his voice, probably to pre-empt a comment that was rising only too noticeably upon his mother's lips at this fait accompli. "I am happy to say that I gave him my blessing, so Agnes — congratulations, my dear!"

In the stunned silence that followed, Charlotte saw Mrs Richmond compress her lips into a tight, straight line until Agnes flung herself in a weeping heap upon her mother, then the lips relaxed enough to utter — albeit through gritted teeth — suitable platitudes.

Everyone else was vocal in their pleasure, Lady Frampton from genuine delight in her granddaughter's happiness, Charlotte from the same, Lily from relief as she suddenly pictured herself one step closer to being sole mistress of the manor.

"When is the wedding to be?" Lily asked brightly. "As you have decreed half-mourning, dear Mrs Richmond, perhaps Agnes could be married quite soon."

"Whenever you please," came the ungracious response. "You are quite correct, half-mourning need be no bar. It will naturally be a most private affair. Arrange it as you wish, Agnes. I wash my hands of the affair and trust you will not live to regret it. Now I am retiring for the night and I suggest that you do too, Agnes. You are quite overwrought. Charlotte, you also have a drained look. I recommend that you go to bed too."

Far from retiring to her room, Agnes hung about Charlotte, trying to fix upon the wedding date, planning her trousseau and wondering if she might make any alteration in the vicarage.

"Of course you can, you goose," Charlotte laughed at her. "It will be your home and you may do whatever

264

you wish. I suppose that as Mrs Richmond has given her consent she will settle some money on you so you may spend it on new paint and papers or pots and pans. The living is a good one, is it not?"

"Yes, indeed," the bovine eyes were moist. "Only fancy, it is worth seven hundred a year! It is wonderful and I can scarcely take it in."

A tap at the door announced the little maid who attended on Mrs Richmond when Old Nurse was absent.

"If you please, Miss Agnes, Miss — Mrs Frampton, the mistress says will you come to her room for a few minutes."

Mystified, the pair hurried to the panelled bedchamber and found Mrs Richmond ensconced in the vastness of her carved oak bed, Barnard and Lily, also looking bemused, at her side.

"Ah, Agnes, Charlotte . . ." She waved a genial hand towards a tray set out on a heavily carved coffer at the foot of the bed. "I have caused champagne to be brought upstairs, so that we may drink good health to Agnes on her betrothal. There, Agnes, you take the old silver goblet from Queen Bess's time. I have a fancy to have your health drunk so, and Charlotte, you take that pewter loving cup, that's it, the one with two handles, that has been in the family since it was given to Eglantine Richmond in 1700. Barn, Lily, you have your goblets also? Now, here is a wish for happiness, health and prosperity to you, Agnes, in your new life."

Astonished but pleased her audience drank from their antique vessels and after a few minutes' desultory talk, when it was decided that the wedding should take place on Agnes's birthday in July, Mrs Richmond appeared to tire and waved them away.

"Off to bed now," she told them. "We can discuss this in the morning."

Agnes appeared to accept without question her mother's astonishing volte-face but Charlotte considered it with astonishment. What on earth had caused Mrs Richmond to alter her views so abruptly? One moment grudging resignation, the next champagne and congratulations? It made no sense.

That night Charlotte's sleep was disturbed by a series of extraordinary dreams, sometimes nightmares, at other times a series of lyrical, floating episodes like nothing she had encountered in sleep before.

Disorientated and confused, she struggled to free herself of the unearthly visions that had possessed her and started awake, slumping back on her pillows with a great gasp of relief.

"Heavens! How — how singular!"

After a few moments, during which she struggled for composure, Charlotte began to feel calmer, the vivid colours and images of her dream, or rather series of dreams, receding as reason and sense took their place.

What, in heaven's name, had caused her to dream so? A rapid review of the previous evening's dinner brought no inspiration: soup, cutlets and a queen's pudding, nothing to disturb sleep. A glass of wine, besides tea, after the meal. Again, that would not have precipitated the strange landscapes she had visited in her dreams. Rags of memory recalled the natives she had known in Australia, whose babies she had herself tumbled with as a child. They had spoken of other worlds, other times, visited when they chewed or smoked their secret leaves. Could I have been drugged? she wondered. Here, on a summer's morning it sounded ridiculous. She dragged herself out of bed, splashed cold water on her face and wandered across to the window where the dawn chorus was already ringing round the garden as the sun rose behind the hills.

The cool morning air was refreshing and Charlotte's innate common sense resurrected itself until she recalled the surprising gathering later last night, in Mrs Richmond's room. At the time she had merely thought that her mother-in-law had repented of her grudging acknowledgement of Agnes's engagement but now she began to wonder.

"No!" She shook her head and scuttled back to bed, thoroughly chilled. Mrs Richmond was quite right: all these fancies and questions must cease. Henceforward Charlotte must play the part she had striven for, a genteel young widow of modest but comfortable means, living quietly in the country with her late husband's family, busying herself about the house and garden, the village and the estate. There must be no more conjecture. If Frampton was indeed murdered, she must accept his death as a blessing and provide no further motive for anyone to do away with *her*. If she threw herself into good works and behaved with seemly dignity perhaps there would be no more little accidents or . . .

At this point Charlotte gave up. If I lie here in bed, she scolded herself, I shall imagine all kinds of nonsense; it's too early to dress and go downstairs, so I'll read instead. If I'm reading I shan't be able to think. She flung her shawl over her shoulders, picked up *The Heir of Redclyffe*, pulled a comfortable chair up to the window and buried herself in romance and drama, arming herself with a handkerchief as she bore in mind Agnes's recommendation that the book was "dreadfully sad".

All through breakfast that morning, Charlotte kept to her resolve and entered eagerly into the plans for a late July wedding, assuring Agnes that she need wear neither black for the ceremony, nor the white figured muslin proposed by Lily as "sweet and suitable".

"Nonsense," Charlotte said robustly. "The amber silk you wore for the Bazaar became you admirably. I think you should wear something in a similar shade. I know your mama wishes the wedding to be a very quiet one but that does not preclude something delectable to wear, or a new bonnet for the rest of us!"

"Oh, Char," gushed Agnes, leaping up to embrace the younger girl and to drip tears of joy onto her neck. "Oh, how generous you are, to put aside your own terrible grief for my sake. You must have the prettiest bonnet of all! That dark emerald becomes you so well and surely amber would suit you also."

"I can see that we shall all have to mount an expedition to Winchester, tomorrow, perhaps, so that we can go shopping." Mrs Richmond expertly manoeuvred her chair through the wide door of the dining-room and took her place at the head of the table, a genial smile adorning her face. "Good morning, Lily, Agnes. Charlotte, you look pale, my dear. Did you sleep well?"

"Thank you, ma'am, I had an excellent night's sleep," lied Charlotte, directing a curious look at her mother-in-law. Was it fancy or was there a sceptical look on Mrs Richmond's face as she surveyed the shadows under Charlotte's eyes?

"I am glad to hear it." Mrs Richmond turned her attention to Lily, who was wiping bacon grease from her lips and eyeing the potted hare and collared tongue with a lustful stare. "You must come on our shopping trip too, my dear. The future heir of Finchbourne must not be disgraced by his mother's apparel." She turned her basilisk gaze on to Lily's bright violet sarsenet dress with its crimson fringes and knots of pink ribbon and sighed. "When I said you might wear half-mourning, Lily dear, I had something a little less . . . *vulgar*, in mind."

Ignoring her daughter-in-law's gobbling rage, the lady of the manor turned back to Charlotte.

"I am glad to observe, Charlotte, that you have resolved to put away those foolish fancies of yours, asking silly questions and the like, and concentrate on more important matters. Perhaps you would like to take over the sewing circle? The members, all very worthy women, have asked if I would allow them to meet here now that the lady whose house they formerly used has retired from public life."

"She began taking off all her clothes," contributed Lily, eyes bright with malicious amusement. "I was in the apothecary's myself one day when she walked in, with her skirts and petticoats heaven knows where and her bodice awry. Her husband has had to put her in the charge of a nurse, with bars on the windows, and the sewing circle has been meeting at different houses ever since. They have been hoping to find a more suitable permanent location for several months."

Lily's intervention and Mrs Richmond's subsequent scathing response allowed Charlotte to bite off the retort that sprang to her lips and to compose herself. Her avowed intention, of putting aside all her suspicions, vanished and she finished her breakfast in silence, lost in thought.

As soon as she decently could she excused herself from the rest of the family and slipped upstairs. Outside Mrs Richmond's room she spotted the little maid hurrying to escape from Old Nurse's strictures.

"Here!" Charlotte beckoned. "In here a moment, if you please, Betty." She cast a wary glance around to make sure they were unobserved and pulled the girl into Henry Heavitree's chamber. The invalid lay against his banked pillows, snoring fit to raise the dead.

"I just wanted to ask you, Betty," Charlotte began. "Last night when Mrs Richmond proposed toasting Miss Agnes, did you procure the champagne from the cellar?"

"Oh yes, Miss Char," came the answer. "Mrs Frampton, I should say."

270

"And did you pour it out? I noticed that the wine was already in the goblets when Miss Agnes and I entered the room. Did Mr Barnard pour it out?"

"Oh no, miss — ma'am. Missus poured it herself while I was fetching Mr and Mrs Barnard and then you and Miss Agnes, m-ma'am. Missus let me have a sip too, but I didn't like it, Miss Char. Them bubbles got up me nose."

Charlotte released the girl and stood irresolute until she was roused by a gobble from Uncle Henry.

"Were you listening?" she asked him, once she had made sure he was not asking for anything. Guttural noises and a cascade of spittle appeared to indicate an affirmative and Charlotte stared at the man in the bed. "But she couldn't have set that trap on the stairs, she can't walk . . ."

Henry began to utter then the gobbling was abruptly halted. Charlotte's narrowed hazel eyes met his bloodshot and bulging brown ones and she gasped as a thought, almost too bizarre to be articulated, entered her head. "She can't *walk*, can she, Uncle Henry?" she asked in a whisper.

CHAPTER
ELEVEN

Charlotte's household duties kept her occupied for the rest of the morning and she had little opportunity for reflection but after luncheon — the collared tongue making a reappearance followed by another cornflour shape, Cook having enjoyed the reception of her previous effort — she could no longer hold back the dark and alarming thoughts that crowded in on her.

A longing to share her anxieties, to be less terrifyingly alone, made her think of the Knightleys. For a moment she yearned to cast herself into the comfort of Kit Knightley's strong arms and sob out her fears so that he could make all safe again. This longing was so strong that she shuddered as she cast it aside. That would never do, she whispered; perhaps I may lay my burden on his broad shoulders but not my head on his broad chest. The smile she attempted at this fancy petered out into a mere twist of the lips but the idea persisted. Mrs Knightley, Elaine, is the person to tell, she determined. Perhaps she could suggest some course of action if, indeed, there *could* be any other course than that decreed by Mrs Richmond — to forget all about it and make a new start.

With Charlotte to think was, after due consideration, to act so she purloined Prince Albert as camouflage, jammed a straw hat on her head and set off for Knightley Hall. That gracious early Stuart house, all mellow red brick and stone mullions, lay in the direction of the heath so she and the elderly spaniel enjoyed an invigorating tramp en route. Skirting the copse known as Cuckoo Bushes, Charlotte entered the drive and, after pausing to set her hat straight and brush the dust off her skirts, she tamed her brisk marching pace to a decorous and ladylike stroll, which was most acceptable to the old dog who waddled beside her.

"Mrs Knightley is unwell, madam," the butler told her with sincere regret, his formal tones softening at her evident distress. "Pray come in, Mrs Richmond, and rest for a while; I will bring some refreshment."

"Who's that?" Kit Knightley strode into the hall from a door at the rear. "Good God, Charlotte! How do you do? My dear girl, come in, come in. What? Prince Albert? Nonsense, of course he must come too. We'll sit out in the sun on the terrace, then His Royal Highness need not feel embarrassed."

With a nod to the butler, Kit ushered Charlotte and the dog out to the raised stone terrace beyond the drawing-room, where several easy chairs were placed to catch the sun.

"Here you are, Char, take this chair and make yourself comfortable." He looked up. "Ah, here is some tea, and something to occupy our royal guest." He handed the spaniel a bone and himself set down a bowl

273

of water while the tea things were placed in front of Charlotte together with some slices of cake and a plate of biscuits.

"I'm afraid Elaine really is not well enough to see you today," he told her. "It was not a diplomatic fiction for the general public. As you know, Elaine gave instructions that you should be admitted even when that edict was in place. Today, however . . ." He sighed and took a cup of tea from her with a nod of thanks. "She really is not well. Dr Perry says it is a symptom of her condition and that — that we must begin to expect more and more episodes such as this."

As she murmured her regrets and sent loving messages to Elaine, Charlotte was uncomfortably aware of Kit's keen eyes scanning her face. Her looking glass that morning had shown her all too plainly the heavy eyes and the frown lines marking her brow, and at the news of Mrs Knightley's indisposition, Charlotte's shoulders slumped in disappointment, in spite of her genuine concern.

"What is it, Char?" he asked gently. "Don't fob me off. I can see that you are unhappy. I believe you had come to unburden yourself to Elaine. Won't you let me help?"

She started to shake her head then halted and threw up her hands in that affecting gesture of hers.

"I think I must," she said in a low voice. "I had made up my mind, as you say, to confide in Mrs Knightley and to ask her advice. I don't think I can go away, back to Finchbourne, without obtaining help from somebody.

274

If you're sure you will not think it too great an imposition?"

A half-smothered exclamation broke from him.

"For God's sake . . ." he began, then reined in his emotion as he sat back and saw the pinched anxiety on her face. "Charlotte," he continued in a milder voice, "believe me, it is no imposition. I would do a great deal to help you. Now tell me what is troubling you."

So she told him.

He listened in astounded silence as she outlined the circumstances of Frampton Richmond's death and the tell-tale threads of silk, rose and black, though she thought it prudent not to mention the precious stones and the 700 guineas now tucked away in her own valise, in Will Glover's secret compartment, or the mysterious ruby which lay in a tiny linen bag on a string round her neck.

As he cleared his throat preparatory to speaking, she hushed him with a gesture and went on to tell him of the opportunities afforded to so many people, of entering Frampton's room and putting an end to his life.

Ignoring the expression of disbelief on his pleasant face, Charlotte related her own experience late at night on the staircase at Finchbourne and ended her narrative with a description of her night's phantasms and her apprehension that she might have been drugged.

Kit Knightley sat in stunned silence when she finished her story. Charlotte knew that in any other woman he might have suspected hysteria, or at the least, a decidedly overactive imagination. But she also knew, for he had laughingly told Barnard so, in her hearing, that Charlotte Richmond was the most level-headed, practical young woman he had ever met. He could plainly see that she was in deadly earnest. After a moment's further consideration he asked: "Whom do you suspect?"

"No-one . . . Everyone . . . I don't *know* . . ."

That night Charlotte sat up in her bed and recalled her cry of exasperation at Kit Knightley's perfectly reasonable question.

"I keep discovering new titbits of information," she had said. "That make no sense and take me no closer to an answer. Lady Walbury may have been in Frampton's room but was she in the house the night I fell? The same applies to Colonel Fitzgibbon, but did he drug my wine or did I merely suffer a nightmare as the result of indigestion? Did Barnard kill his brother then tuck my shawl into a corner so that I could trip on it, or did I drop it myself without noticing? Mrs Richmond does not like me, nor does she wish to have any further discussion of Frampton's death. Is that the behaviour of a criminal or a perfectly normal reaction in a woman who has lost her son? Why should an Indian gentleman haunt the village?"

Charlotte had finished her tea and shook her head at Kit's suggestion that she stay the night, ostensibly as companion to Elaine.

"And tomorrow night?" she asked him, rising to her feet. "And the next night, all the nights? And even if I

276

had incontrovertible proof that someone, anyone, had murdered Frampton and tried to injure me, what then? I am so grateful, you cannot even begin to imagine, just how grateful I am to them all. They've taken me to their hearts and given me the home I always craved. Am I to turn traitor? No, I must do as Mrs Richmond says. It is good advice; I must put nonsensical fancies out of my head and get on with my life and the rest will go away. At least I can throw myself into the arrangements for Agnes's wedding and after that everything should have settled down."

In spite of Kit's demurs and, shaking her head with a smile at his offer of the carriage to take her home, Charlotte had walked briskly across the dusty heath road and set about doing what she had said she would. For the rest of the day, both before and after dinner, she sat down with Agnes and wrote out extensive lists, with some words of wisdom thrown in from Lady Frampton, a few plaintive suggestions from Mrs Richmond and some downright obstructive ideas from Lily who, it appeared, had moved seamlessly from the pale and wan stage of her condition to something even more trying.

Charlotte's brave words had rung hollow to herself, even though she had meant every one of them, so she thought it prudent to make certain arrangements along the lines often employed by her resourceful stepfather. *"God helps those who help themselves"*, was one of Will Glover's favourite maxims and he had certainly lived up to its sentiment, she grimaced, but it was remarkable how very much more secure she felt now, sitting up in bed with her mother's shawl flung around her shoulders, with a stout oak chair wedged under the door handle and a row of pottery pieces guarding the window sill. I must remember to slip out of bed very early, she reminded herself, and put everything in its right place or there will be an outcry when the chambermaid tries to come in.

Nothing untoward disturbed her rest and in the morning Charlotte began to feel slightly ashamed of her fears and to wish that perhaps she had not unburdened herself to her neighbour. She went down to breakfast firm in her resolution to begin her life anew as a dutiful daughter-in-law, a helpful sister-in-law, a companionable granddaughter-in-law and, she fully intended, chief organizer of the approaching wedding.

Breakfast, in contrast to her mood of determination, was depressing.

"Er — what is this?" Charlotte looked askance at the pile of pale grains in the massive silver serving dish.

Agnes peeked over her shoulder. "Oh dear, Cook must have gone to a prayer meeting at chapel last night. That's boiled hominy, Charlotte — maize, you know. It always makes an appearance when Cook has been swayed by the preacher." She lifted some of the lids on the silver serving dishes. "Oh yes, indeed, dear me, I feared as much. She's sent us up some ox eyes too."

"What? Surely not?" Charlotte gulped. "My dear Agnes, I pride myself on having a cast-iron digestion. After all, I've lived in places where they eat crocodile! But ox eyes?"

Barnard intervened with a laugh.

278

"Stop teasing her, Agnes," he boomed, showing his own plate to Charlotte. "These are ox eyes, Char — just eggs baked on rounds of bread, with some milk and a watercress trimming. They are rather well named, though, aren't they?"

"Ughh." Charlotte declined the delicacy and contented herself with hot buttered toast instead. "Well, Agnes, have you come to a decision about your wedding dress yet? I don't believe you can better the amber silk suggestion, it suits you so well."

"Do you really think so?" Agnes blushed purple and would obviously have preened herself had not Lily's scornful eyes been resting upon her. "Percy told me — he said, at the bazaar, that my dress was very becoming. Perhaps I should just wear that one and not go to the expense of buying another?"

Even Lily cried out at this self-sacrifice, although her protest was revealed to contain a modicum of self-interest.

"Nonsense, Agnes," she pronounced with a sniff. "Of course you must have a new dress. If you do not, how can the rest of us justify the expenditure? Naturally you must have a proper wedding dress, and I shall need something new in any case." She cast a coy glance at her waistline, causing Barnard to shy like a startled horse and Agnes to gasp and blush an even less attractive hue.

"Well spoken, Lily," chimed in Lady Frampton. "You get the best you can, young Agnes, and I'll give it to you as a present. What? My only granddaughter to get 'itched in an old gown, the very h'idea! And you too,

Charlotte, and Lily, of course, you can put up the cost of your finery to me. Private ceremony or not, our h'Agnes must be married in prime style, none of this 'ole and corner nonsense, hey?"

In the midst of the clamour of thanks, Hoxton had to cough twice, each time more loudly than before.

"Excuse me, Miss Agnes," he intoned sepulchrally. "Mrs Richmond begs me to tell you that she has important correspondence this morning and that the visit to Winchester will have to wait until tomorrow."

"Oh." Agnes came down to earth then brightened as Charlotte rallied her.

"Never mind, Agnes," she consoled. "We could go over to the vicarage and start packing away Uncle Henry's belongings. I suppose he will stay here permanently now. I know Dr Perry says he is improving and I really believe he is — he almost managed to say my name last night — but he surely cannot live alone or perform any clerical duties. You can make a list of everything that you want to keep."

This plan was decided upon and Agnes loped across the village green after breakfast, armed with an apron, a writing tablet and a pencil, as well as Charlotte's promise to follow when she had paid her morning visit to the ailing vicar.

"Good morning, Uncle Henry," Charlotte said in a breezy tone as she put her head round his door. "How are you today? Sitting up, that's splendid. We'll soon have you up and about."

Experience had shown her that however little Henry Heavitree appeared to appreciate her constant stream of chatter and banter, he definitely sulked if she refrained, so today she told him about the plans for Agnes's wedding and the surprise she herself had received on hearing she was to be offered ox eyes for breakfast. To an unaccustomed ear Henry's grunts and gobbles would have meant nothing but by now Charlotte was attuned to them and knew that her uncle was expressing disapproval of feminine frippery. Besides, as she had told Agnes, Henry's speech was improving daily, if only to her own ear.

"What's this?" She bent to retrieve a fallen pillow and picked up a sheet of notepaper, half covered in vigorous black handwriting. As she went to hand it to Henry, her eye caught the signature: Jas Fitzgibbon, Colonel, and the name of Frampton's regiment. "Uncle Henry? Why in the world is Colonel Fitzgibbon writing to you?"

She frowned and cast a further, reluctant, look at the piece of paper.

"It isn't to you, is it? I don't think I should read this but I'm going to, nevertheless."

The written lines obviously closed a letter, the bulk of which was not on the floor, nor on the invalid's bed. Charlotte sat down and read the note with mounting disbelief.

". . . and so, madam, I reiterate my previous words. In view of the sudden death of your son, the authorities at the War Office have agreed that no good can come out of the disclosure that Major Richmond betrayed his country — and even worse, his own men — by leading them into an ambush, an act for which he had been paid a Judas fee. To make public his earlier gross misconduct and his subsequent cowardice in escaping from India, would serve no purpose. Therefore, madam, you may rest assured that no further action will be taken.

I am, madam, yrs faithfully, etc . . . ' "

A sudden movement made Charlotte look up. In the doorway to Henry Heavitree's bedroom stood Mrs Richmond, on her face an expression of cold fury, in her arms her brother's gun, pointed at Charlotte.

"You meddlesome girl," she hissed in a furious undertone. "I forbade you to continue with your poking and your prying and your foolish questions. Now I shall have to deal with you."

Charlotte sat in frozen astonishment, Henry mumbling and gulping beside her, as Fanny Richmond manoeuvred herself awkwardly into the room, limping with an ugly, halting step, then hanging on to the doorpost to steady herself.

"Luckily I realized I must have dropped part of my letter in here when I read it out to Henry earlier this morning." Mrs Richmond's conversational tone chilled Charlotte to the core as she listened in horror. "I heard you talking to him so I went back to my room and left the chair there." She flashed her teeth in a semblance of a smile. "Do not raise your hopes, my dear. Old Nurse has gone into the village and the rest of the servants are about their duties downstairs. There is nobody to hear."

282

She shifted her position, keeping the gun pointed at Charlotte. "Did you know I could walk? Did your meddling and prying reveal that? Look at me. Do you wonder that I choose to conceal the fact, *I*, whose sporting prowess was legendary; to show myself in public limping like an ugly crab?"

Anguish was plain to read on her face but she shook her head and cast a mocking glance at Charlotte.

"You did not realize that I had relieved Henry of this weapon? The wardrobe was scarcely the ideal hiding place, I am sure you agree."

"You killed Frampton." Charlotte spoke barely above a whisper.

"I had to." For a moment Mrs Richmond's face was ravaged with grief. "What else could I do? That wretched colonel insisted on telling me everything. I, a poor, unprotected female, to be forced to listen to such dreadful charges. I refused to believe his cruel accusations at first but he swore that he was telling the truth. He thrust affidavits under my nose, told me of disgusting practices, threatened me with exposure for my son, until I had to believe him."

"But Frampton . . . You killed your own son?"

"My son?" The brown eyes blazed with anger. "My son? My son was the man I mourned most sincerely, the lost hero, the gallant officer. That poltroon you nursed so assiduously, *that* was not my son — a coward, a thief, a traitor and worse. Oh yes, the colonel took great delight, I could see that, in making me only too aware of the vile escapades that had taken place,

283

what kind of man I had nurtured and on whom I had lavished my love."

She dashed flecks of spittle from her mouth and tightened her lips into a thin, straight line before continuing.

"The Richmonds have been glorious! The line from the first Geoffroi de Richmond, and even earlier, from the Saxon family whose land he seized and whose daughter he ravished and then married. For a thousand years and more my family has been a byword for honour and now — what should I have done? Allowed that gloating soldier to shatter our lives? To sully that hallowed reputation? *Colonel Fitzgibbon!*" As she spat the name, Charlotte became aware of a fleeting shadow at the door but dropped her eyes to offer no clue to the raging, ranting virago before her.

"Colonel Fitzgibbon? What is he to me, or his regiment? Nothing, I say, less than the dust, but I could not allow him to tell what he knew. He went away when I would not allow him to see Frampton but I knew he would return and insist upon an interview. I put laudanum in a glass of wine and told Old Nurse to make sure Frampton drank it, to help him to sleep, I told her; then when the house was quiet I crept into the room and smothered him."

"But how could you?" Charlotte's inveterate curiosity overcame her fear for a moment. "You have been confined to a wheelchair for three years. You cannot be strong enough."

"What? You fool, I have propelled myself about this house for all that time, by my own hand. Can you not imagine the strength I have in my arms and shoulders?

I picked up that gaudy shawl of yours and thrust it down over his mouth and I felt nothing, *nothing at all*, except a desperate desire to protect my family's name. *He was no longer my son.*"

"Did Henry see you?" Still afraid for her life, Charlotte sought the truth. If I am to die, she told herself, I will know everything.

"Yes, of course he did. I told him to get downstairs and not dare to speak of what he had seen and of course he has never done so." She shot a chill, warning glance at the man in the bed. "And he never will," she said in a minatory tone.

"You put my shawl on the stairs to trip me," Charlotte stated baldly, with an accusing stare. "And you put something in my drink — what was it? Laudanum again? That was just a warning, wasn't it, but I don't suppose you would have cared if I had died. But now, if you kill me" — Charlotte strove to keep her voice level — "how will you explain that?"

"Quite simply," came the reply in an almost casual tone. "Henry obviously managed to reach the gun he had concealed in his room and shot you in a tragic accident. His mind has quite gone, poor soul. I heard the shot and by a miracle managed to rise from my chair and walk again!"

She frowned and stared at Charlotte, speaking in a casual, conversational tone. "However, I should prefer not to have to make such an explanation, so I won't shoot you if you give me your word, as a gentlewoman, that you will never reveal what I have told you here today."

"My word as a *gentlewoman?*" Charlotte raised her eyebrow, concealing the amusement she felt in spite of her perilous situation. She was about to agree wholeheartedly to the bargain when Mrs Richmond's mood changed again and she levelled the gun at Charlotte.

"No." She frowned. "It's not safe. You might change your mind and betray me. I shall have to kill you after all."

CHAPTER
TWELVE

Charlotte had scarcely drawn a horrified breath when the door opened silently behind Fanny Richmond, and Kit Knightley reached in to take the gun from her hands.

"I'll take the gun, Mrs Richmond," he said gently, thrusting it behind him into the trembling hands of the butler. "No." — as the lady of the manor opened her mouth to speak — "I heard you threaten Charlotte and so did Hoxton here. Were you about to protest it was a joke? A mistake? That you would never do such a thing?" The woman before him shut her mouth in a tight, angry line and stayed silent, her eyes glinting in frustration.

Kit frowned. "Even if you swore on the Bible, I'm afraid I shouldn't believe you. If I were foolish enough to allow such a thing, and supposing Charlotte agreed to say nothing of this" — he nodded to Charlotte with a smile — "who is to say that you might not change your mind the next time Charlotte disagreed with you? It could be next week, or next year, or even in ten years, but I cannot risk such a thing. Hoxton, send in some tea and cake, and some Madeira, to the library. Is Mr Barnard there? At the farm? Very well, when you have done that, I wish you to send immediately for Mrs Richmond's lawyer and his clerk. Tell them Mrs Richmond has urgent instructions for them."

With a darting, fearful glance at his seething mistress, Hoxton withdrew at speed. Kit handed Charlotte the gun.

"Here, Charlotte, be sure she stays where she is. I'll make certain there is nobody about."

There was no time for anything but compliance although Charlotte was trying desperately hard not to sit plump down on the floor and have screaming hysterics, or at the very least, she thought, I am entitled to a small fit of the vapours. Instead she did as she was told and followed Kit as he carried Mrs Richmond, silent and sullen, down to the library, the wheeled chair remaining upstairs out of her reach. He waited while Hoxton himself served the refreshments, murmuring that the message had been sent to the lawyer, then Kit addressed the lady of the house, who was regarding him with loathing.

"I am a magistrate, Mrs Richmond, and I cannot overlook the fact that I heard you threaten a young woman with murder. However, I am a neighbour and Barnard's friend, so I cannot allow you to be given in charge to the police. I offer you an alternative."

He cocked his head and waited but no reply was forthcoming so he continued.

"You will instruct your lawyer to make over your property immediately to your son Barnard," he told her. "And in return for an agreed income you will go abroad, taking your brother with you. The reason given out will be that you wish to try the cure for the vicar as well as for yourself. It will be assumed that your absence will be for a stay of some months only but it will be announced after a reasonable period that you have benefited so much that you intend to make your permanent residence on the continent."

He turned to Charlotte. "Does Mrs Richmond have a relative, or friend, do you know, who would agree to travel with her as companion and, in some degree, nurse?"

She nodded. "I believe Agnes has mentioned one such, a middle-aged second cousin who lives in straightened circumstances in Putney. Barnard would furnish you with the address, or Hoxton."

"Thank you. I'll telegraph when I have interviewed the lawyer."

A difficult silence fell and neither Charlotte nor Kit Knightley seemed inclined to break it. The woman at the centre of the situation did not speak either then or when Hoxton nervously ushered in the lawyer and his clerk. Kit, informing them that he was speaking for his neighbour and her son, his friend, Barnard, outlined the proposals he had already made to Mrs Richmond.

The lawyer gaped anxiously at his client but, receiving no assistance from her, made haste to comply with Mr Knightley's instructions, knowing him to be a man of the utmost probity.

In less time than Charlotte would have believed it possible, the document was written out, signed and witnessed, Mrs Richmond appearing to have yielded to the inevitable. Kit Knightley then issued instructions that his hostess be taken to her room and that a maid should begin her packing.

"Just enough for a day or two," he added to Hoxton. "The rest can be boxed up and sent after her." He turned to speak, not unkindly, to Fanny Richmond, who had still uttered not a single word though her baleful gaze spoke for her. "If you have no preference when it comes to choosing a spa," he said. "I should suggest you try Carlsbad, in Bohemia. My wife and I visited the town some five years ago and found it charming; the waters spring up out of the ground all along the valley floor and are said to be beneficial to many different ailments. It also boasts a large contingent of English people so there is plenty of opportunity for pleasant society. I'm sure you would speedily feel at home there."

Charlotte took a bowl of soup in her room for luncheon, feeling herself quite unequal to the task of making polite conversation. Kit had hastened first to telegraph then back to Knightley Hall to pack a bag as he proposed to accompany Mrs Richmond to London, accompanied on the journey by Betty, the young maid who would relinquish her charge to the attendant Kit had recommended the obliging cousin engage.

At half past three he reappeared at Finchbourne and asked to see Barnard in private, suggesting, however, that Charlotte might be included in the interview. She had wondered how much he intended to reveal to the estimable Barnard, whose character was as admirable as his brain was slow, but she need have had no fear — Kit's explanation was lucid and brief.

"So, Barnard," he concluded, frowning as his friend's honest face shone with astonishment and incomprehension. "Do you understand? Your mother feels that she must have a period of complete rest, far away from the distressing memory of your brother's death, and that she will be accompanied by the vicar, whose health should benefit from the spa treatment. She has also arranged to travel with her cousin, Miss Cornelia Richmond, who will be at the hotel in London to meet us." He made haste to explain himself. "I have taken it upon myself to offer my escort," he said solemnly, brushing off Barnard's cries of gratitude. "My dear fellow, it's the least I could do. You must not leave your wife at this time, you know. I beg your pardon but I had the news from my own wife and I congratulate you heartily. No, no, I beg you will say no more; it will be my pleasure."

It was accomplished with so little ado and in so short a time that Agnes and Lily, as well as Lady Frampton, were given a scant ten minutes' notice of the momentous departure. Such was the exclamation, lamentation and speculation that Charlotte was spared the rigours of a tender farewell with her mother-in-law, though when Agnes had been dragged weeping away from her mother, who uttered not a word throughout, Charlotte approached the carriage.

"You will not believe me," she spoke in a low voice, "but I have always been most heartily grateful to you, Mrs Richmond, for offering me a home. I wish it had not turned out as it did, that you could have been left with your memory of Frampton as a gallant, fallen hero. I am most sincerely sorry about that."

There was no response. She had anticipated none, and she fell back to allow Barnard to embrace his mother and uncle, with many a manly tear and a great trumpeting into his red spotted handkerchief. With a violent pumping of Kit Knightley's hand, Barnard too stood back and the assembled family watched as the lady of Finchbourne left her ancestral home for ever, or so I devoutly hope, breathed Charlotte, before she put a comforting arm round Agnes's heaving shoulders.

The next three days seemed strangely unreal.

"It feels like it did when I came home from school," Barnard said reflectively, the day after his mother's abrupt departure. He glanced down at Charlotte, who was standing beside him as he surveyed the stable yard. "You know, or at least, I suppose you don't . . . *Then*, I kept expecting the beaks to jump out and bark orders at me — went on for a week before I got it into my head that I was rid of them. Well, same thing now. I keep thinking Mama's going to wheel herself up behind me and tell me I'm doing it all wrong."

He let out a loud guffaw, which he hastily covered with a guilty hand.

"Ah, ought not to say that, d'you think? God knows what put it into her head that she should hand over the whole concern to me. What do you think, Char?"

Charlotte thrust her arm into his and gave him a reassuring smile.

"You must allow for the effect of Frampton's death," she reminded him gently. "Think what a shock it was to the rest of us, when he reappeared like that. You must remember how overjoyed your mother was, then to lose him so quickly, it must have been terrible for her. And don't forget Uncle Henry. Agnes has told me how devoted Mrs Richmond is to her brother. I think you must just accept that everything suddenly became too much to bear, but don't fret, they will be well looked after."

"Yes, of course." Barnard was comforted. "Kit Knightley said that Cousin Cornelia was overjoyed to be asked to travel with Mama and Uncle Henry and when she learned that she was to remain with them always, he said her transports were a sight to see." He chewed thoughtfully on his bottom lip. "Let's hope she doesn't drive Uncle Henry into another seizure. Cousin Cornelia can be excitable. M'father always said she was an elixir to be taken only in small doses and only as a last resort."

Charlotte smothered a grin and turned Barnard's thoughts towards a more pleasant prospect — his proposed reforms and repairs. Kit had snatched a moment on his return, to confide that he had directed Miss Cornelia to an agent known to him, and to whom he had earlier covertly telegraphed instructions, and that the respectable middle-aged woman engaged as nurse and dresser to Mrs Richmond had spent some time as an attendant in an asylum for wayward women, a fact that had not been revealed to Mrs Richmond, her brother, her cousin or her son. I almost feel sorry for her, thought Charlotte. She also felt truly sorry for Henry but was reassured when she spoke to Kit.

"No need," he had smiled. "I provided him with a reliable ex-soldier as nurse and servant. He'll keep the vicar safe and let me know when he improves sufficiently to be brought home."

By the fourth day the waters had closed over Mrs Richmond's head and the household was settled in its new routine. Agnes, Lily and Charlotte had spent an exhausting day in Winchester visiting every silk merchant and linen draper in town and communing with the dressmaker and milliner about dresses and bonnets. They had also allocated a few hours to sending out cards to their neighbours and acquaintances to inform them of Mrs Richmond's departure and adding, with some scepticism on Charlotte's part, that she would be writing when she had a settled address. Lady Frampton and Charlotte had spent some time closeted together, just the two of them at first, then latterly with Barnard, but they had not yet apprised Lily or Agnes of their conclusions.

Charlotte was in the old lady's room when a summons came, if she was at liberty, to the library, where Mr Barnard Richmond would be glad of a word. She entered the room swiftly, somehow managing to combine decent and decorous respect for a house so recently in mourning, with a lightness of step that clearly conveyed her relief at the end of the strains of recent weeks.

"You wanted to speak to me, Barnard?" She moved across the heavily patterned carpet then paused as she noticed the other occupants of the room: Kit Knightley and another man. "Is there something wrong?"

"No, no." Barnard hastened to reassure her as he set a chair for her between his own and that of Kit Knightley, who shook hands with a friendly nod then sat down again. The other man was introduced as Colonel Fitzgibbon; he had also risen at her entrance, bowed gracefully over her hand, then resumed his seat with a grave expression on his pleasant, sun-browned face.

"Kit has informed me, Charlotte, of the incredible tale you had from Mama, about Frampton's behaviour," Barnard said heavily. As she started up in her seat, he shook his head. "Aye, you did not know I had been told, but Kit was right, I had to know. I telegraphed at once to Colonel Fitzgibbon and he has been good enough to come here with all speed."

Charlotte breathed a sigh of relief. The colonel plainly intended to keep his promise to Mrs Richmond and she, as well as Barnard, scarcely relished the thought of her late husband's perfidy being bruited abroad in the newspapers. Although she had read his fateful letter to Mrs Richmond, she was glad to meet the colonel in person and receive his assurance. She nodded gratefully as the colonel took up the conversation.

"There is another matter that I must pursue," he told them. "I have been given to understand that rumours have been flying thick and fast concerning the presence of an Indian gentleman of some mystery? And that he is widely suspected of criminal intent?"

Kit Knightley looked at Charlotte and Barnard and gave a slight shrug. The colonel continued.

"I should be most grateful if you could, between you, give the lie to this mischief. Perhaps a tale of friendship between Major Richmond and this man's master; kind enquiries on his behalf, that sort of thing. Close enough to the truth, I must say, and yet how far from it!"

As the colonel appeared to sink into a fit of abstraction, Charlotte was grateful to Barnard who, with a look of incomprehension, prompted his guest to further revelation.

"I beg your pardon. Before I lay my tale before you I must have, though I am sure I need not ask, your solemn assurance that you will keep this information a secret, guarded with your very lives. Indeed, Mrs Richmond, you are so young a lady, I shrink from the very notion of sullying your innocent ears with such matters."

"My dear Colonel Fitzgibbon," Charlotte informed him in a dry tone, "I may be young but rest assured that any woman who had the misfortune to be married to Frampton Richmond could find nothing surprising in anything you can have to say."

The colonel nodded, his expression grave. He cleared his throat portentously while Charlotte looked up curiously at an involuntary movement from Kit Knightley. For a moment she thought he had clenched his fist but when she looked again, she knew she must have been mistaken, for his strong tanned hand lay relaxed upon his knee.

"Very well," embarked the colonel. "Here is my tale and a disgraceful story it is so I will make it as brief as I can. Major Richmond was known to indulge in

296

liaisons with young men. This, as you know, is a criminal offence in this country and a reason for instant dismissal from the army. However, as long as it was done discreetly a blind eye was turned. We were suffering a shortage of European soldiers, three regiments fewer than normal, disaffected native troops, the government at Calcutta ignorant and incompetent; we could not afford to lose a seasoned officer like Richmond. However, he overstepped the mark and an ultimatum was issued. He might resign with no repercussions, or he must, if he wished to continue his career with the regiment, marry and reform his way of life. The third alternative offered to him was that there would be no alternative but to cashier him and dismiss him with dishonour, not to mention the threat of criminal proceedings."

He harrumphed again and took a turn around the room, hands clasped lightly behind his back. "As we know, the timely arrival of the Reverend Mr Glover and his stepdaughter, together with the sudden death of the former, offered a solution to Major Richmond. It is not difficult to comprehend the reasons why a penniless young woman, so grievously bereaved and alone in a country in the turmoil of bloody rebellion, would accept his offer."

The gruff soldierly tones and kindly smile almost overset Charlotte and she lowered her glistening eyes, gripping her hands tightly in her lap.

"Well, as far as the regiment was concerned, honour — such as it was — was satisfied. However it seems Major Richmond had no intention of discontinuing his affair, nor of pursuing his other avowed quest, to acquire a fortune while he was in India." He glanced at Charlotte once more before continuing in a level voice. "Two nights before the massacre, Major Richmond and his lover were inadvertently discovered in flagrante delicto by his sergeant, Walter Appleton. He was disgusted; there were very young boys involved, I will say no more, but he promised to keep silent when Richmond spoke to him the next day."

"The sergeant's promise was not sufficient guarantee for the major, however, and he plotted with his lover, agreeing to lead his men into the fateful gully. In return his ally would ensure that *dog's* safety and spirit him away, then as soon as he could do so unobserved, Richmond, in disguise, would make his way to the coast, take a steamer to the Malay Straits and wait there for his . . . friend, when they would set up a cosy nest until it was safe to set sail for America."

Colonel Fitzgibbon paused, took a sip from the brandy glass Barnard had thoughtfully placed at his side, and carried on, while his audience sat, enthralled.

"You might ask how I know all of this? Unfortunately for Major Richmond the one soldier who survived the ambush, albeit with almost mortal wounds, turned out to be Sergeant Appleton, who asked urgently to see me (or rather my late predecessor) as soon as he regained consciousness. The other stroke of bad luck, if one may term it so, came about when the young Indian, his paramour, was *persuaded* to reveal everything to his father, the Maharajah, who was appalled. He is a most honourable man and was involved in delicate

298

diplomacy at the very instant of the ambush, efforts that were brought down by his son's activities."

"What finally proved unforgivable was that in the youth's passionate admiration for Major Richmond, he was inspired to shower him with jewels stolen from his father's treasury, including, and this, above all, is the greatest infamy in his father's view, the fabled ruby, known as the Heart of the Goddess. The mysterious Indian gentleman who has occasioned so much discussion amongst your townsfolk is none other than a very high official at the court of the Maharajah of — But no, I must not say his name."

He shook his head in weary disappointment.

"Alas, although I carried out a thorough, if clandestine, search of Richmond's room on my visit here, the turncoat was delirious or I should have questioned him on the spot, so the missing jewels were not brought to light, and I must report failure and hope that we can avert further diplomatic disaster."

Abruptly Charlotte rose, all three men rising automatically with her, their eyes agog at the purposeful expression on her face.

"One moment, if you please, Colonel," she said and left the room, to return a few minutes later.

"I think this is what you are looking for," she told him, dropping a large and glowing ruby into one of his limply outstretched hands. "I can't . . . I won't say where Frampton had concealed it," she told him calmly, following the ruby with a shower of glittering stones. "I'm glad you came today, Colonel. You have saved me the trouble of trying to find out what to do about these. Pray return them to the rightful owner with my profound apologies."

Later, as she and Barnard hastened the colonel on his journey, she recalled the way the colonel had blown his nose vigorously, muttering, "Brave, plucky little woman," and patting her hand. The hoard of gold sovereigns weighed heavily on her mind but her entire life had been lived from hand to mouth and habit was too ingrained. Perhaps . . . She salved her conscience with the notion that perhaps she might "discover" the coins at a later date. But not, she said firmly to herself, until I am so securely established that nothing can touch me.

"So?" Elaine Knightley, gallant but frail as a dandelion clock, gazed at Charlotte with dancing eyes as she poured tea at Knightley Hall the next day. "What is the latest news since I rose from my bed? So much that is startling, and frankly unbelievable, has emerged from Finchbourne these last few days, that only something sensational will suffice today."

Charlotte took her cup and smiled as she shook her head, knowing that Kit, like herself, had been sworn to secrecy.

"Oh come now. Frampton dying like that, so suddenly, when he was thought to be on the mend. One can only be glad — what a dreadful thing to say! And following upon that the vicar's apoplectic fit and Mrs Richmond's truly astonishing decision to take him to Bohemia instanter for the cure. I must have done her an injustice, poor thing, she is obviously distraught at her son's death. But what becomes of Finchbourne and even more importantly, dear Charlotte, what becomes of you?"

"Mrs Richmond was upset," confirmed Charlotte. "But I believe she lately found herself able to move a little more freely and had been considering a long stay at some pleasant watering place. Frampton's death and her brother's affliction have merely spurred her into action. As for Finchbourne, everything is very well arranged. Barnard will make a perfect squire, he has such a good heart, and Lily can queen it over everyone as lady of the manor to her heart's content. Percy Benson is to take the living and he and Agnes are to marry in July, Barnard giving her away with Lady Frampton, Lily and me as supporters. We can scarcely call ourselves bridesmaids."

She broke off abruptly when Elaine gave an involuntary gasp of pain as she shifted in discomfort. As Charlotte hastened to help her to a more comfortable position, she became painfully aware of the thin shoulders, the wasted frame. Her gaze sought Kit in anxiety and saw that he was pale, with new lines engraved on his pleasant face. For a moment their eyes met and she read Elaine's fate written there, and, beside that agony, something else. He turned away from her.

Elaine, settled once more, waved them aside. "Thank you, that will do very well, I assure you. Do go on, Charlotte."

"But what about you, Char, what will you do?"

It was Kit who spoke and she glanced at him through her lashes but turned to Elaine to answer.

"Oh, I shall do very well, I assure you. Lady Frampton and I are to set up house together after the wedding, in Rowan Lodge, near the vicarage. It belongs to the manor, you know, and has apparently been empty since the death, last winter, of some elderly relative. It has taken all this time to remove her cats, I understand, and it is being set to rights, but it will be perfect for Gran and me. We can leave Lily in undisputed charge at the manor and we will take with us Hoxton's daughter, the widowed one, as housekeeper, together with young Betty, her daughter and Tom the boot-boy, her youngest son. We shall be very snug, believe me."

A sudden downpour prompted the offer of the carriage to take her home and as Kit saw her to the door he gazed down at her, anxiety visible in his expression.

"Did Frampton Richmond leave you well provided for?" he asked abruptly.

His question startled her and she strove for balance.

"Not really," she admitted frankly after a moment. "His fortunes were in a parlous state, that's why he stole the mess funds, but please don't be concerned. Barnard has insisted on making a settlement upon me and it seemed a real kindness to allow him to do so, he has been so mortified by his brother's conduct. Beside that, the colonel wrote from London that he has restored the Heart of the Goddess to its master's agent and that there will be a reward forthcoming, so I shall be perfectly comfortable."

302

He said nothing but continued to look steadily at her, his face pale and drawn. She felt impelled to fill the silence.

"You must know," she told him, trying for a lighter note, "that from the moment I married Frampton I prayed to be a widow and here I am twice blessed." She hesitated and added, more soberly: "When I came here I had nothing. I desperately wanted a home and a loving family, security and respectability; now I have it all, everything I ever wanted."

For a moment her words sounded hollow to her own ears, then a ghost of her usual mischievous chuckle surprised him out of that unnatural introspection as she leaned out of the carriage window.

"Perhaps it was as well that Colonel Fitzgibbon mentioned the ruby for I had earmarked it to provide for my old age. I fully intended to take it to London and see what Asprey's would offer me for it."

"Charlotte! You *cannot* have been in such dire straits for money. You must know that I would do any . . . Oh God, Elaine is . . ." His voice tailed away and when he spoke again his voice was roughened with tears. "Elaine is dying. There is nothing I can say or do. Dr Perry says it may be a year, it may be two, or it might be next week, but I . . ."

His hand clutched convulsively at the window sill. Charlotte covered it, just for a moment, with her own gloved hand.

"Don't say anything, Kit," she told him gently. "Don't say a word."